NOT EASY BEING GREEN

SUSY GAGE

ABOUT THE AUTHOR

Susy Gage is the pen name of a physics professor who hopes to remain anonymous until tenure, retirement, or death, whichever comes first. *Not Easy Being Green* is the second in a series featuring Lori Barrow. The first, *A Slow Cold Death*, was published by Bitingduck Press in 2012. Visit Susy's website at grosorange.com or tweet @SusyGage.

Afterword

This is a work of complete fiction. None of the characters or events are real. Nonetheless, the science is based upon real possibilities, and just as the book was going to press, a few events highlighted just how real the events in this book could be. The first was a tragic complication of unapproved stem-cell treatment of spinal cord injury, which caused a patient to grow nasal tissue within the spinal cord. The scientific reference for this is found here: "Autograft-derived spinal cord mass following olfactory mucosal cell transplantation in a spinal cord injury patient," *Journal of Neurosurgery: Spine* Vol. 21, No. 4, 618-622 (2014). There are also many discussions in the popular press, such as at popsci.com and in *New Scientist*.

Another major theme of this book is lab safety, and the rather cavalier fashion in which many scientists treat pathogens. I don't think there is any malice involved; it's more just a case of familiarity breeding contempt, or maybe a lack of belief that viruses are actually real. In 2014, a variety of instances of safety breaches occurred at high-level containment labs, with true "hot agents" such as smallpox left out in cardboard boxes. These events led the CDC to close two labs, ban movement of infectious agents, and purge the biosafety board.

See, for example:
"C.D.C. Director Admits to Pattern of Unsafe Practices," *New York Times,* July 16, 2014.
"From anthrax to bird flu – the dangers of lax security in disease-control labs," *The Guardian*, Friday 18 July 2014.

www.ingramcontent.com/pod-product-compliance
Lightning Source LLC
Chambersburg PA
CBHW070846250626
47159CB00003B/960

NOT EASY BEING GREEN

Susy Gage

Bitingduck Press
Altadena, CA

Published by Bitingduck Press
ISBN 978-1-938463-98-3
© 2014 Susy Gage
All rights reserved
For information contact
Bitingduck Press, LLC
Montreal • Altadena
notifications@bitingduckpress.com
http://www.bitingduckpress.com
Cover art by Pedro Veliça

Publisher's Cataloging-in-Publication
Gage, Susy [1971-   ]

Not Easy Being Green/by Susy Gage –1st ed.—Altadena, CA: Bitingduck Press, 2015
p. cm.

[1. Barrow, Lori (Fictitious character)—fiction 2. Laboratories, Scientific—fiction 3. Virus diseases—Transmission—fiction 4. Detective and mystery stories] I. Title
ISBN 9781938463983

LCCN 2014920797

PROLOGUE

THE SUNDOWNER CONVALESCENT HOME was in a part of downtown L.A. so sketchy that there wasn't even any traffic. The building was low and dusty, with a carved wooden sign outside that proclaimed *Welcome!!* (two exclamation points). The June Gloom hung dank over the city. Oriol Ortiz shivered and reached for his jacket as he emerged from his car.

It made him nervous to leave his new Mercedes in the parking lot unsupervised, even if only long enough to go inside and find a security guard to keep an eye on it. He didn't see a guard right away, either—in fact there was no one at the splintery wooden front desk at all. He rang the small desk bell over and over until a receptionist hurried up. She looked as though she'd been sleeping.

"I need someone to watch my car while I see my patient," he explained. The receptionist looked blank, so he steered her towards the door. "Just keep your eyes open, and call 911 if anyone does anything. This won't be long." He realized he didn't know where his patient was. "I'm here for Alexander Zimmermann."

The receptionist stammered a bit, but eventually recovered and pointed him down a narrow hallway, where strong disinfectants failed to cover the aromas of incontinence. The old man was propped in a plastic chair in his room, trying to close his mouth but failing, dribbling down his bib in the classic expression of moderate-to-late dementia. Progressive supranuclear palsy had given him all of the symptoms of Parkinson's and Alzheimer's rolled into one.

Oriol sat on the end of the bed and glanced at his watch, waiting for the old man's caregiver. "Where's your nephew?" he asked, knowing he wouldn't get a sensible reply.

The old man tried to say something, but Oriol didn't bother to listen, wondering why he'd spoken to someone in the first place whose brain was tangled with tau protein.

Then the old man shrieked, a cry from deep in his limbic system that caused echoes of response from other patients beyond the thin walls. He continued to wail, rocking, until the nephew came through the door and clasped the old man's arm; the noise subsided to a lobotomized moan.

The nephew was surprised to see Oriol. "You're late."

"There was traffic. Why is he vocalizing like this?"

The nephew looked uncertain. "That's what I wanted to ask you."

"Clearly a complication of his illness. Not unusual."

Over renewed shrieks, the young man took out a battered manila envelope and handed it to Oriol. "Can you look at these, please?" When Oriol made to shove the envelope in his briefcase, the words became more firm. "Here. Now."

Oriol sighed with exaggerated tolerance, and glanced at his watch again, this time to show his impatience with the suspicion. He was prepared to equivocate on what he saw, but the x-ray films left him no choice. "God," he burst out. "The guy has a huge brain tumor."

"I know." The young man took his uncle's arm again, but this time the screaming didn't let up. "He didn't have it before. Shh, Uncle Alex..."

"I cannot speak in here," Oriol winced, "with this din. What is it that you want? The diagnosis is obvious. Just because he suffers from one brain disease does not stop him from coincidentally developing another."

"Coincidentally?" the nephew echoed with more than a hint of sarcasm. "It's hard to believe this is by chance, since you did brain surgery on him less than a month ago."

"It was not brain surgery. A series of injections." Oriol stood to go.

"Wait." The young man went to the door, blocking him.

"I cannot bear this noise. If you want to have a discussion with me, it will have to be elsewhere. If your uncle needs further treatment, he must return to Mexico."

"Is there nothing you can do for him?"

"Do?" Oriol wondered. He gestured at the dying man. "I can tell you that his chances with traditional treatment are zero. I can make no promises, but if you bring him down to my clinic, there are several things we could try."

The screaming finally stopped. Oriol was about to say something further, but a sickening smack made him pause and look over the nephew's shoulder to the back of the room. His patient had slipped from his chair and fallen headfirst onto the tile floor. Mr. Zimmermann's breathing came harsh and ragged and then, before either of the others could move, it ceased.

Weekly Interaction

Superior Technological Institute

California's oldest student newspaper
weekly@sti.edu

Volume 137, #23   Los Angeles, CA   June 6, 2008

Biology Welcomes Rising Star

Ellen Drake, Contributing Writer

When Oriol Ortiz was 16, he was helpless to stop his grandfather's descent into Alzheimer's disease. Now, barely a decade later, he may be in a position to make sure we all face our golden years with our memories intact. A recipient of a 50-million-dollar grant from the LOBE Foundation for Regenerative Neuroscience, Professor Ortiz joined our faculty this month, occupying the entire second floor of the Integrated Biology Complex. Ten members of his research group are moving in definitively this week, including six transferring PhD students who will take their places in STI's Departments of Biology and Biochemistry.

Dr. Ortiz received his B.S. and M.D. degrees from the Universitat de Barcelona and his Ph.D. from Harvard University. After a whirlwind postdoc, he was hired as an assistant professor by our Eastern rival just over three years ago, where he rapidly became the star of the new Medical Biology program. Over the past year he has published an average of one

Science or *Nature* paper each month and won numerous prestigious awards, among them the Society for Neurosciences Young Investigator Award, the American College of Neurosurgeons Best Discovery Prize, the AMA Translational Medicine Award, and the American Physiology Society's Top 30 Under 30.

He admits that there's one Prize that still eludes him, but he has a long career ahead of him to work on it. "It's time to bring biology pride back to STI," he announces, reminding us that it has been over thirty years since one of our faculty has won science's greatest award. Dr. Ortiz sees the Biology Complex as only a start to a new era of the biological sciences at STI. Cross-appointed in Biology and Biochemistry, he intends to build a lab that will span the disciplines and interact seamlessly with local hospitals, where discoveries can be taken immediately to the clinic.

He is looking forward to the beginning of rotations in August. Although his group is already substantial, he hopes to hire at least four or five more PhD students this year. He is happy to admit that the quality of our graduate students was one of the biggest attractions of STI, though he confesses there were other factors, too. "I'm Spanish," he says, laughing. "I hate snow."

ONE: NOT A CREATURE WAS STIRRING

BIOLOGISTS ARE SLOBS, LORI grumbled to herself, on her hands and knees amidst the mutant HIV. She balanced a roll of paper towels and a spray bottle full of bleach, sweat pouring down her face in the heat. The biosafety Level-3 laboratory was not even big enough to swing a cat in, and it was a mess. Incubators teetered precariously on top of each other, inviting the wrath of the earthquake committee; tubes of pink liquid and pipette tips littered the floor, and under the tissue culture hood, someone had crammed a bulging bag of biohazard waste. She should have dealt with this months before. Now the semester was starting, and she'd be too overwhelmed with teaching and grad-student wrangling to come in here and keep things clean.

She tried to think of herself as a victim of her own success, but it rang hollow. This past summer she had earned her tenure at the Superior Technological Institute—the youngest ever in physics and only one of three women in STI history. Together with her colleague, Lou Maupertuis, she'd been awarded a five-hundred-million dollar NASA grant. But she had no postdocs, no students from biology, nothing but a bunch of physicists who liked to muck around with neuron-eating viruses. The one real biologist who used the room was either a sloppy experimentalist or a liar. Oriol Ortiz was a young superstar, which Lori had thought would make for fruitful collaborations, but every piece of DNA he gave her was different from what he claimed.

Done sweeping, she turned on the germicidal lamp inside the tissue culture cabinet, idly removing her gloves and holding her fingers up to the light for examination. All of the approved viruses encoded a green fluorescent protein, so anything infected would glow under UV or blue illumination. She wasn't sure what she'd do if she did have green fingers, but so far she'd been clean.

She then did everything she was supposed to do: put her dirty lab coat into the autoclave, disposed of the outer pair of gloves inside the containment area, then walked into the outer vestibule and closed the door against the negative pressure. The second pair of gloves went into a biohazard bin next to the personal cubbyholes that held people's watches, keys, and cellphones. She didn't collect her stuff, since she'd be coming back, just gave her hands a spritz of alcohol and stepped into the hall to meet yet another clueless, unqualified would-be user of the lab.

They'd never met before, but there was no mistaking the newest addition to the mathematics faculty. Dr. Kathy Greenwood was standing in the hall, waiting, with a confused but eager look and an inability to meet anyone's eye. Instead she was fixated on the sign on the door, the one that said

BIOHAZARD

Containment Level: 3

Specific Hazards: HIV-1, recombinant lentivirus

Responsible person: Professor Lori Barrow, Office SRB 312

"Oh!" she exclaimed as Lori emerged. "You must be Lori!"

Aw, shit, Lori thought undiplomatically. At five feet one and three-quarters, she rarely got the opportunity to tower over anyone—but Kathy looked as if she'd been scaled down in Photoshop to three-quarters size. Every part of her was delicate and frail, from her long thin nose, to her size-three feet, to the clammy narrow hand she presented with limp social ineptitude. She was not quite thirty, fresh from her PhD at NYU, but looked older, her skin dry and freckly and veins showing in her neck. On this blistering Southern California September day, she was dressed head to toe in thick black textiles. Her sweatpants were black, her Doc Martens were black, her hair was black—with an inch of strawberry blond at the roots—even her brand-new lab coat with its shiny row of skull buttons was black.

After recovering from her initial shock, Lori found herself fighting not to be sarcastic. "And you're Kathy. Here for the BSL-3 training?" No response came.

At last Kathy leaned in and lowered her voice. "That old lady in the room next door has the worst essential tremor I've ever seen."

Lori explained, taken aback by the mathematician's slack-jawed fascination at the poor technician's twitch. The woman in question had been there, in the DNA sequencing facility, for close to sixty years. Before anyone knew acrylamide was a neurotoxin, molecular biologists would stir huge tubs of it with their bare arms, leaving them tremulous and possibly demented.

"Oh, wow," Kathy breathed, showing the braces on her teeth. "Is that the same acrylamide that's in French fries?"

"Presumably," Lori sighed, and changed the subject by pointing to Kathy's lab coat. "I didn't know they made goth lab supplies."

Kathy giggled. "Oh, they don't. I made the coat myself."

"All right, then. If you use it in this lab, it has to stay in this lab, and it has to be autoclaved before you move it from the inside room to the outer room, so make sure those buttons can withstand the baking. I see you've read the sign—the first rule is, you must get Safety Committee approval before you use any new type of virus or cell in this lab that is rated Biosafety Level 2 or higher. No bacteria or fungi of any kind. The Safety Committee starts with me, so tell me *everything*. Got it?"

Kathy nodded distractedly, noting everything in a small black lab notebook. She craned her neck gawker-style when they went into the vestibule, then sucked in her breath as Lori ushered her into the lab itself. "It's noisy," she whispered. "And it smells."

"The noise is from the negative pressure and the laminar flow hoods," Lori explained. "The smell is from—well, we try not to think about that." There were no Smalls in the pile of glove boxes, so she handed Kathy two sets of Medium, one blue nitrile and one latex.

Kathy pulled the blue ones on first, her tiny hands swimming in the excess rubber. "It just looks like a normal lab," she observed, sounding a little disappointed. "I was expecting space suits."

"You're thinking of Biosafety Level 4," Lori corrected. "A BSL-3 lab is just like a regular bio lab, except it's under negative pressure and has double doors. We're free to wallow in the viruses—they just can't leave this room." She cast a disapproving look at Kathy's clumsily gloved hands. "That's why it's important to be extra careful with everything you do. The first rule is that your gloves are considered contaminated. Do not touch anything sterile with them, and whatever you do, keep your hands away from your face."

"Ooh..." Kathy dropped her hand to her side. "My nose itches."

"Yeah, it will do that. The next most important rule is that it's almost as important to protect *it* from *you* as *you* from *it*. The cultured cells, especially the neurons, are extremely sensitive, and any contamination will spread through everyone's experiments and ruin them. Once I caused a fungal infection by going for a hike in the woods and coming back in here without washing my hair. I took a bath, but you have to shampoo. My colleague Lou once spent the weekend making bread—and by Tuesday, all our cells were teeming with baker's yeast and we had to autoclave everything."

Kathy held her gloved hands out in front of her, seemingly afraid to touch any surface. "I didn't know that. I thought you were trying to get individual neurons wired up to fly a spacecraft. How can they do that if they're full of fungus?"

"NASA doesn't know much about biology," Lori replied. "So that's what they fund us to do, and we try to do good science despite them. Now, I'm going to show you a run-through of how to handle cells with sterile technique. We'll start with dishes of water so you don't wreck anything."

Kathy was left-handed, so things were in the wrong place for her, and she was also a klutz. Her feet didn't touch the floor when she sat on the lab stool, so every time she bent over to dispose of a used pipette, she'd slide around—usually jabbing something in the process. Lori stood next to the hood, sweating in the stifling heat, biting her lip to refrain from commentary, and praying something would be left of her day after she finished Kathy's orientation. It was Lori's favorite kind of day outside, the kind of Los Angeles late-summer weekend that made people swarm to the beach, or else line up at hardware stores and then shoot each other in the parking lot when they found out the air conditioners had already been replaced by plastic pumpkins. An hour's mountain bike ride into the mountains would bring cool, clean air and perfect solitude.

"No, that's still not right," she scolded patiently. "See, your pipette touched the back of the hood, so it's dirty—you can't stick it back in the cell dish. Throw it out and get another. Since it's just water, try it once without the gloves. We'll get you some smaller ones tomorrow."

Things went much more smoothly that way. Bare-handed, Kathy was able to pull a pipette from its plastic sleeve, suck up water from a Petri dish, and then transfer the water to another flask without touching the pipette tip to anything else. She did this a few times, proud of herself.

"Good," Lori said at last. She glanced at her wrist, but her watch was in her cubbyhole. "Why don't we continue tomorrow? We can try some real cells then. Just toss away that dish."

She closed her eyes for a moment, trying to blink away the salty perspiration, until she heard Kathy scream.

Kathy's hand was in the overfull biohazard bag where she'd tried to jam her pipette and Petri dish. It wasn't clear what the problem was—something seemed stuck to her finger. She pulled her hand out and stuck it back into the culture hood, then whacked her fingers several times against the stainless-steel surface.

A soft brown, dazed-looking field mouse detached itself from her hand and staggered away across the metal. Lori quickly reached for a wide-mouthed beaker and upended it over the creature, trapping it, then turned her attention to Kathy. "Did it bite you?"

Kathy showed Lori a bleeding index finger. "It clamped right on. It didn't hurt a lot, but it sure was a surprise."

Lori glanced at the mouse, struggling under the glass. "Let's get out of here. I think you need to see a doctor."

TWO: BRAIN DRAIN

THE NURSE AT THE walk-in clinic laughed at the thought of sending Kathy to the emergency room. She just wiped the mouse bite off with disinfectant, covered it with a Band-Aid, and sent the mathematician on her way.

Lori had to admit that the BSL-3 sometimes made her imagination run wild, but she still had to do one last thing, even if it meant missing the last mountain bike ride of the weekend. As soon as she was sure Kathy would be fine, she sprinted back across campus and once more put on all her lab safety gear.

The beaker she'd used to trap the mouse had a lip on it, so plenty of air could get in, but still—the mouse was dead. It looked as if it had died in agony, lying on its back with its mouth gaping open. *Maybe it died of the heat*, Lori thought as she removed the jar and pinched its tail, just to assure herself that it wouldn't leap back to life and attach itself to her finger. But the animal was cold and had already started to stiffen.

It was hard to tell whether it was a wild mouse or a lab mouse. Most of the lab mice on campus were brown or black instead of white, and enough had escaped from various labs that all wild rodents on campus no doubt carried a large dose of laboratory strain.

Either way, it should not have been here. Animal experiments were completely forbidden in this lab, and disposal of animals in a plastic autoclave bag was about the most disgusting thing she could imagine—but the alternative was scary, too. If a wild mouse could get into the lab, then it could get out, potentially carrying their genetically engineered viruses everywhere. The users of the BSL-3 all pretended the lab was sealed, but they knew it was an illusion. Crickets and grasshoppers were regular visitors, accompanying the late-night experiments with trills and chirps. Lori had succeeded in deluding herself that the insects had set up a colony there and that they couldn't get in or out. Anyway, they were just bugs. A mouse meant a big hole, maybe a hole that was being enlarged by gnawing incisors, and it also meant mammalian tissue for which their viruses were a target.

The door creaked open, making her jump. Her usual BSL-3 jitters were amplified by her mistrust of Oriol. Despite his own messiness, he was constantly taking her to task for alleged failures in her sterile technique. She hadn't yet figured out how to stop acting like his personal maid.

She could hear the whoosh of the rubber gasket that was supposed to protect the world from them, and then a squeak of wheels that told her it wasn't Oriol but her closest collaborator, Louis Maupertuis. "Hi, Lou," she called over the hum of the containment hood, drawing a sigh of relief. "What's a theorist like you doing in these parts?"

"Ah, merde," grumbled Lou, who prided himself in being silent and discreet even though he'd used a wheelchair since Lori had known him, legacy of a spinal injury that had left him paralyzed from the waist down. The chair he used in what he called the "pus lab," though, wasn't his usual ultralight, and it badly needed new bearings. "I'm here because none of your experimentalists can change the mercury bulb."

"Can I borrow your scissors?"

"What for?"

"Well..." Lori hesitated, but only for a second. "There's a dead mouse in here. I want to dissect him."

"Nasty. Not with my good microscopy tools you don't!"

Lori turned around to find that Lou was perfectly serious, scowling at her with a look of disgust. She scowled back.

"You're so squeamish, but look at you—no hairnet, one pair of gloves, I bet you even have a cell phone."

"The hairnet is for contamination, and I promise I won't open the incubators." Lou gave her a look of scornful indifference, like a cat being reprimanded. The lab coat he was wearing was rumpled and shrunken from being autoclaved, barely reaching his elbows and giving off a burned smell. It was free of engineered viruses, but not of dust and caramelized culture medium.

"We'll never solve our problem with spores if people keep breaking the rules," Lori insisted.

"Then teach your students to change a fucking light bulb." He set about his task with great care; she could see why it would be hard to turn such tiny screws with two pairs of gloves on. Soon a powerful beam of white light came out of the box in the back of the microscope, emerging from the objective lens and scattering onto the walls of the room. Lou adjusted the eyepieces to his face and reached around back to twiddle the three knobs that centered the beam's x, y, and z-axes.

It wasn't like him to be taciturn and grouchy. "Is something wrong?" Lori wondered, getting up from the lab bench and going over to stand by the microscope bench.

He finished centering and sat back with a sigh. "Our best postdoctoral candidate just called to say he got a faculty position and isn't going to be interviewing here."

"Oh," said Lori. "...Merde."

"Yeah." He went to wipe his forehead with his sleeve, then thought better of it and tried to blink the sweat from his eyes. "Why is this so difficult? How can there be so many completely worthless people with PhDs?"

"Part of the problem is your standards are too high," Lori replied although she knew he didn't want to hear it. "You don't want to send geniuses to the South Pole; you want to send basically competent and practical people who can see that the job gets done. Of course, most of the problem is the

South Pole—anyone who is willing to spend nine months cut off from humanity has got issues."

"Well, I know who we could send, then," Lou muttered. "His name begins with *O*." He reached around the back of the microscope to turn off the lamp, but Lori stopped him.

"Wait! I wanted to look at the mouse."

Lou understood immediately, and hit the button to turn the filter wheel until the light that emerged was blue. He was picky and arrogant and often insufferable, but he was the only person Lori knew who never needed anything explained. "Fine, put him up here and we'll see if he glows green."

Lori fetched the mouse and laid it, whole, over the microscope objective. The ears and the tail had no obvious fluorescence, but the rest of the mouse was too furry to tell. It was indeed a he-mouse, the belly flat and bare—male mice had no nipples. "I wanted to take out the stomach," she explained. "If he's been eating the viruses, the fluorescent protein should be in there."

"If the virus can't reproduce," Lou reminded her, scooting the mouse over and turning up the objective lens to a higher power. "If it somehow managed to replicate, it could be anywhere."

"How could it do that?" Lori wondered. "This is supposed to be the safest HIV-based viral vector out there. It doesn't have any of the genes for replication. I'll be right back."

Now it was her turn to break half a dozen safety rules, as she left the containment lab in her full gear and dashed into the lab next door, which was held at a constant 4 degrees C that felt immensely refreshing.

Lou looked surprised when she handed the rusty old dissecting kit to him, but set about opening the mouse without complaint. "What do we really know about how viruses reproduce?" he wondered, staring into the eyepieces as he slit the animal lengthwise. "Couldn't it just pick genes from somewhere in the environment?" His voice was calm, almost teasing; he was playing the devil's advocate to be difficult, the way he did when he talked about physics.

Unlike physics, there weren't any quantitative answers. "In principle, I suppose," Lori answered, thinking fast, "but the scenario is pretty far-fetched. If one of us had HIV, and happened to hemorrhage all over the experiment, then..."

"Then the HIV recombines with our construct and unleashes a supervirus?" He scooted over to let Lori look at the stomach.

She took the forceps and scissors and settled herself in front of the microscope. "A terrorist's dream."

"Yeah, well, I'm not a terrorist—and I certainly don't want to be known as the moron theorist who killed Los Angeles by playing with something he didn't understand."

Lori had to laugh at how stupidity was always the greatest crime in Lou's world. "You understand it as well as anyone else. Our students are about the first ones ever to use this vector." The mouse's stomach was lined with even columns of perfect epithelial cells, all entirely regular and non-green.

"That's even more terrifying." Lou gazed at the butchered remnants of the mouse. "You know, I've never really liked cats, but I think I'm starting to understand them. Mice come apart so nicely."

"Why don't you take the brain out?" Lori suggested, continuing with her inspection of the esophagus and the duodenum.

"How do I open the skull?"

"A mouse's skull is very thin, like your fingernail," she replied distractedly, finding nothing of interest in the gut and turning to the liver just for the hell of it. "Make a little hole in it with the scissors, then peel it back as if you were peeling a prawn."

"Mmm, yummy." Lou set to work as Lori continued her microscopy, but after a second he laid the scissors on the table and made a noise somewhere between a gag and a yell.

Lori peeked over and saw a bloody clump of un-brain-like cells spilling out of the mouse's head and onto the lab bench. "Ew! What did you do?"

"I didn't do anything!" he objected, like a kid who's broken the window. "I peeled back the skull and this poured out. That's not normal, is it?"

"God, no. No wonder it was staggering." She guided the glop onto a slide with the forceps, and placed it under the microscope, where there emerged a ray of green fluorescence so powerful they didn't need the eyepieces.

"*Tabarnak!*" exclaimed Lori, who had lived in Quebec for five years.

"*De saint-ciboire de câline de binnes*," added Lou, who was Parisian but who had developed a taste for Quebecois movies. "Let me see! Can you put on the video so we can both watch?"

"Just a second." Lori laughed nervously, reaching around the scope with a hand that shook slightly. "I can't see that well and I'm afraid to wipe my eyes."

As she fumbled with the scope, Lou changed his gloves, then reached over with a lens paper to dab her eyes. She pulled away, instinctively repulsed by the latex, and sneezed explosively.

"Oh, great," she snuffled, feeling a trail of stickiness down her face. "Now not only are my eyes full of sweat, but I'm covered with snot."

"Er, Barrow," said Lou cautiously, "it's not snot. Your nose is bleeding."

"Well, fug it, it's just going do hab to bleed." She sniffed as hard as she could and turned back to the microscope. She twisted the objectives up to the highest power, projecting on the TV screen the clear image of a single green neuron, axons and dendrites extending past the field of view. Around it, a mass of multi-nucleated, bloody, misshapen cells gave off the same fluorescent glow.

Lori and Lou were silent for a long while, subdued by the anarchy of cancer and how it had apparently been sparked in the poor little creature that had somehow crawled under the door, or fallen through the ceiling, or gnawed through the wall. "How did it get into his *brain*?" Lori wondered rhetorically, snapping a picture. A trail of bloody snot dropped onto her lab coat. She needed to get out of here—but she wanted these pictures. "Why can't I save the files?"

Lou snorted impatiently. "Because your best graduate student didn't replace the hard drive before he went to the conference, like he was supposed to do. If you have a CD, that works, but this computer won't take USB. What time is it? I have to be in Malibu by five o'clock."

"Don't ask me. The computer says it's November 17, 2077."

"Wow! My hundredth birthday. Funny, I feel so much older." He studied the unsaved image intensely, fiddling now and again with the computer settings. The infected neuron came into crisp focus, little blebs on its membrane showing that it was dying. The misshapen cells scattered around seemed to be straddling its dendrites to attack it.

"Beauddiful," Lori sniffed. "Don't you wish you'd become a wildlife photographer after all?"

"It would certainly be less dangerous. You know, I'd like to know the *provenance* of those small, misshapen cells." Lou's speaking franglais meant that he was very, very nervous. "I mean, are they neurons?"

"They have to be glial cells or cells from the meninges or something, or even some kind of immune cell..." Lori started to add that neurons didn't divide, but caught herself. It really wasn't necessary to emphasize that point to a guy who hadn't walked in more than three years because of one tiny disruption of axons somewhere just below his rib cage.

"But that one looks just like a neuron—and I have all the antibodies to the neuronal differentiation markers," he reminded her suddenly. "Remember, my vegan student was trying to convince us he could make neurons from precursors instead of having to kill a mouse, so he wanted to track all of the stages with antibody staining. Can I slice this brain and stain it?"

"Of course you can—first you just have to drop it into fixative. But I'm going to—AH-CHOO!" Catching the blood and snot in the shoulder of her lab coat, she finally decided something had to be done about her nose and removed both pairs of gloves. After washing her hands carefully with ethanol, she blew her nose into a giant Kimwipe and stuffed sterile gauze into both nostrils. Then she went to measure out a fifty-milliliter tube of formaldehyde while Lou gathered up the bits of tumor to place with the rest of the brain.

Taking the tube with exaggerated care, Lou eased the organ from its fragile skull into the liquid using the blunt end of the forceps, then handed it back to Lori because he clearly hadn't done this before and didn't know what to do. Lori wrapped the tube in foil, labeled it "Louis M., DON'T TOUCH!!" and placed it on a little device called a "rocker," where it would be cradled in gentle oscillations to allow the formaldehyde to soak all the way through.

"Let it go at least overnight," she instructed. "Then you can embed it, slice it, and stain it. It's true that retroviruses integrate into the genome, so maybe our virus managed to get into an oncogene and cause a tumor. Still, I can't believe that even an oncogene would make a neuron divide like that."

Lou was quiet for a long while, then pointedly changed his gloves, turning the used ones inside out and placing them into a fresh autoclave bag. He then began wiping down the microscope stage, the lab bench, and the tools with bleach. "If those are neurons," he said quietly, "then this is not our virus. It's something else."

THREE: THE WHEY OF THE GOAT

THE STONY SILENCE SAID everything. Claudine spoke twenty-one languages, and "sullen grad student" had not been a difficult one to learn. Nor did it seem that the sullen grad students ever grew up. "I am *not* dotty," she responded to Lori's wordless reproach. "You only have to come up here to see how beautiful this house is."

The lull that followed was spoke volumes: *You're not my mother-in-law anymore, not since Roger died. And anyway you never were, because we were Just Friends.* "Not this week," Lori admonished. "School has started."

Claudine knew she was the very antithesis of dotty—indeed, she was trying to save them all from insanity, but she couldn't get the temperamental science divas to listen. Lori might have been at the pinnacle of her career, but she was living in a dormitory with a bunch of undergraduates, alone and unable even to acknowledge the years she had spent in Montreal with Roger. "It's a short flight. You could ride your bike here from the airport."

"I have classes. And research. And service. Usually you get a sabbatical after tenure, but since I've only been here a year, I miss out on that. I'm practically the most senior member of the department right now, since the Head resigned and our Nobel-prize patriarch quit on us."

"Now that you're a star, don't you have minions to do your work for you?"

"Sorry." Lori laughed harshly. "Fresh out of minions."

"I saved all of Roger's stuff for you to look through. There's a cabin that's set up just for you."

Lori choked, and obviously had a hard time coming out with, "How thoughtful. Look, I can't get away. Why now?"

Claudine equivocated a bit, finally admitting that she had finally got reservations from VIP guests—and she wasn't ready for them. "My so-called chef is a nut. I think she's using me as a front for growing weed. Last time I had a group visit, I had to pretend it was Detox Week and give them nothing but fruit juice. There are goats in the guest rooms..."

"Sounds like you're the one who needs minions." And with that, she was gone.

It was always like this. Even when Roger was alive, it had been a chronic refrain of "No time," with an undercurrent of dread as if Lori feared being made to speak of things best kept silent... or feared two days with nothing to do, two days during which her competitors could inch her out in that cutthroat race known as science.

So Claudine was on her own to make the place respectable for the famous Hollywood agent and his personal physician, due to arrive first thing Friday morning. That gave her less than two days to sweep, wash, cater, furnish—even paint.

The tasks swirled in her head as she paced the grounds, trying to decide where to start. Twenty acres of meadows, rolling hills, orchards, secluded ponds, and a view of distant mountains seemed a tropical paradise after thirty-four years on a farm in Alberta. The original owner had stamped his vision of aristocratic living on the buildings, and the main house in particular had reached such a state of splendid, dilapidated ruin that Claudine didn't want to touch it. At the same time, its "Turn me into a spa for the stars" command was as unambiguous and compelling as a "wash me" plea on a dirty windshield. The outbuildings instantly became guest cottages, and the barn the restaurant. There had already been animals there—sheep and goats, rescues from a shelter, kept as pets—and she had already found the perfect name for her resort: *The Whey of the Goat*.

She was ready for a guest or two—her daughter, or Lori, even a few physics nerds who wouldn't notice the décor—but not for real Hollywood stars. Her dream was suddenly all too real.

Like the French, goats would eat anything. That slut Brigitte was sitting in the middle of the bed in the super-deluxe suite, shreds of a sheet costing $950 (400 organic cotton threads to the inch) hanging from her grinning mouth. Claudine grabbed a broom and chased her out into the pasture, then went back into the cabin to use the broom on the poo-spattered floor. It was a good thing goat poo was innocuous; it reminded her of the French chocolates *crottes de chèvre*, and she wondered if her raw-vegan guests might appreciate the real thing. She hung some curtains, cracked a window to air out the place, and cut a few roses to place on the coffee table. It would have to do.

That was her best room, and it wasn't big enough for two. It seemed that all of a sudden, people had decided to spend the last gasps of summer in Clonic, California. The only cabin large enough for a guest and his doctor was what she had officially baptized the Two Suite, complete with hand-watercolored sign. But in reality she had avoided it, because it was the haunted suite, where all of her dead son's worldly goods were stacked in boxes that she couldn't bear to open.

Roger was within two weeks of his fortieth birthday before one of his suicide attempts was finally successful. That was maybe a horrible way to look at it, but Claudine was resigned. Exactly fifty percent of the men in their family committed suicide; that was how it had been since that first *maudit* ancestor had brought his tainted gene over from France.

"Moe Deet," agreed an ethereal voice from the darkest corner of the room.

Claudine jumped. "You're back," she said, without looking around from the box of books she was sorting onto shelves in careful alphabetical order. "Since you only show up when you disapprove of something, I can hazard a guess."

A snorting noise came from the dimly lit recesses of the cabin. It was the first time she'd ever heard a ghost laugh, which allayed her curiosity about that element of spectral existence anyway. "It's not easy to make a ghost laugh, Ma," agreed the protoplasm or whatever it was, "but somehow you manage."

He had always been able to read her thoughts, so she didn't know if that was another ghostly attribute or just her son. A change in energy waves in the forcefield around her head perhaps? What were the differences between Roger dead and Roger alive anyway? Were there fewer differences the higher your IQ climbed? Maybe that explained why so many geniuses died young. It didn't make all that much difference to them anyway, being as they were used to inhabiting higher realms and all that. But it made a difference to the people left behind...

"Stop it, Ma. You were almost onto something and then you lost it. As usual. I am here for a reason though, and I'm not mad at you. See if you can guess."

The thought she had been suppressing leapt unbidden into her mind, and though she didn't need to blurt it out she did anyway. "It isn't my VIP guest, who calls himself Moe Deet?"

"He's really Morris Dietrich, but rumor has it that he's stuck with his current moniker since it was given to him by Gérard Depardieu. And he *is* a Hollywood agent with a gargantuan A-list." The ghost spoke in a subdued voice, another first. "That is rather goose-bump making. But that isn't what I wanted to talk to you about. You have another guest coming." He waited. "Abby."

Claudine fumbled in the pocket of her apron for the guest list. Sure enough, just below Moe Deet, she saw that the second-most-luxurious accommodations were taken by a name she recognized.

Absinthe McRae had been another of Lori and Roger's classmates once upon a time, in that emotionally charged first year of graduate school when every test was the end of the world. Abby had called the farm more than once, sobbing as she choked out the details of Roger's latest episode. If Abby hadn't been around, Claudine never would have learned the truth; his other friends were protective of his privacy with the natural distrust of college students for parental involvement. All the same, Abby's concern had had overtones of tattletale. She'd never been accepted into the "genius" circle, and had lasted less than a year in the program, leaving to marry a banker and move to Manhattan.

It was a superficially different Abby who had surfaced at Roger's funeral—divorced, successful, living in California. She gave all of her classmates a wide berth, except to brag occasionally about how intellectual property law brought her more money than they would see in their lifetimes, while at the same time letting her determine the fates of all the scientists she loathed.

She had also more than once stated loudly that Lori had "killed Roger" and Claudine had backed away, unable to go there. In the year since, she had avoided Abby's calls, even though there was something touching about someone who would carry a torch for her son beyond the grave.

Chronically condemned to dating men who resented her for being smarter than they were, this time Abby seemed to have found herself a Frenchman, who had signed her up for the three-day Birthday Special that included two facials in Claudine's special treatment room. The Frenchman himself wasn't coming—just his name, Louis Maupertuis, made Claudine imagine a reclusive 86-year-old sugar daddy lurking at the Malibu billing address.

"I never liked Abby," said Roger impatiently. "You know how I felt about being treated like there was something wrong with me. I wasn't crazy, but that used to drive me nuts."

His mother knew better than to get suckered into an old, incredibly painful argument. Oh no, *he* wasn't schizo—everyone else might be, but never him. She knew that his classmates, too, had had flaming rows with him over his refusal to take his meds. Abby'd described multi-colored bunny pellets tucked away under cushions that reminded Claudine of the way kids tried to hide their peas under mashed potatoes rather than eat them. "So what am I supposed to do?" she asked hastily. "Just keep her out of your room?"

Claudine watched objects blur and grow solid in succession; the ghost was pacing. "There's something more than that. She works with Lori."

Lori again. Suddenly Claudine shook with a rage she couldn't control, as much as she knew it was unfair. It was NOT Lori's fault that Roger had plunged into the deep end of the trough. And even though she knew that, knew it intellectually anyway, a little part of her agreed with Abby that Lori was the source of Roger's woes. Lori had an uncanny knack of losing rivals and enemies to mysterious, bloody deaths. Her own parents had been shot on a street corner when she was not quite thirteen, which seemed to please her no end. Her nickname in grad school had been *Killer*, which was funny if you saw it in a Jack Russell terrier kind of way, but not so funny if you took it more literally.

The blurry places had come to a halt, and now they were coalescing into a tiny cyclone from which little sparks were flying. Just once Claudine would like to have just a little privacy inside her own brain, and now the ghost was mad. No, not mad, angry. Okay. It was time for her to act like a mother.

"Abby loved you, *mon fils*," she said quietly. "She never got over it."

The ghost was savage now. If Claudine got to see a side of Abby no one saw, the same certainly held true for too-good-to-be-true Roger. He dismissed his old friend cruelly. "Abby was nothing. The only one who ever meant anything to me was..." he stopped, unable even to say her name. "was a kid," he finished after a long, fraught silence. "She was sixteen. Sweet. Sweet and clueless and so goddamn brilliant. She was the only one who ever *saw* me, Ma. The rest of you, all of you, including my own mother, just saw a pathetic nutcase. But that lost the power to hurt when she was with me. You all were moping on the ground while we two danced among the stars."

The ghost began to take on vaguely human outlines. Evidently emotion was an energy source so powerful it could even organize molecules. Whatever the bonding energy was it was significant, and someone like Roger could perhaps calibrate it...

The ghost resumed its habitual tone of faintly sardonic tolerance. "Confronted with raw emotion, the true St.-Pierre begins to confabulate, retreating behind half-baked theories made up out of whole cloth. Ma, I just came back because I heard that Abby was coming for a spa weekend. Can you find out from her how Lori is doing? I'm sure you can broach the subject without hurting Abby's feelings."

"And you can't go find out yourself because..."

"Because I'm stuck here, that's right. We've been over this. I have not been allotted travel privileges yet—it's very complicated, *ma mère*, but I am not unhappy. Really. Or rather, no more unhappy than I ever was. But if you could get Lori to come up here it would improve my situation considerably. I wasn't going to mention this but...oh, never mind. Forget it. I'd just like to find out how she is. If she's happy. If she's found someone she likes..."

A knock on the door coincided with all the lights in the room suddenly going on. A voice from the other side of the door informed her the blown fuse was fixed, and Claudine murmured a vague response. By this time Roger had, of course, vanished.

FOUR: RELUCTANT EXPLORERS

Lori's only teaching was on Tuesdays and Thursdays, but the first Monday of term still managed to run her ragged. At least a dozen undergraduates came in wanting to become physics majors, or to stop being physics majors, or to drop out completely and go to a school that offered things like art, music, Russian literature, or kinesiology. Each request for an add/drop signature was accompanied by a long personal tale usually involving weeping. She often thought she should dispense with the box of tissues on her desk and just get a huge shaggy rug to absorb all the tears. Between her constant bloody nose and the emotions, she went through a big box in less than one day.

Then there were the students who were already unhappy with their Undergraduate House assignments, and most of these were Buboes from Lori's own House, so she was responsible for re-housing them. It was admittedly true that Pasteur House held the freaks and misfits of a school that specialized in freaks and misfits, but she hadn't expected so much desertion already. Most of the defectors were female—maybe they had been fooled seeing Lori as their Residential Associate, thinking she was normal and would sympathize with them. They were wrong, and now they would have to choose between Ferrier, Calvin, and Snodgrass houses, each weird in its own way. Ferrier Ferrets had to spend their undergraduate years dressed entirely in black, and the Calvin Thorns did not wear shoes. The only thing that distinguished a Bubo was a refusal to obey any rules of any kind.

The graduate students had been around all summer, but even they were stressed out and running screaming down the halls. In the confusion caused by the loss of their department head and secretary last year, no one had assigned teaching assistants for the six different levels of first-year physics. Being the smart and resourceful bunch that they were, the physics grads had just assumed they'd all do the same thing as last year—except two of their number had graduated, and one had run off to Australia to work on a banana farm. That left the whole section of Physics P without TAs.

The worst part was that "Physics P" was the bonehead section, designed for pre-meds, biology majors, and other losers from Snodgrass House—whose official motto really was "Yeah, We're the Dumb Ones." No one would ever admit to being willing to teach Physics P.

Finally Lou just snorted, "Why don't we cancel Physics P altogether? It's for fools," and Lori realized that she could, with one stroke of a pen, do exactly that. All of the biology majors were now enrolled in plain ordinary Physics 1, where they would have to sink or swim. And if they sank, they could go crying to someone else.

All of this educational nonsense interfered with the real business of being a professor, which was getting research money and spending that money hiring galley slaves to spend long hours in the stinky biohazardous basement, where they could discover garbage-bag mice and fix light bulbs. She was sitting at her desk, waiting for their second-choice postdoctoral candidate to come for his interview, when yet another head poked in to her office. This one was topped with a familiar ruff of black curls and peered at her through negative-eight diopter lenses. "Is it safe?"

"There's no one else here, Sam."

The door opened a crack and Lou's best graduate student bounded in. Just starting his fourth year, Sam already had a single-author paper and two papers co-authored with others in the group. Lori often forgot he was a student and told him things she shouldn't, in part because her brain stubbornly insisted upon confusing him with Lou. The only physical resemblance between them was big eyes and lots of curly hair, though Sam was very dark while Lou was blond. But Sam had a funny way of imitating the voice and gestures of anyone he was around, so it was sometimes hard to think of him as his own person. Some people, especially the Chinese students, were insulted by his mimicry, but it was completely unconscious.

When he was alone, he spoke with a Brooklyn accent. "I can't do it, Barrow. I can't go to Northern Canada all by myself."

Lori sighed, her one respectable space-science project now betraying her along with everything else. "Sam, we've been planning this trip all summer. Everything's ready. You know that the planes don't even fly after October."

"I know that, but I *can't*. I mean, even if I were willing. That instrument you want me to take has four lithium batteries that you're not allowed to check, you have to carry them on, and the limit is two per person."

"Right." Lori tried to pretend she hadn't forgotten this. "Well, look, we'll just have to get someone to go with you. It's not too late."

Sam stopped pacing and looked her in the eyes. "I heard you had a postdoctoral candidate to interview."

"We do. He should be here any time."

"Well, unless he has horns and hooves, take him."

"Horns and hooves might do well in the ice and snow," Lori argued. "Honestly, this is harder than I ever imagined. We've been looking for postdocs all summer, and we've tried everything: ridiculously high salaries, ridiculously low ones, and everything in between. We've put ads in all the science journals and had a booth at the summer Particles conference. And everyone who's responded has been like the guy who was here last week."

"Oooh, he was creepy," Sam admitted. "It was bad enough when he asked if there was a brothel at the South Pole, but then..."

"I just about called the police and told them to search his crawlspace," Lori finished. "We can't afford to send freaks into the field, or people who screw around and drink vodka and accomplish nothing. We need at least one who will actually work."

Sam heaved a deep sigh, hugging his laptop to his chest. "Lou doesn't even want me to go to Canada. He thinks I'll freeze to death or get stuck."

"He just wants to keep you here so he can drive you nuts. Want to know about his latest obsession?" Without leaving out a detail, but lowering her voice slightly in case any undergrads happened to be around, Lori described what had happened that morning in the BSL-3.

She had forgotten how squeamish Sam was, and his eyes got bigger and bigger as she spoke. He finally pulled over a plastic chair and sat down heavily. "Oh my God, Barrow," he breathed. "That's scarier than hell. Now I want to go to the Arctic just to get away from the green mouse brain."

"We thought Oriol might have done it," she suggested.

"Don't be dense," Sam exclaimed. "If Oriol had done it, he wouldn't have left it in the garbage for you to find. That mouse sneaked in, drank your virus, and it went straight to his brain and he died horribly." He turned to leave and emitted a bloodcurdling scream.

Lou's face was visible through a crack in the door. His mouth was covered with foam, and he was making a very convincing low, choked growl. After pausing for a maniacal laugh, he pushed the door open and wheeled in, cappuccino cup held in his teeth. "I've been thinking," he announced, taking a long drink from his coffee as if it were the elixir of life and picking up more foam. No matter how hot the weather was, he declared any form of iced coffee an abomination. "*Rabies.*"

Sam had backed up against the opposite wall, no doubt certain that his boss had finally snapped, but Lori understood right away. It was what had been worrying her since this morning. "It's true that rabies virus goes straight for the brain. It's also true that that lab is full of vials of frozen rabies. And that mouse was acting pretty strange before it died."

Lou squinted suspiciously at her. "You said it staggered. What else?"

"Well... it bit Kathy."

"Kathy who?" he demanded quickly.

"Greenwood, you know, the new—"

"—The mathematician I found and hired because she works on the Standard Model? What was she doing in that lab to begin with? And please, by whatever's holy, tell me it bit her through two pairs of gloves."

Lori sighed, really not wanting to have to endure what she knew was coming, but she told them everything anyway.

There was a long silence when she had finished.

"Nice one, Killer," said Sam at last. "The university's first female math professor, and you've murdered her already."

"Now, wait," Lori protested, the hyperbole bringing her back to reason. "Kathy's not dead yet, or even green. I might advise her to get rabies shots, but only if we find evidence of rabies in the lab."

"But how would we find it?" wondered Lou.

"We should test the mouse brain," Lori began slowly, thinking, "and we should steal some of Oriol's cells from the incubator and test them, too. If there's rabies virus there, someone had to grow it and clone in the fluorescent protein—it's not just going to happen by chance."

"Why not?" Lou demanded, in a voice that showed he was trying to catch her in a contradiction. "Can you tell me how our virus works?"

"Well, sure," Lori began, wondering if the dogma in biology was going to get her into trouble. "We have three separate plasmids—pieces of DNA—that encode different parts of the virus. One makes the genome, one makes some of the internal structure and enzymes, and the third one makes the envelope. All the pieces pack into the envelope to make the working virus."

"Right. And how do the other things get into the envelope?"

"Well...the genome has a packing sequence on it, so that it stays in the form of RNA and gets bundled up without being transcribed into proteins."

"Bundled up into any old envelope that happens to be floating there?" Lou drained his coffee cup and tossed it into the trash, wiping a couple of stray drops off his *Entropy Isn't What It Used To Be* T-shirt.

"Yuck!" groaned Sam. "If there happens to be rabies around, the genome goes right inside like some kind of biohazardous hermit crab, and now you have HIV in a rabies coat? Ew. Ew. Ew."

"That's extremely unlikely," Lori insisted. "Even if the rabies viruses were just lying around and happened to infect our dish of cells, there would be a lot fewer rabies coats than our usual coat protein. If someone has been making a huge amount of rabies coats in the same incubator, though, then all bets are off."

"So how do we know if someone's been doing that?" Lou asked.

"With PCR—the polymerase chain reaction."

"Right," Lou agreed eagerly, showing his pointy teeth in an evil grin. "Where do we do this, though? There's no room in the BSL-3 for all this stuff."

"Nope. And that's my news for you guys," said Lori calmly. "Because we won this grant, the Life Sciences Center is giving us the entire third floor of the complex for our wet labs and microscopy. I've already ordered a dozen PCR machines."

"Barrow, you're a genius!" cried Lou, clapping once. "I knew you could do it!"

"She's not smiling," Sam warned, backing away from both of them.

"Yeah, you're right." Lou squinted in Lori's direction. "So what's the catch?"

"The catch is that the NASA inspectors are coming next week to check up on our results," Lori admitted. "And if we don't have anyone working there yet, we're in big trouble."

Just then here was a knock on the door, and it took two shouted invitations from all of them before a young man of ineffable nerdiness shuffled in. He was almost medium height, but his hunched posture and scrawny shoulders made him appear shorter, and he had bristly, tabby-patterned fur on his upper lip as if he had just eaten a kitten. "Um, I'm David Snavel," he informed them in a timorous voice. "The postdoctoral candidate from NYU? I'm looking for Dr. Barrow or Dr. Maupertuis." He did a better job than most with Lou's last name.

Sam grinned and pointed at his two supervisors one at a time. "That's one, and that's the other."

David looked taken aback, unsure of whether he was less shy around a girl or a guy in a wheelchair. To be safe he split the difference, looking between the two professors at a spot somewhere on the wall.

Lou and Lori peeked sideways at each other, suddenly shy themselves. They were nerds too.

Lori started sneezing, so Lou apparently decided he had to speak. "Well," he declared finally, "I just have one question. Have you ever wanted to kill someone and hide his body in a glacier?"

Lori and Sam snickered, remembering the creepy candidate from last week, but of course poor David was completely at a loss. "Um... well, I don't think so?" he responded, as if unconvinced that this was the right answer.

"Good," said Lou. "Then you're hired."

FIVE: THE CASE OF THE MISSING MOUSE BRAIN

"BARROW! MY BRAIN IS gone!"

The cord to the old black phone stretched dangerously as Lori rolled over in bed and peeked at the clock through her eyelashes, refusing to wake up. It was 1:20; she'd been asleep for just over an hour, and she had to teach at 8:30. "Yeah, that's about right," she murmured, hoping the shrill ring hadn't awakened the rest of the House.

"Seriously." Lou's whisper was almost drowned out by the airflow of the containment hood. There he was, using a cell phone in the BSL-3 again. "Somebody took the mouse brain."

"Who would take your vile green mouse brain?" Lori mumbled, but she was becoming more alert. "Did you check the sign-in sheet for the biosafety lab? Anyone who uses the lab without signing in is in big trouble."

"There's no one besides us in the morning and then you again two hours later. Did you run the autoclave?" He barely waited for her to assent before he breathed a sigh of relief. "Good. I didn't want to rummage through that stuff. Yuck."

"Especially since the mouse brain wouldn't be good for much if it had been baked at 121 degrees C for two hours." Lori sat up, finally awake. "Look, Lou, maybe it fell behind the containment hood. Things roll back there all the time."

"I know," he said darkly. "I lifted the aluminum cover and saw some horrible things—but no mouse brain. I think you-know-who took it."

"Oriol Ortiz? Assuming he did, do you think it's to cover up or to publish?"

Lou was silent for a moment, then laughed. "I hope he publishes it! He doesn't need to sneak around to do that—it's not as if we care if our names are on a mouse brain paper."

"I know, but that's just how he is. He lies to me about everything." She sighed and swung her legs over the edge of the bed. "Should I run over there and see if there's someplace you haven't thought to look?"

"If you don't mind," Lou replied eagerly.

There were lots of night owls at America's most prestigious science university, so Lori had to wend her way past a sprawl of Buboes as she exited her apartment through the common area. Some were doing homework already, on this first night of term, but most were debating the scientific plausibility of the plot devices in an old *Star Trek* movie. She thought about interrogating them about the mouse brain, but decided it was premature. Best not to get the Buboes riled up about nothing.

Pasteur House opened into a grove of olive trees and a small Zen garden, no doubt intended to soothe the savage beasts within. Fully one hundred percent of Buboes registered as physics majors when they entered, and eighty percent left with a degree in physics. The other twenty percent switched into biology or went the way of madness, drug abuse, suicide, or painful performance art designed to convey to the world how much it hurt to be a misunderstood geek.

The role of the professors, the grad students, and the administration was to make sure that the successful eighty percent left without significant damage to their bodies or criminal records, and by and large they succeeded. After a tumultuous four years of pranks and classes and competitions, ninety percent of successful graduates went on to finish PhDs. Of those, a few select few came back to stay. Lori was one of sixteen faculty members, half of them in physics, to have been a Pasteur House Bubo. She was also the youngest by almost twenty years, which she thought reflected on the declining quality of the university's physics department on every level. She wasn't alone in thinking that; alumni donations to the department had fallen by half over the past decade.

She was a big part of the problem, too, contaminating the purity of the physics department with viruses and mice. A few people had even objected to her being den mother to the Buboes since she was no longer a "real" physicist.

The sad thing was that she saw their point. But who else would take the job?

The walkways by the dorms were deserted, and only the bright lights in the Chemistry building testified to the graduate students' hard work. The campus gardens gave off a cool sweet scent, as if the flowers were recovering from the heat of the day by releasing their perfume once the sun went down. Bullfrogs—or were they escaped *Xenopus* from the biology labs?—croaked in the ponds, sitting on fat lily pads that almost choked the water with their leaves and flowers.

Nostrils full of calm, fragrant air, she recoiled in disgust from the pestilential reek of the autoclave. It was open to the vestibule, but whoever had opened it hadn't bothered to take the bags to the biohazard disposal box next door.

Two bags. Without bothering to dress for the confinement lab, she peeked in the door and announced, "OK, you're right. Someone else was here. I only autoclaved the bag in the hood, not the one by the microscope."

Lou was using a broom to sweep out stuff that had fallen behind the incubators. He had a small pile of plastic tubes, but no mouse brain. "I told you someone took it! Now you know I'm not crazy."

She'd come this far, so Lori pulled on her lab coat and booties and entered the lab. All she could do was confirm that the rocker where she'd put the brain was indeed empty, and there was no obvious nook or cranny where a tube that size could have rolled. It was hard even to think it might be a Bubo prank—why would Buboes run the autoclave? Only four people knew the secret of shutting the ancient rusty autoclave door: two of them were in the room right now, and one was Lori's student, Walter Waddles IV. Even if she would otherwise have suspected him, Walter was currently in DC at a conference. The fourth, of course, was Oriol.

"At least the floor is clean now," Lou grumbled, sweeping the tubes into an autoclave bag.

"Change your gloves quick," Lori advised. "That looks like that stuff from fifty years ago."

"I kind of have a sore throat," he admitted. "Is that a symptom of yellow fever or rabies?"

"Either or both." She noticed that he looked pale and exhausted. "Did you drive in?"

"No." He put the trash bag with the sweepings next to the microscope, where their previously half-full autoclave bag had been before it was taken by the mystery intruder. "I was afraid the engine would wake Abby."

"If you didn't date a science-hating lawyer, you wouldn't have to sneak out to do experiments in the middle of the night," Lori scoffed.

"If I wasn't dating someone from the legal office, we wouldn't get our safety protocols approved so quickly," he countered.

"So you do actually like her, or are you a whore for the cause?"

Lori regretted her question when Lou just shook his head and murmured "No idea" in a faraway tone, as if speaking of an event long ago. They were both silent for a moment, listening to the crickets, and then he pulled open the door, bending to inspect the rubber gasket as if he expected it to be chewed by mouse teeth.

Lori had only her coat and booties to remove. She put them with the clean clothes, since she hadn't touched anything, and then waited for Lou. He did everything in order of contamination: the first pair of gloves into the biohazard trash, then his lab coat onto the semi-contaminated rack (to be worn only in the containment lab), then he transferred into his everyday wheelchair. It was his own rule to have a separate chair that he used only in the BSL-3 and that he would never touch without gloves on; as he put it, "Everything that falls on that floor ends up on my hands. Ew." When he was done touching anything potentially infectious, he took off the last pair of gloves, wadded them into the trash, and sprayed his hands with disinfectant.

They both sneezed upon emerging into the clear windy night. Lou looked so tired that Lori asked, "Do you want me to borrow the Bubo Wagon and give you a ride?"

He shielded his eyes as if something were falling from the sky. "I'm looking for the flying pigs," he explained. "Did you just offer to drive a motor vehicle?"

"I *do* know how to drive, you know," Lori snorted. "And Pasteur House has a car for emergencies."

"It's hardly an emer—" *sneeze* "—gency. I just have a little cold." He took a deep breath, banishing the stench of infected air and burnt plastic. "I love this campus. Everything is so—"

"Green?"

Lou doubled over in coughing fit. When he sat up, his pants were spattered with blood.

"Oh, yuck." Lori dug in her pockets for a tissue. "Wipe your nose."

"What? You expect me to put that on my mucous membranes after it's been inside that pus lab? Ugh!" Instead, he chose to wipe his nose with his bare arm, leaving a trail of goo.

"Oh yeah, that's a lot more sanitary, I'm sure." Lori used the tissues herself, sneezing a few times before she started walking up the ramp past the library. "Are we ready to do our PCR yet?"

"Not really." He cleaned his arm on his pants before

following. "This sounds dumb, but I'm actually not sure how to start."

"What do you mean?"

Lou sneezed. "The polymerase chain reaction works because DNA has two strands, each complementary, so it encodes its own copy. You separate the pieces of DNA by heating them up, and then copy the strands using a polymerase enzyme and free bases—those are the A, C, G, and T. Then you separate them again, and so on, so you amplify two to the nth times for n cycles." He paused at the top of the little hill by the library to catch his breath and draw DNA strands in the air. "What I don't understand is how you get that complementary piece to the known sequence, from rabies or whatever?"

"You order it from the facility on campus, from the woman with the terrible tremor," Lori explained, amazed somehow that Lou had never done PCR. "It's called a `primer,' it costs three dollars, and it takes a day to get it."

"Oh boy!" Lou exclaimed. "So I could get primers for all sorts of gnarly diseases?"

"Sure, why not?" Lori wanted to laugh, even though she was a little bit worried about his mental state. "Then if you die, I'll give them to the doctors who take out your brain tumor so they can test it for stuff in our lab."

"Ha, ha, Barrow, you asshole." He started chasing her down the ramp, but he was not going as quickly as usual. She barely needed to jog to stay ahead of him.

She was happy to have a convert to her human-powered vehicle obsession, but she didn't want to kill him. She wasn't even sure if any of her hand-powered bikes made the three-mile climb to his house any easier. "So, what device do you want?" she wondered. "And should I come along?"

"That thing with the battery is good," Lou suggested. "And you can come along if you have a funny vehicle, too. Maybe the unicycle?"

"Oh no! I'm *so* over that. I almost got creamed three times trying to get downtown." She thought for a moment. "I have the off-road rollerblades. I don't even know if they work."

"Perfect!" Lou laughed cheerfully, as if it weren't two in the morning with a missing green mouse brain. He waited outside while she went in to the human-powered-vehicle club storeroom; when she came out, he'd wiped the blood off his nose and arm, and looked OK again.

He attached his "device," which was a crank with twelve gears attached to a BMX wheel with a battery underneath, while Lori sat on the walkway and put on her skates. She had designed them herself—they had only two wheels each, inflatable and bumpy, conceived for fire roads but completely untested. Just in case, she shoved her running shoes into her messenger bag.

There was no one on the tree-lined road that led east from campus through the movie-star neighborhood, and still no one on the side street that headed north up the hill. Once they crossed the main avenue through town, there were no longer any streetlights, so Lori pulled out a headlamp for each of them. It was really just an excuse to rest her increasingly chewed-up feet.

"How are the skates?" asked Lou.

"Kind of horrid, actually," she panted. "The wheels rub against the frame."

"What? No five-thousand-foot mountains this weekend?"

"Not like this." She kicked the front wheel into the sidewalk in some vain attempt to loosen it up, then started off again.

Lou was giggling. He was just pretending he liked this so he could watch her suffer. *What an asshole*, she thought. *After he got me out of bed, too.* "Next time wait until after dawn to call me about mouse brains, all right? Have you ever even used the cryoslicer?"

"No, but I was going to follow your lab book."

"The hardest part with brains is lining the axis up right," Lori commented. "If you cut off-axis, you can't tell what you're looking at."

"So how do you get the mouse brain to sit on one of those aluminum holders in the first place?"

"Superglue." Lori imagined herself trying to explain this on the phone in the middle of the night. "A drop on the cerebellum and a drop on the olfactory lobes."

He snickered as if that were a joke, but burst out laughing when he realized she meant it. "Science! We do some weird shit, don't we?"

"To think, a year ago you were a pure theorist." Lori waited at the eternal traffic light of Washington Street, wondering how she was going to say this. Finally she asked, "Do you mind a bit of criticism?"

"No, of course not," he responded, as if surprised.

She was flattered. The only other person he'd taken advice from was Solomon Rose, who had the Nobel Prize. "OK— you're driving your students nuts."

"They're driving *me* nuts!" cried Lou with excessive vehemence. "They don't do anything. You do realize that I'm now the only un-tenured member of the department? Every dumb thing they do is a nail in the coffin of my career."

"You just need to micro-manage a little more." The light finally turned green and she fought the sticky axles to get rolling again. "Experimentalists aren't like theorists. You can't say 'Go away and come back when you have cool data.' They need a lot of hand-holding."

Lou upshifted fast, too many times, until he could barely turn the crank at all, then swore as he downshifted. "But I'm in the lab all the time!" he grouched. "They can come find me when the bulb is burned out, rather than waiting two weeks until I discover it for myself."

"I don't know what to say," Lori shrugged. "That's just how

it is. If they were as good as we are, they'd have our jobs, so you just have to learn to deal with it."

Lou made a grumbling noise like a dog about to start barking. "I can't stand working with idiots who can't do anything. How can you be too stupid to change a light bulb?"

"They're not stupid—in most cases—they're just scared. And if you act stressed, they get more scared."

They were already most of the way up the hill. It was cool and quiet and the air smelled clean and floral. Sometimes being awake in the wee hours had its privileges. Neither spoke as they navigated the last long block, which was the steepest, rolling to a stop just under the farthest branches of Lou's carob tree. The perfume of his clump of kahili ginger filled the air, and their headlamps shone off the silvery fronds of the jelly palm.

"Bleah!" Lou put his hands on his head, waiting for his breathing to slow before he spoke. "I *am* stressed. Solomon Rose was supposed to do all of the recruiting and bureaucracy, and leave us to do the science—and then he quit."

"That could have been predicted. He was over eighty years old." Lori worried suddenly that she was supposed to play the role of mentor. She had a few years' more experience than Lou, but she'd only recently become an experimentalist herself, and the ink on her own tenure letter was still drying.

"And he left me to teach his class." Lou laughed nervously. "General Relativity was legendary. All the theory students are going to throw tomatoes at me."

"How do you think I feel? I'm now the effectively the leader of the department. None of the others do any research."

"Yeah, but at least the arrogant Nobel-Prize assholes we're trying hire won't get to vote on *you*."

Lori sighed. He sounded exactly the way she had eight months before. "All right, all right, go ahead and panic. It's natural. But you can't give up now that you have everything."

"Including—" He sniffed, then sneezed, spattering his pants once more with blood. "—rabies."

Lori had a sudden vision of Lou on an autopsy table, green neurons pouring out of the top of his head. "Take care of yourself. Get some sleep."

"Yeah." He glanced down at his pants. "Do you think it's safe to get into bed with Abby? She'll be annoyed if I'm not there when she wakes up."

For once, Lori repressed any number of sarcastic comments about the hazards of Abby. "I'd throw your clothes into the washer with hot water and some bleach," she advised. "Bleach will kill viruses very fast. I really have to go to bed now. Do you want to keep the device?"

"Sure. The long wheelbase is useful on the downhill." He wiped his nose, coughed. "Goddamn it, I am so fucking tired."

About to turn around, Lori came a little closer instead, and spoke in a low voice. "If you have any weird symptoms—I mean, anything that's different from a cold—just let me know, OK?"

He grimaced in disgust. "Do you know something you're not telling me?"

"No, I don't," she exclaimed. "I promise. I've just never had nosebleeds like this, and now yours is doing it, too."

"It's the Santa Ana wind," he replied, voice sounding a little desperate. "The Santa Ana and a cold. Christ, Barrow, thanks for scaring me to death." Sneezing one more time, he pedaled off.

As soon as he was safely onto the sidewalk, Lori spun around and headed back to a few hours of oblivion among the Buboes. Unlike all her usual speedskates, these were fine on the downhill—slow enough that she never had to brake or crash into the grass.

All of her undergraduates were still awake, of course, so before going into her apartment Lori let them know that there was a missing mouse brain in an orange-capped polyethylene tube upon which the reputation of the physics department might depend.

SIX: DOUBLE AGENTS

WHEN LOU EMAILED THE next morning to say he was too sick to come in to work, Lori called the Centers for Disease Control.

It rang once, and then she hung up, realizing how silly she would sound. It was still just a cold, even if her desk was splattered with blood from the relentless sneezing. She wanted to go back to bed herself, but there was too much to do; now that they'd finally succeeded in hiring a postdoc, the last thing she wanted was for him to run screaming from a mystery BSL-3 disease. She swallowed a few cold pills and tried to look perky as she went to meet with the latest addition to their team.

It didn't help that the words *Have You Seen Me?* stared down over the conference room—with, naturally, a picture of a mouse brain.

Fortunately it was a normal pinkish brain color. "Did you guys do this?" Lori inquired, hiding a cough behind a fake laugh.

Sam shook his head with exaggerated innocence. The new postdoc, David Snavel, just looked blank—as well he ought, since he'd only been there for two days.

It was much too hot and sunny of a day to think of Eureka, Canada, but she started describing it all the same for David's benefit. At more than 80 degrees North latitude, the settlement, if it could even be called that, was on a fjord at the western edge of Ellesmere Island, right near the very top of the landmass before the polar ice caps began. Farther north than Svalbard, farther north than the highest point in Siberia, Eureka had only two permanent residents but as many as fifteen researchers who stayed for extended periods in winter. The astronomy and physics laboratory there had been well-funded in the nineties but had fallen into disrepair, with nothing but an old building and a bunch of broken spectrometers covered with plastic tarps to keep off the endless Arctic dust.

Sam had spent all summer collecting instruments to help fix up the station and do some of the experiments Lori had planned before she left Canada. She had just been funded for her first experimental project in the Canadian High Arctic when Roger died, and she could no longer face so much as another month in Montreal. Thanks to her old advisors, she had an open offer at STI that she'd been refusing for two years—so she'd suddenly stopped refusing, dropped off her parkas at the Salvation Army, and taken off for Southern California without so much as cleaning out her office. It had been just over a year, and she had not been back, nor did she have any intention of ever returning for any reason. "Your goal is to make my colleagues forgive me for quitting," she told them bluntly. "No one expected me to just pack up and leave, but, well, that's what I did, and left a lot of things hanging."

She showed them where everything was packed, emphasizing where all of the instructions and user manuals were arranged in their own separate baggies. They would have contact with the outside world only by iridium phone.

If she'd had time, she would have made them put everything together and take it apart again, to demonstrate they knew how—but of course there was never enough time to do things right. She felt as if she were speaking to pair of kittens, with Sam indifferent and sullen and David making idiotic jokes. He wouldn't shut up about the poster, so finally she tore it down, crumpled it into a ball, and threw it into the trash.

"I need to talk to Lou before I go," Sam insisted. "He'll kill me if I don't finish this paper."

"He's out sick. Call him on the phone."

"What's wrong with him?"

"Nothing too serious. He's kind of irritable and has a sore throat... Not drinking much."

It took a second for Sam to catch on, but then he got mad and kicked a Pelican case. "Dammit, Barrow, you're such a Bubo! The safety office goes on and on about keeping Buboes out of the pus lab, and then there you are giving people rabies."

"It wasn't me, it was the guy Lou calls That Bastard—" She stopped herself and clapped her hand over her mouth. Standing just inside the door, where he must have slipped in unnoticed sometime in the last few minutes, was Oriol Ortiz.

Oriol was tall and tanned and muscular, kind of a Miguel Indurain in glasses and an impeccable white lab coat, with a large crest of black hair moussed back over his head. "I am looking for Louis," he said in his Barcelona accent, which everyone had learned not to refer to as a "Spanish" accent in case, God forbid, someone were to infer that Oriol was Mexican. He despised all North Americans for the way they butchered their official languages, almost as much as he loathed the teeming hordes of what he called "Eurotrash."

"He's out with a cold today," said Lori.

"Well, I am not available tomorrow," Oriol griped. "Are you sure it's just a cold?"

Yeah, you tell me, Lori thought. "Well, I suppose he could be out with green fluorescent protein," she replied sarcastically.

Oriol looked down his perfect Roman nose as though she were the biggest fool ever to usurp the title of doctor. "I just meant that Louis doubtless suffers from complications of his spinal cord injury of which you are not aware," he sneered.

"There's nothing wrong with Lou of which I'm not aware," Lori replied, "unless it has something to do with what *you*'ve been doing in the BSL-3."

Oriol looked her up and down as if searching for the right insult, but collected himself in time. "We work with the same viral vector," he responded smoothly. "Could you please ask

Louis to contact me as soon as possible." He spun on his heel, lab coat billowing, and stalked out.

"He was *so* spying on us," Lori muttered.

"Think he took the mouse brain?" asked Sam.

"More importantly, did he turn it green in the first place?" She could hear shuffling outside the door. "We know you're listening, so why don't you just come in?" she called in a loud voice.

The door opened, but it wasn't Oriol—it was Kathy. "Oh," the mathematician stammered, glancing around the room as if expecting someone. "I'm sorry to interrupt. I just thought we were going to finish my lab training."

"Good, so you don't need me," rejoiced Sam, who suddenly sounded as if he were from New York. "I'm off." He gathered up his duffel bag, expedition backpack, and Pelican case, and so burdened, walked slowly from the room.

David Snavel stayed standing among all his gear, watching Kathy with his eyes wide. Kathy was all prepared for her next molecular biology lesson. She had a cloth shopping bag filled with XS gloves, the smallest possible cleanroom booties, and her own hairnets—black, of course. "I practiced at home," she admitted. "I put grape juice into a Petri dish and carried it around."

"Why grape juice?" Lori wanted to know.

"So I could see where it spilled. But come to think of it, I made a mess on the carpet."

Lori peered into the bag. "Have you written your safety protocol yet? I don't think I even know exactly what you want to do."

Kathy nodded, squared her shoulders, and launched into what sounded like a speech. She claimed to be interested in the kinetics of viral binding and entry into cells, and especially of how HIV got into the nucleus of a non-dividing cell, such as a neuron. "Your lab is almost unique in the country, you know," she praised, face flushing. "You have the facilities to handle the viruses, the cultured neurons, and the optics to do fast imaging."

They'd only had the cultured neurons for a couple of months, so Lori was instantly suspicious. "How'd you know about this?"

"A guy with a funny name told me at the new faculty retreat," Kathy replied. She obviously could tell Lori wasn't satisfied with that response, so she added, "Sparrow or Wren or something."

"Oriol," Lori corrected, trying not to laugh at the idea of what he would do if they all started calling him Sparrow. "Without the 'e.' Look, Kathy—that lab is a mess. I need to clean it up before anyone new starts using it. I'm sorry. Can you come and find me next week?"

Kathy looked much more bummed than she should have, given that she had classes to teach and research to do. "But you said—"

"I don't care what I said!" Lori pulled a tissue from her sleeve and sneezed into it. "I don't have time right now. And frankly, I don't really buy your story. Why don't you go do some math?"

Sneezing again, she stomped out, hearing an "*Ooooh....*" from David Snavel behind her and then a series of whispers and giggles. She didn't care. She was going to talk to the safety office about the BSL-3 and then go sleep for a long, long time.

She cursed the incestuousness of their tiny school as the safety officer referred her to Absinthe McRae. Abby was everything Lori didn't want to deal with. She was the administrator on Lori's NASA grant. She had been an enemy from their first year of graduate school. If that wasn't enough, she was sleeping with Lou.

Abby and Lou had traveled together to Denver for business last year. They'd left hissing and spitting at each other, and returned making goo-goo eyes. Lori found this less ironic than just plain creepy. What could an avowed physicist-hater possibly see in a guy who was the biggest physics geek west of the Charles?

Naturally, Abby made her wait all afternoon for an appointment, too. Lori tried to rest at her desk, but if she put her head down, her sinuses immediately filled with something hot and viscous. She wondered if Lou had had the chance to figure out what a "primer" was and design a few for their experiments—she had some ideas for what she wanted to look at besides rabies and green fluorescent protein. But she never got around to sending him a message, what with people in and out of her office all day and repeated futile attempts to clear her head with drops, pills, and lozenges.

She made no effort to hide her sorry state in front of Abby, who went "Eeew" and sat at the opposite end of the long table in the legal office, keeping two meters between herself and Lori. "Why aren't you in bed?" Abby demanded.

"Because..." Lori sneezed, but before she could reach for her tissue, Abby slid a huge box down the table to her. Lori imagined that Abby saw just as many tears in her office as they did in Physics. "Because this is what I wanted to talk to you about," she managed at last.

"Huh?" Abby rolled her bright green eyes all the way up until only the whites showed. "Your gross head cold?"

"It's just that—" Lori plugged her nose with a tissue to stop the dripping. "I'm worried about that BSL-3 lab. It's a disgusting mess and there are too many people using it. It's full of viruses whose properties we don't even know for sure. So what if someone has a cold, and the cold virus recombines with some experimental construct, and we all end up expressing green fluorescent protein?"

"Is that bad?" Abby wondered.

"It could be. A lot of these viruses can cause allergic reactions or even cancer."

"Hm." Abby was out of her element, and it showed. "Is

that even possible? Wouldn't you have to be working with something similar to a cold virus?"

"Maybe. But I'm not even sure any more who's working with what. Oriol Ortiz has about ten people going in there, and none of them have had my safety training—I tried to insist, but he told me I was wrong about sterile technique and shouldn't even wear gloves!"

"Isn't every virus you work with required to be listed on the door?" Abby seemed a bit uncertain.

"Well, yes, in principle it is. But I don't trust Oriol or his students."

Abby stopped looking concerned and put on an infuriating little smirk. "Have you seen Ortiz's lab?"

"His main lab? No. Why?"

"It's immaculate. We just had a press conference there, and you could *eat* off those benchtops." Abby lowered her voice. "He also runs the place with an iron fist. Those students aren't going to do anything without his say-so. I'm not saying I approve of this approach, but..."

Lori glanced up, forgetting her misery. "So maybe he's forcing them to do something unethical."

Abby's confiding tone snapped off like a light switch, and the smirk returned. "I think *you're* the one who's had problems with trainees running wild. Not to mention that you live with Buboes, and you were one yourself not all that long ago. You do know what happened in 1974, right? The undergrads thought it was just some pink liquid, and it was really—"

"Rabies virus, yes, I know." Lori sighed, which made her cough. "I've not seen any sign of Buboes getting in, and I have only one student who uses that lab."

Abby tapped the table. "Walter W. Waddles IV?"

"Right. And you know if he did anything wrong, his whole family would be down on him. His grandfather is the Dean of Students. It's not my lab that's the problem."

"No, but it's your name that's on the door, so you're responsible." Abby stood up dismissively. "Why did you come to see me about it? Just clean the place."

"I think we need to do more than that. The safety office should put a sign on the door and then we can sterilize the whole room and start again. Autoclave all the cells and viruses and bleach every surface."

It was a reasonable recommendation, but to Lori's astonishment Abby's eyes grew large with what looked like terror. She collapsed back into her overstuffed armchair with a squeak that could have come from the leather or her attempt at speech. "You don't..." she began, and drew a long breath. "Do you have any idea what this university did to recruit Ortiz?"

Curious again, Lori sat up straight and listened, arranging her face into what she hoped was a look of innocence as she shook her head.

Abby planted her hands on the table. "Well. I figured you'd know this. Superstars like Dr. Ortiz don't just leave Boston and come out here for nothing. One of his absolute requirements was a BSL-3 lab. They're building a whole new one next door, but for now your lab is all he has, and he has several grant reviews and site visits coming up. There's no way we can shut that place down for even a day."

"Fine. Let him be responsible, then."

"Sorry. The room belongs to Physics, and honestly—is there anyone else in Physics even remotely qualified to deal with rabies and HIV?"

Lori was reaching the end of her patience. "Oh, so that's why Oriol thinks I'm his personal cleaning service?"

Abby's mirthless grin was downright evil. "It's hard not being the only superstar in town, isn't it?"

"My grant's still bigger than his," Lori muttered.

"Yes, and as I recall, you also have a site visit coming up. Maybe you should worry about that and not about a little sneezing." She stood up again, and Lori knew it was time to leave.

"That's what I'm trying to do," she admitted, struggling to her feet, "but my team is all getting sick. If I were you, I would avoid kissing Lou for a while."

"I'll do that," Abby agreed, and Lori couldn't tell if she was being sarcastic or not. "If only because I'm leaving for Clonic this afternoon, because I appear to be the only one who cares about Claudine St-Pierre."

Before this could turn into a lecture, Lori nodded politely, replaced the box of tissues, and at last headed back across campus to her apartment.

SEVEN: A THIEF IN THE NIGHT

LOU WAS USED TO being stared at in the gym. Usually it didn't bother him—the tech geeks just wanted to check out his arm bike and the ergometer that Lori had made for him at the human-powered vehicle club. But that person in the corner had pale eyes glued on him, staring and then hiding back behind a pillar, then peeking out again. Wanting to concentrate on his intervals, Lou closed his eyes and pedaled, willing the exercise to burn out the last remnants of his fever. But in the near emptiness of the gym it was hard to ignore whoever it was, growing nearer, breathing a bit stuffy.

At least let me finish my zone 3 interval before you talk, Lou thought, but when the voice came, he immediately forgot all about the workout. The pedals spun slowly to a stop with his hands still attached.

"I can get you a green mouse brain," it said.

Lou opened one eye, squinting in the direction of the voice. It was Kathy the mathematician, clearly not here to work out, swathed as she was in black fleece and Doc Martens.

"You know where it is?" he hissed over the sound of the decelerating flywheel.

"Oh, yeah, there's a whole bunch of them!" she cried for the whole room to hear. "That guy, Oriol, he has a roomful—"

"Oh my God, shhh! Not here!" He pushed some buttons on the bike, making it beep, hoping no one had heard. There were only a few people here, but he didn't know any of them. The NASA visitors for the inspection next Monday could be on the next treadmill, for all he knew. Was she an idiot? "I'm going swimming," he declared, hoping she'd get the hint to follow, though she'd have to pass through the women's locker room first and at least take off her shoes.

The pool, as nearly always during the semester, was deserted except for the lifeguard, who waved at him cheerily. Lou's first instinct was to avert his eyes, since the gym had apparently hired a cross-dressing lunatic to keep people from drowning. Then he recognized the kid, a junior from their department, and realized that his pink miniskirt must be an homage to the dearly departed Tutu Man.

One of the campus's most enduring legends, the Tutu Man had sued the university for intellectual property theft back in the twenties and won. For the next eighty years he couldn't be fired, and wandered from classroom to classroom wearing a vintage women's bathing suit and swim sandals, accosting people at random intervals to tell them about his inventions—one of which, apparently, was the outfit. As he approached his hundredth birthday, campus legend also held that he was immortal. Sadly, he was not, and he had died the year before Lou was hired.

Somehow Lou didn't think that the tan, buff twenty-year-old lifeguard quite captured the effect—but it was a nice try. He waved back, somewhat guiltily, knowing that the guy was failing vector calculus and that some member of the faculty would have to tell him he couldn't be a physics major.

The water looked blue and sparkly and cold; he dipped his fingers in to make sure it was heated to its usual 78 degrees before plunging in, sinking nearly to the bottom and as usual fighting panic at how the buoyancy of the water made him feel as if his lower half had simply disappeared. He gulped a mouthful before he managed to paddle his way to the top and hold on to the edge. He'd give Kathy five minutes before he started swimming.

But in less than thirty seconds, she was there, still with all her clothes on. She sat cross-legged by the edge and bent over to speak. In the reflection of the water, her eyes were oddly colorless; he wondered if she were wearing contacts.

"Oriol Ortiz has a secret room so he can infect the mice and not have to take them back to the Mouse House," she half-whispered. "It's in…"

"I don't want to know! I shouldn't even be hearing this. Don't you know who I'm dating?"

"Yes, and she's out of town."

Damn this place, he thought. *A thousand busybodies with IQs of 180.* "How do you know their brains are green?"

"Oh, they're green all right. Ten o'clock tonight in the pus lab?" She leaned in so close that he could see the rubber bands on her teeth. "And *don't* tell Lori."

It was a difficult request. He'd been out for two days, and Lori had all sorts of things for him to do. She'd been sick, too, and they were both scrambling to get the new lab in order for the NASA visit and to put together their presentations.

Also, just by looking at his face, Lori could tell that something was up and stayed stubbornly in her office all evening. Lou could hear her through the shared wall of their offices— typing, printing, sometimes cursing at her computer. It was past eight when he finally decided he had to leave to throw her off the track, but he didn't want to go home, where he'd probably find himself confessing to Abby on the phone.

So, after a bowl of pho and a strong coffee in town, he took refuge on the biology floor of the library and tried to understand some things.

It had been a long time since he'd looked at paper journals, but some of the articles he wanted went further back than the on-line archives. They were bound into large, dusty tomes, hidden far back in collapsible stacks alongside other quaint antiquities, such as *Photographic Atlas of TB* and *Surgical Injuries of the Great War*. Surprisingly—or maybe not so surprisingly—there were a lot more students here than could ever be found on the physics floor. Some were hunting for gnarly pictures, others were doing real work; a few slept fitfully in armchairs, homework piled on their bodies. Mostly they were quiet, until just a few minutes before his rendez-vous with Kathy.

"He's going to kill you," hissed a furious whisper, one stack away from where Lou was browsing *Human Gene Therapy*.

"I know." The reply came as a sob of indeterminate gender. "I can't figure out how it could have happened. It must have been during the conversion to pdf—"

"He's going to kill *all* of us." The first voice, male, trembled a little. "You'd better leave now and try to get a job flipping burgers, because once he finds out, you won't even be wel-come at the Ptomaine Palace."

"But no one saw it. I mean, it never even got sent to re-viewers. It was just the editor..."

Unable to contain his curiosity, Lou inched aside a volume of *Molecular Therapy*. He saw the marbled gray of a T-shirt, which then slid down until he was face-to-face with a wet brown eye behind a convex lens. He pushed the book back, but it was too late.

"Someone's here!" came the sobby voice (a woman, surely?) and then there came a rustle of papers, a few thumps, and scuttling of footsteps like giant sand crabs. Silence de-scended once more; no one seemed to be coming to peek into the stack and find out the identity of the spy.

They'd taken all of their books, but a few papers littered the floor. Lou picked them up one by one, checking to see if any of them had names on them. They didn't; what he saw in-stead was a pseudo-handwritten memo with the bold header

***
WELCOME TO THE ORTIZ LAB
***

Congratulations! You have been accepted into the fastest-growing and highest-impact research group at STI (which means the best in the WORLD!). I want all of you to succeed, and every one of you can be great. But remember the equation:

$$***$$
$$SUCCESS = TALENT \times EFFORT$$
$$***$$

I did not get into medical school at 18, or get my MD/PhD by 22, by working 9 to 5.

How many hours do I need to be in the lab? you may ask. Think of it this way: If I am looking for you, I expect to find you.

You can take one of Saturday OR Sunday off. The other is expected to be a normal workday. Tell me your choice at the beginning of term, and if it changes, it must be cleared with me first.

Of course, working hard does not mean that you should neglect your health. Proper nutrition and exercise are essential to health and happiness. We also all need to "unwind" once in a while. But while you are a student in the Ortiz lab, the following are strictly forbidden:

1. Binge drinking. This has been shown to kill up to one billion neurons per event! (See: Adolescent Health 8(1): 121-124)

2. Motorcycles. Where do you think our human brain tissue samples come from?

3. Dangerous sports. If there is any ambiguity, check with me first.

My trainees, from undergraduate through postdoc, have the highest rate of success at finding positions at the best universities in the world. I want every one of you to succeed and make the ORTIZ LAB proud.

It went on in this vein for several more paragraphs. *I should have known*, Lou thought, folding up the note and sticking it in his pocket. Now all he had to do was figure out which of Oriol's students was farsighted. But first, the mouse brain.

He half hoped that Kathy had just been putting him on, but she was already there in the basement, waiting outside the lab. She hadn't showed up with a mouse brain. Instead she had a live, squeaking, dashing-about mouse in a plastic cage, and no idea how to take the brain out. Lou very nearly told her to give up and go home—but all of the unanswered questions teased him. Why were the brains green? How did she know they were green? How had the first mouse ended up where it did?

Against all conscience and reason, he stayed. They sat there for almost half an hour arguing half-heartedly about whether the stolen mouse was staggering or breathing funny, knowing that they had to work up the nerve to kill it. Somehow it would be less horrible a task if it were already dying of a green brain tumor.

"Don't kittens have to learn how to do this from their mothers?" Kathy wanted to know.

"No one's asking you to bite its head off," Lou replied with a shudder, thinking that he wouldn't put it past her.

"That's probably less cruel than the mini-guillotine that Oriol uses. Then how do you get inside the skull?"

"Barrow taught me how to do that. What I don't know is how we get the brain ready for PCR." He squinted at the screen of his iPhone, searching for instructions on how to do PCR starting from something the cat dragged in.

"Oh, right. Isn't there something you add to cells to digest them?"

"Yeah, but we have the whole brain, not just cells. We'll need to squish it up somehow, and I imagine we have to do something to get all the fat out."

"A mouse brain is full of fat?" Kathy asked with eager distaste.

He was beginning to think she was very, very weird, but he had fair number of gnarly anecdotes about the CNS to share with her. "The brain is thirty percent by weight cholesterol. That's why it tastes so delicious spread on toast."

"Ew! I'm sure the GFP would add a certain *je-ne-sais-quoi* to your pâté."

Using a sterilized stylus to operate the touchpad, he typed in *Whole mouse PCR kit*. It would have been nice if Lori hadn't been excluded for unknown reasons, but if he had learned anything from her, it was that everything in molecular biology could be done with a kit.

Lou and Kathy giggled like kids looking at underwear catalogs as they scrolled through the many ways of scientifically smushing a mouse brain. You could put it in a tube with some sand and centrifuge it; you could push it through a cheesecloth-looking filter; you could sonicate it with a probe; or you could use a mortar and pestle much like the one Lou had in his kitchen.

"I vote for the tubes and sand," said Kathy.

"It sounds easy enough," Lou agreed. "Then we digest it overnight with an enzyme. We won't get to see the results before the NASA visit."

"I don't know how to do the PCR."

"First things first," said Lou, who didn't know either—although he did have a lovely sack of primers from the campus BioBar. "There's a tank of CO_2 next door that we can use to... you know." He glanced guiltily at the mouse, then picked up the cage. It was fortunate that they weren't that cute and didn't have large, soulful eyes. "All of the enzymes are in that lab, too."

They were both dreading the killing so much that it was more relief than shock to go into the cold room and find that the supply cabinet he and Lori had just stocked had been raided. The PCR tubes were down to a handful, the A, C, G, and T were nowhere to be found, and the tube of DNA polymerase was still in the freezer but sadly empty.

"Well," Kathy announced with a sleep-deprived mad giggle, "I guess someone else is illicitly screening mouse brains, too. Hopefully they're not going to show up right about now and catch us!"

"*Tabarnak*," Lou swore over the squeaking from the cage on his lap. The mouse didn't appear to like the cold room either, even though it was nowhere near so cold as it had been last year, when Lori had used it to slice Antarctic ice cores. "I'm out for two days, and the supplies are gone. What has Barrow been up to without telling me?"

"Maybe it's not Barrow," Kathy reminded him, banging open drawers one by one. "Hey! Look what I found."

She held a hot-pink cardboard box labeled *MR. GREENGENES Instant Tissue DNA Kit*. Inside was some kind of magic buffer for instant brain solubilization and all sorts of homogenizers, each individually wrapped in a sterile packet. While that would save them eight hours of enzyme digestion, it also proved beyond a doubt that someone was using this lab to do things that their NASA grant explicitly forbade, and they weren't even making the slightest effort to be discreet about it.

He was so furious he almost didn't want to continue. No one should be invading their cold lab with illegal green mice. "How can they be doing this?" he hissed. "Could it be Oriol and his gang?"

"I don't know," Kathy replied insouciantly, "but if you can go get some polymerase somewhere, I can—you know."

There was no stopping now. "You're going to murder the mouse? Without using your teeth, right?" He went over to the CO_2 tank by the electron microscope, finding the rubber tube that led from the nozzle that usually terminated with a pipette tip. This time, though, it had something that looked distressingly like a nasal cannula stuck onto it.

Despite her supposed ignorance of biology, Kathy picked up on this immediately. "I just had a terrible thought," she exclaimed, with a cackle that suggested she didn't think it was terrible at all. "What if when Oriol's injections fail, he helps people—" She gestured at the cannula.

"Off themselves?" Lou responded automatically, then froze with his hand still on the tank. "Wait. What do you know about Oriol's injections?"

"Huh?" She tried to act innocent, but he wasn't buying it, glaring at her until she continued. "Oh—well, everyone knows about that, right? He has a clinic in Mexico."

"Everyone does *not* know," he protested. "He's not licensed as a physician in the U.S. His job here is in neuroscience research, and he's allowed to do up to twenty percent time `consulting' elsewhere, but the whole business is at least a little bit sketchy. I doubt that he'd advertise among the faculty here that he's doing experimental treatments on people."

Kathy moved over towards the tank and took the hose, inspecting the cannula closely, not looking at Lou. "Well, all right. I found out about it on the Internet." She fiddled with the hose, still with her face averted. "I'm sure you know by now that I was an undergrad here, but I had to drop out and move back east to take care of my grandmother. She had Alzheimer's. It took her over ten years to die, and I kept searching, hoping there would be something..."

This was clearly a load of bullshit made up on the spot, but it didn't really matter. There was only one thing he wanted to know. "So, do you think Oriol's injections have something to do with GFP?"

She could finally meet his eye, but only briefly. "I don't know. I doubt it. I mean, he's not going to put HIV in a rabies coat into a person, is he? I thought his Mexico treatment was something else altogether."

"So did I," said Lou, but all of a sudden he was not too sure. "Anyway, he hasn't come up with any miracles yet."

"That's why he's got this!" She waved the cannula.

"In here? How would he hide the bodies?"

"I don't mean he's actually blowing CO_2 up their noses," she sighed impatiently. "But he could be giving them a kit."

The image of Oriol shrugging helplessly at dying people and handing them a final exit kit was so absurd that in spite of himself, Lou burst out laughing. "As long as he's not buying the kits with my NASA dollar, who cares?"

"Do you really mean that?"

"Yes." He snorted impatiently. Unlike Barrow, who would run the other way at the mere mention of suicide, it appeared this was one of Kathy's favorite subjects. She was even more excited about offing oneself than she was about brain squishing. "Most of his patients wouldn't have been able to do it themselves, anyway."

"Aren't you Catholic?" she pursued, looking as if she were about to pull out a notebook to record his response.

"No one in my family has been inside a church since the French Revolution," he replied dismissively. "That's enough of this shit. Don't you ever talk about what you're supposed to be working on, like non-abelian gauge theory? I'm going over to Biology to try to find some polymerase. Good luck."

He got out quickly before she could attach the cannula. Maybe he was a hypocrite, but if there was going to be a botched inhumane mouse-gassing, he didn't want to see it. He couldn't take too long, either; Barrow had said you had to cut off the head quickly because the mice often came round after carbon dioxide exposure, even if you put them into the freezer.

The problem was that it was after hours, and his ID card didn't let him into the Biology complex. For a few minutes he waited out in the increasingly chilly evening near the front door, hoping for some nocturnal grad student to wander by.

The moon was full, the sky crystal-clear, the Big Dipper lurking just at the edge of the horizon.

A tall thin figure sprinted from behind the building and through the patch of palm trees in the parking lot. Moonlight gleamed off of his white lab coat, billowing behind him like the sheet of a friendly ghost. It was a dreamy image, and for a crazy moment Lou felt as if he could spring up and run after him, disembodied and free in the light of the moon.

He smiled, enjoying the vision, until he realized he was freezing cold and still had no polymerase. He looked up some lab numbers on his phone, dialing at random until at last someone answered—one of Oriol's students.

The girl came downstairs to meet him, out of breath and nervous. She wore glasses, but they were concave; she wasn't the eye from the library. "I can only give you enough for sixteen reactions," she whispered. "I hope that's enough." She pressed a cold cup into his hand, containing a single tiny tube. "Can you bring this back tonight? Because Dr. Ortiz…"

"…is going to kill you?" he prompted when she trailed off.

"Uh huh." She nodded vigorously, chin trembling. "He threatened to fire us all over…well, I can't say. Just bring it back, OK, please, Dr. Lou?"

It was better than nothing, and they would probably fuck it up anyway, so he assured her he'd return the cup and went back to find Kathy.

The BSL-3 was quiet. Too quiet. There was no squeaking… and there was also no sound of air from the cell culture hood. The lights were off and everything was shut down.

"Kathy?" he called pointlessly, and was about to turn to leave when, as if by instinct, he flipped on the light switch just to be sure.

Kathy was sitting in a lab chair, her upper body slumped into the culture hood, with her face on the metal surface where rabies, HIV, yellow fever, contaminated culture media, and other nameless horrors were regularly spilled. The mouse cage sat next to her head, empty.

"Kathy!" Lou yelled. He shook her shoulder, got no response, then shoved his hand up the sleeve of her lab coat to feel for a pulse. It was hard to tell anything through two pairs of gloves, but the idea of removing them was horrifying. Not to mention the idea of giving her mouth-to-mouth after she'd been facedown on that bench.

When he pinched her wrist harder, it pulsed, and she drew a long, ragged breath. The pipette she'd been clutching fell from her hand and rolled under the culture hood. He didn't want to leave her in the confinement area, afraid that she'd fainted from some problem with the ventilation. His own heart seemed to be pounding, too—but maybe that was just panic. He gently tilted her backwards against the back of her chair, then turned the chair around and pushed it towards the door. It was a bit of a wrangle getting the inner door open and the lab chair over the lip, but Kathy was almost frighteningly light; she couldn't have weighed ninety pounds. He supported her head as he maneuvered her out into the vestibule, then shut the door and ripped off his gloves.

He had to rest for a few seconds, catching his breath, before he could retrieve his phone from its cubbyhole and dial 911. The whole time he kept shaking her, calling to her, urging her to breathe. He wondered if somehow she had inhaled too much carbon dioxide while trying to kill the mouse—but then why wouldn't she be next door? And for that matter, where was the mouse?

His earlier vision leapt to mind and continued to evolve—the creature bursting from its cage and transforming into a tall, thin man, disguising itself with a lab coat before tearing off at full speed across the campus. The image was so real that he checked the labeled racks, seeing if anyone's lab coat was missing from its hanger.

There was just time to notice that Walter Waddles IV's hook was empty, when sirens sounded outside the building and the pounding feet of the EMTs descended into the basement.

EIGHT: AN UNEXPECTED GUEST

MOE DEET, MOE DEET," muttered Claudine as she ambled down the path. The man was assuming the dimensions of Fate in her mind, and with that name she was not inclined to think it augured a benign one.

At least the Dreaded One had been delayed a day, apparently because his doctor had had an emergency. Abby, on the other hand, had shown up right on time to help. She'd flown in early this morning and promised to find a caterer to keep Moe provided with the organic caveman diet he had so carefully requested. As useful as she was, it was hard not to compare her unfavorably with Lori, who would have set up winches to move statues, hauled rocks in a rickshaw, and programmed a robot to sort Roger's books by title and theme. All Abby could really do was talk on the phone—and Claudine's spa was set up to be the most phone-unfriendly corner of the modern world.

She could hear Abby now from inside the office, yelling unnecessarily loudly into the old black handset. "NOT vegan, caveman... What does that mean? Darned if I know! ...Fine, send us the steaks. Somebody will eat them." The receiver clicked, and a moment later Abby came out of the garden, stretching her arms to the sky.

To the untrained eye Abby hadn't changed a bit—her surface was smooth and perfect as an egg, her hair gleamed, she was at her ideal weight, and her muscle tone was excellent. It took special perceptive abilities to note the stress lines lurking just below the epidermis, waiting to fracture at the application of some unknown pressure at some unknown future date. Upon seeing Claudine she jumped, interrupted her stretching, and started to scold like an old-fashioned schoolmarm.

"Claudine, your no-EMF policy is really making my life difficult. All I have is this landline and a two-year-old phone book. Plus, no one in this town has heard of the caveman diet. They're going to send what they send, and Moe's just going to have to deal with it."

"*Du calme, du calme.*" Claudine ushered the younger woman into the recesses of the office, where she dug up a teapot, teabags, cups, and some shortbread cookies. They both fumbled around for a while picking out teabags and pouring and getting settled. "I have a plan," Claudine pronounced at last.

Abby crammed a cookie into her mouth as if it were the last survival biscuit on a life raft. "Oh, no."

"If Moe doesn't like the real food, we'll tell him we're introducing the 'Whey of the Goat thankfulness regimen.' Everything he eats, he has to pick or kill himself outside, giving thanks to all the plants and animals. If he's not very fast, he'll have to settle for slugs and snails."

Abby shuddered. "Sounds like the things Lou's family fed me in the south of France."

Claudine decided not to expound on her theory that their predilection for slimy things gave the French nice skins and first-class mathematical minds. Look at her kids, for example—they were both brilliant and her daughter had a lovely complexion. She was sure Roger would have nice skin, too, if he weren't dead, but she had to admit the beneficial effects began to backfire on the male side of the family at some critical point. Maybe they were actually allergic, and in the way of allergies they actually craved what was killing them. She would have to ask Roger next time he visited if he had been eating unusual amounts of escargots before he...

She jerked out of her woolly thought-knitting to listen to Abby gripe about France, the world-famous all-truffle restaurant where everything tasted like "mold," and the glacial pouring rain that ruined her visit to the seashore. She mocked Lou's family with a French accent that was much improved since the last time she and Claudine had met, though with a somewhat comic mix of Parisian and Quebecois that no doubt had an interesting story behind it.

"Lou booked you into a single. I'm surprised he's not coming," Claudine commented cautiously, trying to hide her eagerness to have another body she could put to work. If Abby's Frenchman wasn't actually 86, maybe he could be of use up here.

"Lou is busy." Abby rolled her eyes. "He had to do some kind of *experiment*."

Claudine's ears pricked up. After a miserable time with financially successful dull-normals, it looked as if Abby had returned to her native element and joined up with a scientist at last. She'd had a love-hate relationship with nerds ever since she dropped out of graduate school, but it was inevitable she'd end up with one. No one else had sufficient brainpower—but of course with the brainpower came the fatal flaws, as Claudine knew all too well.

"What kind of science does he do?" she inquired.

"He's supposed to be an origins-of-the-universe theoretical physicist." Clearly this had hit a nerve, because Abby was ranting now. "But he got himself mixed up in some kind of virus thing, and sent me up here for my birthday weekend alone so he could search for a rabid mouse."

Claudine couldn't help it. She had to laugh. "Sorry, Abby, it just sounds so familiar. The good ones are all crazy, you know." As soon as the words were out of her mouth she regretted them, but if Abby was about to launch into a heartfelt confession—and she was screwing up her forehead in a way that portended an emotional twister—Claudine had only herself to blame.

"Including your wonderful son," Abby gulped, the gale-force winds heading closer. "I feel so guilty. I've kept this from you a long time, because...because I thought I should bear the burden alone."

Claudine looked around furtively, but saw no storm shelter in sight. *Crottes de mouton*, she thought, bowing her head like a penitent to allow Abby to dump a load of pent-up, guilt-ridden fantasy all over it.

"When I left grad school Roger promised me he would go with me. We were going to get married," she wailed.

Claudine felt terrible. She hadn't realized Abby's delusion ran that deep. She knew that Lori and her "genius" circle had rejected Abby with all the cruelty of booby hatchlings elbowing their siblings from the nest; Roger must have stood out from the pack just because he was kind to her.

"I could have kept him on his meds," Abby was snuffling now.

Claudine flashed back to Abby's sobbing phone calls in graduate school. She could feel Roger's spirit bristling, but she wasn't about to bust the poor woman's balloon, not so many years later. In fact, how would it hurt to play along? Her son wasn't around to contradict her, after all. "I know he loved you," she murmured, patting Abby on the shoulder. This set off a fresh torrent of tears, but Claudine kept the anodyne platitudes coming—there was nothing you could have done, you did everything you could, the disease was too much finally, *gnan-gnan-gnan*.

Finally, Claudine had had enough. She pointed out that all that crying was causing inflammation, which was damaging to the skin, and Abby pulled herself together. She looked up and gave Claudine a long, measuring look, a glint of determination in her eye.

"At least I can help you, Claudine," she announced firmly.

Great. Well, lord knew she needed all the help she could get, and besides, Abby would keep the ghosts away, ha-ha.

"No, I mean it," the young woman insisted. "I just saw someone walk by and I'm just hoping it isn't who I think it is. But he looked an awful lot like Moe Deet's doctor. Sort of unmistakable with that ruff of hair..."

"*QUOI*?" Claudine leapt from her seat, spilling her tea in a puddle around the ancient phone, which started to make a zapping noise.

"So much for our one link to the outside world," Abby mumbled.

"Moe Deet! Is the Cursed One here?"

"So what if he is? The cabin is ready. Wait!" Abby stepped in front of the door to keep Claudine from barreling through it. "This is important. Remember how you said Moe was bringing his personal physician?"

"That's what he told me. He apparently suffers from all sorts of conditions, I don't know."

"Listen." Abby lowered her voice. "I just saw someone who runs a clinic, and he's one of our professors. He has an MD from somewhere, but he's not licensed to practice medicine in this country. His name is Oriol Ortiz, and my job is to keep him happy, but he's been making it increasingly difficult. He came into our office the other day with some kind of crisis, and absolutely refused to talk to me, saying it was a 'conflict of interest' because I'm dating Lou. But Oriol's work has nothing to do with Lou's. Their only link is that they both use the BSL-3 lab. So what I think..."

Claudine finally managed to push by, barely heeding the words. She was dismayed at having missed her VIP guest's arrival. Had he come by goat cart, as he was supposed to—or had he done the unthinkable and driven to her spa?

She sprinted down the garden path, craning her head for signs of life. She'd put Moe and his doctor in a section of the resort she called "Queen's Bath," intending someday to model it after the swimming hole Queen Liliuokalani used to splash in on the Big Island of Hawai'i. The Queen's Bath suites were a short trail away from a swimming hole surrounded by ferns and eucalyptus; all that was missing were a few fruit trees of the tropical variety, mangoes and guavas, maybe passionfruit vines.

"*Hola*, Miguel!" she hailed a goat cab driver who was pulling up in front of the Halema'uma'u Suite. A rapid exchange of Indio-Spanish assured her that their famous guest was on his way. Walking. Claudine helped Miguel unload the luggage onto the veranda, joking about the ten pieces of luggage for a two-day stay, then waved him off. She was about to conclude that Abby had been wrong about the doctor when she spotted a white Mercedes parked just around the corner from the suite.

Blood pounded in her temples. Ambulances and fire trucks were the only motor vehicles allowed at her spa. Whoever the jerk was who thought he could bring his reeking Nazi machine into her haven of green silence was just about to learn a lesson.

Before she could take another step, she was enveloped in a billow of white cloth, and addressed in musical European Spanish. "Claudine, if I may presume?" The white cloth dropped away to reveal a spotless lab coat over a light grey summer suit, and a thick head of perfect hair above the most classic Roman profile she had ever seen. "Dr. Oriol Ortiz. My patient will be here any moment, but while we wait, we must discuss the potential of this location." He made a sweeping gesture towards the as-yet-unimproved grounds. "A spa for the stars! I can see every inch of it. Work with me, Claudine, and I will make you rich and famous beyond your dreams."

NINE: FROM BAD TO WORSE

THE NASA INSPECTORS WERE coming in twelve hours, and everything was a disaster.

Fortunately, Lori had managed to pack Sam and David off to the airport early Friday morning, before they found out that Kathy had been found unconscious outside the BSL-3. Since then, everything had gone from bad to worse.

Walter Waddles had called later that day to say his flight from DC was delayed. That meant that Lori was all alone in setting up the new lab to pass NASA inspection. Oriol refused to take part, instead sending an incredibly rude email saying he was out of town on business too important for her to understand. When Lori responded in kind, he retaliated by sending over an even more arrogant and condescending minion, who told Lori she "seemed to be doing things mostly right," stuck his name on a bench with the label-maker, and left. Lou was spending all his time over at the hospital with Kathy—hopefully with a lancet and plastic tube tucked in his pocket so he could sample her blood, or at least her snot.

Lori should have worried when Lou didn't call her all day Saturday; she had been too busy unpacking boxes, setting up equipment, and arranging supplies on all of the shelves of the new lab so that it would look bustling and inhabited. On Sunday she woke up past noon, sick as a dog, feverish and with her sinuses packed with what felt like curing cement. She gulped a shot of DayQuil, topped off with smuggled

Canadian Sudafed, and dragged herself into the lab to finish the preparations.

Some Buboes offered to help, but kept insisting upon hanging up pictures of mouse brains, so she finally banished them all and worked alone. She had just hung the banners— *Welcome To the Polar Artic Research In Astrobiology (PARIA) Project!* they declared, tastefully decorated with the NASA meatball—when Lou showed up.

He shut the door. Then he closed the blinds. Then he ushered her into the corner behind the thick black velvet curtains, where they kept the microscope.

His eyes were red and he seemed to have trouble getting words out. "Kathy just..." he mumbled.

"What?" Lori demanded, a bit annoyed that he'd not even looked at the decorations.

"...just died," whispered Lou.

Lori staggered back a step and grabbed the curtain, meaningless words like "What?" and "How?" pouring from her mouth. She flashed back to the mouse, stiff under the glass beaker, incisors bared in its death throes.

He shrugged. "I wish I knew. They wouldn't tell me anything—I'm not family. Apparently she has no family. I've been trying for days to..." He broke off, exhausted.

She tried to press him, but gave up quickly. He didn't have any of Kathy's bodily fluids, and it sounded as if he didn't know any more about how she died than Lori did. "Did she have any neurological symptoms?" Lori pursued.

"She was in a coma. I guess that's neurological."

"But you don't know—"

"Not really. They think she might have bumped her head in some way. I found her passed out in the hallway on Thursday night. I don't know if she'd been in either of the basement labs, or what she'd been doing." He cleared his throat. "I think we need to shut that BSL-3 lab down."

Lori tried to shout her agreement, but a fit of sneezing cut her short. "Didn't Abby tell you that we're all slaves to Oriol?" she managed at last.

"This is different," whispered Lou. "This isn't a weird cold."

"I know, but I still don't think—I mean, I can't believe it was the mouse bite. Even if the mouse did have green rabies, that's much too fast. Besides, if she wasn't in the lab, why do you think it's even related?"

"It has to be. Doesn't it? I mean…" He stopped himself with a cagey look.

Lori was just about to accuse him of lying about where he'd found Kathy when there was the scratching of a key in the lock, and they both grew silent. Lori pulled the curtain open just a slit, so they could see who was invading their new space—and then she drew a long snuffle of relief.

Walter W. Waddles IV was not only the best graduate student in the world, he also knew more about the university and NASA than just about any other living person. His great-grandfather Walter Waddles Sr. had been STI's first president, and his grandfather Walter Junior was the Dean of Science and a practicing physical chemist. His father, Walter III, had once been head of the physics department, but had stepped aside from his position to become the Chief Scientist at the university-controlled NASA Lobo Peak Rocket Lab.

Apparently that made Walter Senior a pariah: once he moved to NASA, his own father refused to speak to him for years. Even Lori hadn't quite understood this at first, even though she'd known since her undergraduate years that the employees of the NASA lab were treated like STI's deformed brother in the basement, the moniker "LEPER" much more than a funny acronym. She'd just always figured that they didn't know they were LEPERs, or didn't really care—after all, didn't they get to send things to Mars?

"Walter!" Lori exclaimed. "You're back!"

"I sat in the airport for twelve hours to get on standby," Walter yawned. "I'm dying."

"We're all dying," Lori retorted, flinging aside the curtain. "Sit down. We have some things to tell you."

It was so great to have him back. Rather than barf or faint at the tale of the green mouse brain, he just pulled up a lab stool, grabbed a notebook and a pen, and listened intently. As Lori and Lou told the story of the mouse brain, Walter murmured several times "HIV in a rabies coat... HIV in a rabies coat" while scribbling, a bit of tongue showing in the corner of his mouth. Finally he pushed the notebook over to the others with a picture on it:

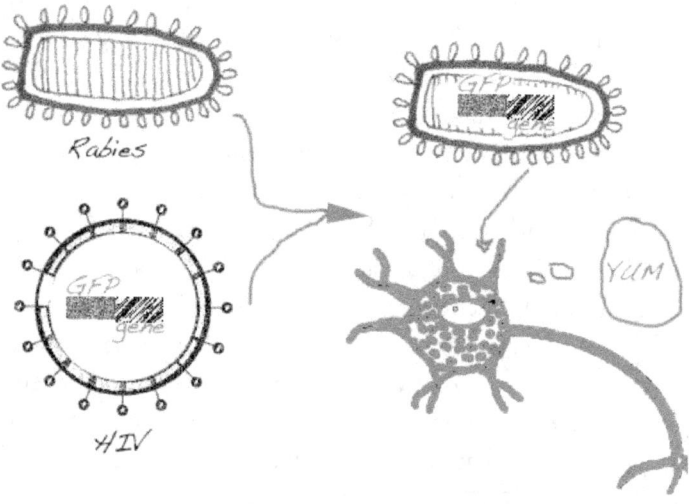

Lori wasn't in the mood for mysterious messages. "You *want* HIV in a rabies coat?" she demanded.

"Oh hell yes," Walter hissed. "Neurons hate all viruses. I'll try anything if it works."

Lou narrowed his eyes. "You haven't already been trying this, by chance?"

"Huh?" Walter looked so thoroughly baffled that Lori believed him. "Of course not. I wouldn't know how to find the rabies virus if I wanted to."

Lori wasn't entirely convinced. "All right, then, but your cells died again—and they all had a pretty rabid look, if you ask me."

"My cells died?" Walter hung his head as if it had been his puppy. Then his nose twitched, and he reached up his sleeve for a huge cloth handkerchief, sneezing violently into it several times. Lori could see spots of blood on the hanky.

"All shriveled and dead," she confirmed.

"Show me." Walter headed for the door. "I need to see."

All three of them trooped next door and down into the basement. As they passed the DNA sequencing facility, the twitchy technician smiled and waved, making Lori feel inexplicably guilty and sad.

Walter looked glum as he emptied his pockets and reached for his coat hook, where there was a size XL lab coat with a message written on it in Sharpie: *This is Walter's STOP taking it*. "Did you guys forget to feed the cells?"

"I just fed them three days ago," Lori promised. "They looked bad then, but then this morning..."

Walter didn't even bother about sterility as he took the cells from the incubator, popped off the lids, and stuck them into the microscope. Projected onto the computer, they looked even worse than Lori had thought—broken, grainy, and fractured, with no long axons or dendrites coming out. Walter turned up the magnification, but there weren't any bacteria or yeast to explain the problem. The medium was a healthy pink color, not the yellow it turned when contaminated. The neurons were just dead. "Do all the dishes look like this?" he asked.

"Every last one."

"Why don't you turn on the fluorescence lamp?" Lou suggested.

Walter looked startled. "Why?" He grabbed a spray bottle of dilute bleach and jetted the cells; the medium slowly turned colorless. "No point. They're dead."

"Autoclave them all," Lori ordered. "Whatever got in there, I don't want it in any new cells. Let's toss out the bottle of medium, too."

"Another two weeks of work." Her student slumped in front of the microscope, tired and defeated, then got up slowly to get the rest of the dishes from the incubator. Halfway back to the bench, he was seized by a fit of coughing and had to whirl around to put the cells safely on a shelf. Afraid to touch his face, he coughed at the floor, gagging.

"It's not a big deal to make more cells," Lori reassured him. "What might be a big deal is that we're all sick."

Walter giggled through his cough. "It's a cold—not rabies. You're not biting each other, I hope? Why don't you PCR your snot for GFP?"

It was said half-jokingly, but Lou responded in all serious-ness. "We plan to, but we got distracted. First the mouse died. Then your cells died. Then a faculty member died."

"What?" cried Walter, slamming his notebook closed and peering at them. When no further details were forthcoming, he pursued, "Not Dr. Ortiz?"

"No," Lori responded suspiciously. "Why would you think of Oriol?"

"Well." Walter tittered. "You know. He works with some scary stuff."

"That he doesn't list on the safety protocol?" Lori persisted.

"I don't know." The student's voice became a whine. "But tell me, who died?"

Lori listened again to Lou's story about how he'd found Kathy, which really didn't make any sense to her. She decided she would believe him that he'd found her outside the lab. After all, Kathy didn't even know how to pipette culture medium from a dish—what would she be doing in the BSL-3 alone? She must have been doing something else, maybe com-pletely unrelated to the BSL-3.

"Well." Walter shook out his thin, nearly white hair. A film of sweat had broken out on his forehead. "This is a lot more serious than some sneezing. You can PCR your boogers if you want, but I don't think it's going to tell you very much. What we need to do is take some of Oriol's cells from the incubator, the ones you think might have rabies, and feed them to a mouse and see if we can reproduce the green brain effect."

Lori peeked at Lou to see if he was as outraged as she was. He was—maybe even more so. "I hope you know you can't really do that," she told her student as seriously as she knew how.

"And I hope you realize it's more than your life is worth to breathe a word of that to the inspectors," Lou added.

Walter denied it vehemently, shaking his head with a look of wide-eyed innocence. He retrieved the platter of cells and made it to the benchtop with them, where he began bleaching them one by one.

"I think it's a brilliant thing to test on cells," Lori continued, "but we can't use mice, and there's simply no way around it unless we write another grant. The NASA money specifically excludes any and all human or animal experimentation."

"Dr. Ortiz has mice," Walter attempted as if he'd just thought of that. "Can't we just borrow some extras from him? Nice, fresh ones, straight from the Mouse House so we know they're not infected."

Lori sighed, pulling over a lab stool so she could sit down and try to explain some things to her now second-year grad student. She supposed she should write all of this down for the group, but hadn't expected the issue to come up so soon. Trying to appeal to ambition first, she told him that he wouldn't be able to publish or include in his thesis any animal experiment that hadn't been approved by the Ethics Committee. For their part, the Ethics Committee wouldn't approve a project not supported by a reputable grant, and they knew perfectly well what NASA policy was.

"What if Oriol adds it to his project and gets it approved by Ethics?" Walter wondered.

"I doubt he'd be able to," Lori replied. "He'd need to have a special place to house the green mice—once they're infected with a BSL-2 or greater agent, they can't go back to the Mouse House."

"What?" Walter sounded as if suddenly he believed nothing she was saying. "That's crap! People put them back there all the time."

"I know they do, but it's against all regulations and can get you in a lot of trouble. *Especially* if anything happens or anyone gets sick."

"Oh, and one more thing," Lou added. "Who's the person who signs off on all Ethics approvals? Absinthe McRae."

"Oh, *shit*," whimpered Walter. "I can't hide anything from you guys, can I?"

"You really can't," Lou agreed, reaching into his microscope tool drawer. "Here—blow your nose into this tube."

Walter obeyed without protest, and almost seemed disappointed when Lori reminded them that they didn't have time to do the PCR tonight. "Business first," she declared, putting his tube into their new upright cryogenic freezer. "I want to hear the presentation you're going to give NASA tomorrow. When that's over..."

"When that's over," Lou reminded her with quiet irony, "we need to plan a funeral for someone who was only a professor here for six weeks before she died. And only then will we bother to check whether we all have what killed her, too."

TEN: SAM'S DIARY, PART 1

From: sjroth@its.sti.edu
To: lab@its.sti.edu
Subject: what now?

Hi Lori,

Well, we're here in Montreal. I must say your colleagues think you're NUTS for sending me to Eureka in October. Even here "down South" the trees are all well on their way to being orange, and a frigid lashing rain is descending.

With that said, they admitted it's a lot easier/cheaper to get plane tickets this time of year. I hope you realize you don't fly straight to Eureka—first you have to stop in a place called Sqalid, the capital of Nunavut, which is already well off the top of all normal maps. Then you go to another stop called Desolute Bay, which is as far as jets will take you. After that you have to wait for a Twin Otter charter to take you to the station.

We're trying to arrange all of this here right now, but I need help from you. I need to know if there's any equipment you want us to bring from your Montreal colleagues' labs—one guy here thinks he knows but he's not sure. Also, do we have to actually unpack it or just leave it up there in boxes? This guy says most of the stuff is kept in "Weather Haven" tents that might not keep it warm in winter. Also, apparently your Polar Continental Shelf research grant should be paying for the stay, but I can't find the number, and no one answers the phones at the Polar Shelf office.

By the way, each time I say "we," I mean me. David is of no help at all. He is enjoying the night life—found some place called "The Village" and comes back at all hours smelling of cigarettes & alcohol & mumbling in franglais.

We're going to go to some molecular cuisine restaurant now. Last gasp of civilization! Too bad about the lashing rain.

Sam

ELEVEN: MOE DEET'S TRUE COLORS

IN JUST A FEW minutes, Claudine would finally have Moe all to herself, and she was determined to find out what made him tick. The beauty business was 99% psychology, and this was the area in which she knew she shone, evidence of a mad son she couldn't save to the contrary.

The consultation room overlooking the garden soothed even Roger's perturbed spirit. When guests threw open the tall French doors in the back and walked into the luxuriant greenery, they were stepping into another time and place. Elephant ferns towered overhead, and other water-loving plants thrived in the moist climate to such an extent that all of the yard art left by the previous owners was draped with leaves and moss. One sculpture of a female figure had been placed on an old couch that now sprouted with wild grasses, reminding Claudine of Rousseau's *The Dream*. The reclining lady was flanked by a fountain on the other side that spurted water into a pool from various spigots on a sculpture group of Myrmidons wearing helmets and nothing else. Tasteful though, no pissing parts, with the exception of a single fat cherub. A haphazard collection of LEDs backlit the statues and led the way to what apparently had once been a pond.

Abby had shed her princess patina at last, reverting to her farm girl roots and donning a pair of waders to try to clean up the muck and weeds from the rectangular concrete basin to see if it was, in fact, a serviceable pond. She claimed to see traces of an artificial waterfall, but it was so buried under asparagus fern that Claudine was not convinced. Hands protected from the spines by big rubber gloves, Abby pulled organic matter from the basin and piled it up around the outside. "It's great fertilizer," she explained as Claudine appeared, pausing to remove one glove and wipe her brow. "If you can get me some seedlings, I can plant flowers in a circle—" She stopped and leapt a foot in the air as she was interrupted by a low BAAA. "But first," she grouched, slipping back into pedantic mode, "you need to do something about this creature. He's going to eat the flowers before I even get a chance to unpack them, and Mr. Collie here is not doing his job." The dog stretched up to lick her face, oblivious to the large sheep trampling around the pond, munching the flowers and greenery.

Claudine stepped forward to take the collar of her favorite sheep to lead him back to the meadow. Nothing could discourage Bracegirdle from sneaking into the garden. He was a wandering sheep by nature and he just loved the area around the reclining lady, for reasons known only to himself and his Ovine Creator. It wasn't just the foliage either; his favorite activity was to push his long face up against the glass of the treatment chambers, especially when Claudine was giving a facial. Perhaps he was a watcher, like Chauncey Gardener. Or maybe, Claudine mused as she stroked him on his ski-slope snout, he had appearance issues, and if he could talk he'd plead for a nose job.

She still had Bracegirdle on her mind as she hurried back to the office and waited for Moe Deet. He was a few minutes late; when he arrived, he fumbled around the room until he finally found the consultation chair and settled gingerly into it. Like a veterinarian, Claudine watched him carefully for signs of stiffness or pain, knowing his body would tell the truth even if his mouth did not. As long as people had ovine characteristics she got along with them just fine. She was okay even when they didn't, but those folks were rare. Scientists, good ones anyway, tended not to be sheep, maybe because they could handle statistics...but here she was wool-gathering again when she needed to be attending to her very first VIP client.

"I have blemishes," Moe was saying, pointing to an invisible spot on his face, "and large pores on my nose and wrinkles around my eyes." If she had a nickel for every time she'd heard this litany she wouldn't have to work for a living. She tuned out again as he continued describing his "problems" and scrutinized the facial and body language that would tell her everything she needed to know.

"My chin is receding," Moe went on, "my neck is getting folds in it, and last week..." he paused, and suddenly his entire body contracted ever so slightly, like a snail horn receding when touched. This alerted Claudine to listen attentively to the next bit: It was confession time. Sure enough, his head twitched slightly from side to side as if he were afraid someone was listening in, then he lowered his voice to whisper. "I went to a store and got asked if I wanted the senior discount."

He adopted the penitent pose, head bowed, shoulders slumped, of a supplicant not daring to hope a miracle might intervene in his own hopeless cause. It was the same pose of resigned patience bovines exhibited before they were slaughtered. Claudine studied him through the longish pause that came next, thinking that Moe was, like all her clients, hiding something. But she suspected he was hiding something that was causing him considerably more distress than just looking his age, devastating though that must be for someone in his profession.

"The first thing we need to do," she said gently, "is list what sorts of treatments you've had in the past year. Then we'll go from there."

The list was staggering. He'd had collagen injections, poly-acrylamide injections, not just Botox but "variant" Botox, hyaluronic acid at a French clinic that used HA from cockscomb, two series of human growth hormone injections at a

Swiss clinic, human placental injections at a Bavarian clinic, and a series of highly experimental injections from Oriol Ortiz in Mexico. And all this within the last six months! When he wasn't being poked he was undergoing skin resurfacing treatments of various sorts, including galvanic, laser CO_2 resurfacing, microdermabrasion, intense pulse light therapy, and radio frequency resurfacing. When he wasn't being poked or sandblasted he was on the operating table for more serious stop-the-clock procedures, but so far, thank goodness, his plastic surgeries had been limited to an eyelid job and modified forehead lift, and a liposuction or two. Hair implants of course. He hadn't seen the sun in years and would have been paler than Andy Warhol except that he routinely used a self-tanner containing dihydroxyacetone, which gave him the rusty-brown color of a desiccated orange peel. He reminded her of how fruits and vegetables grown on a *biologique* farm differed from supermarket produce; a natural apple, say, that glowed from rude health as opposed to one that had been sprayed, force-fed, artificially colored, waxed and polished. It might look good from a distance but close up it looked suspiciously perfect, and when you bit into it you got mealy, tasteless mush.

Even if Moe chose organic food for his fad diets—veganism, macrobiotic, Atkins, and South Beach were among the many that had preceded his current caveman—the benefits, if there had any to begin with, were undermined by detox procedures. The upper colonic irrigation had ensured that not a single bacterium was left in the gut to digest the carefully selected food items. Top this regimen off with a tremendous amount of pill-swallowing (he was taking 89 a day, he told her) and it was no wonder he was having stomach problems and beginning to show signs of wear and tear. Claudine's "miracle cures" for the most part were nothing more than an application of that least common of all senses, common sense.

Just for starters, this human guinea pig needed a good meal and surcease from prodding, poking, scraping and starving.

After listening to the full recital she took him into the treatment room, settling him onto the reclining couch for his facial. "The body," she continued soothingly, "is the miracle worker. Once it has what it needs to take care of itself, it is a fabulously resilient healing machine. But you must be careful not to abuse it. My therapies are all about giving the organism what it needs to heal itself. And my sense is that your attempts to improve your health, all unbeknownst to you, have depleted you of resources. You have been trying very hard to improve your health status, but you haven't always been given the right information."

She started by giving him a facial cleanse, which to no surprise rinsed out a murky shade of orange. Then she fell back on her old traditional Alberta recipe, "A New Ewe," which no one had to know was simply mutton fat scented with lavender. A thick layer of this had protected her skin from the ravages of three decades of Canadian winters, and Moe's cracked skin drank up the soft cream. He started to relax under Claudine's massaging fingertips as she explained gently that it was no virtue to work oneself to madness. What everyone needed was a chance to tune out, pet a goat, eat a peach, and sit in the grass under a warm sun.

"Benefit from seeing how animals live their harmonious lives," she advised. "When I'm sad, I bury my face in a sheep's woolly coat—the lanolin will also do wonders for the skin. When you have trouble sleeping, watch a housecat as he takes a spontaneous nap. If you're allergic, I even have a pet snake you can try."

Moe purred as Claudine kneaded his skin over the bones. She was just thinking about which animal she could pair him up with when suddenly he reared upright on the recliner, crying, "Christ on a skateboard, what's that *monster*?"

Given the not-so-random appearances of her dead son, Claudine was quite relieved to glance through the window and find a perfectly normal, though perhaps somewhat nosy, visitor. Bracegirdle had his wet nose pressed against the window and protruded his tongue thoughtfully in their general direction, his broad nose and wide brown eyes almost too-human in his glabrous face.

"Why, Moe, he's just a sheep!" she explained quickly. "Just lie here quietly. I'll only be a moment," she called over her shoulder as she ran out of the treatment room and out to the garden to find the culprit.

Abby was still out there, standing in the pond in her waders, testing out the lights. She pushed buttons, one at a time, causing bright flashes of blue and white to come from the garden and inside the water. Attracted by the spectacle, the sheep approached her, bleating.

Claudine stepped forward to restrain her pet, leading him away from Abby's carefully prepared garden plot. As she headed once more to the meadow, she turned around to see a strange sight. Moe had followed her out of the treatment room and now, with clumsy motions, was patting the statue of the reclining lady à la Rousseau. She dropped Bracegirdle's collar and hurried over to him, wondering if he were hallucinating.

At Claudine's approach he tilted his head sideways to smile at her. "He's colder and harder than I thought he would be, but he's very docile," Moe confided. "I was afraid of him at first, but you were right, there's something very soothing about communing with an animal."

"Er, yes. Moe, why don't you come with me now?" Claudine took his arm and led him back to the real sheep. Bracegirdle, who ordinarily enjoyed being the center of attention, began flaring his nostrils and edging away in the direction of the fountain, evidently anxious to get as far away from Moe as possible.

Oblivious to the animal's distress, Moe approached and clutched at his wool. Bracegirdle shifted nervously from one hoof to the other while edging ever closer to the fountain; when he reached the edge he gave an agonized bleat and dived into the pool, carrying Moe with him.

Abby looked in as if she were going to try to help Moe and the sheep out, but then recoiled in horror. "Oh my god," she cried. "Why is Moe's face all blotched with green?"

TWELVE: MOMENT OF TRUTH

THEY PUT ON A good show, but NASA wasn't fooled.

Walter Waddles started out with a sanitized history of the project—nothing at all about how the STI team had won almost literally over the LEPERs' dead bodies, or how Lou and Lori had fired the LEPER director out of pure spite. He showed off the poster he'd presented at the conference in DC, spotted in key places with the NASA meatball, and then exhibited their refrigerators and freezers full of mysterious, scary implements of "gene cloning."

"Astrobiology research requires infrastructure and institutional support for technically difficult and dangerous biological experiments," Walter explained. The NASA visitors cringed as he opened the sash of a completely virgin containment hood. "This was why the PI of this project decided early on that all of this type of science would be done here on campus, rather than the L-P-R lab." Walter was careful to say each initial separately. "We also benefit from a substantially decreased overhead rate—only fifty percent on salaries, and nothing on capital equipment. This has allowed the project to hire several people at less than the cost of a single L-P-R employee." He gestured towards some hastily borrowed third-year grad students, who pipetted dutifully. "We've also established a collaboration with Dr. Oriol Ortiz, the newest member of our faculty. This allows us to obtain primary neurons and biological expertise that we ordinarily wouldn't have."

It was a little funny, Lori had to admit, to hear the word "cloning" from a guy who looked exactly like the first president and the Chief Scientist. Either the female Waddles line was uncannily similar, or they had found some way to duplicate themselves without remixing.

Next it was Oriol's turn. He had no obligation to be here, but he had promised to lend his presence, and he acquitted himself well. Rather than talk about his mouse-torturing, he mentioned the arrays of neurons that were going to pilot spacecraft, and the methods he had up his sleeve to make them cleverer and less susceptible to infection. He also had what sounded like a disgusting plan to use disembodied cricket heads to control a rocket ship. Insects weren't protected under any ethics regulations, so no one minded if he snipped off their heads and wired them into an array. "I've gotten it to chirp in synch," he declared proudly, playing a recorded sound on his laptop.

Lou wasn't there. He had left precipitously for the airport the previous evening, saying something about Claudine, Abby, and "green cells." Lori really didn't want to know—and was kind of relieved he'd taken his pre-tenure nerves elsewhere. His theory students took over after Oriol, doing a beautiful job of describing the astrophysics side of the project, with early-universe modeling, lots of Feynman diagrams, and no mention of any molecule more complex than helium.

Then they broke for lunch, and when the fat men in suits returned, they accused Lori and Oriol of doing illicit animal experiments, hiding mice in places outside the Mouse House. They ran all around campus looking for secret mice, even barging into Oriol's lab where they had no business being. Lori hated them so much she even felt sorry for the arrogant biologist, flapping about in his lab coat and opening his rooms one by one to show that there were no animals hidden in unapproved places.

Then the inspectors decided that any use of cells taken directly from animals was a violation, even if Oriol was killing the mice anyway. They finished by suspending the entire project until the next formal reporting date in January, at which time the investigators had to demonstrate substantial progress without the use of mice.

In a daze of cold medicine, Lori could barely process what was happening. All she registered was that all of a sudden, the sky was darkening outside and everyone in the room was mad at her.

"This was a setup," Oriol declared.

Walter whirled on him. "What do you mean?" he demanded, too canny for his years.

"Funding agencies care about results, not petty rules." Oriol got up from his lab bench, uncharacteristically putting all of his pipettes away on their designated hangers. "You made a lot of enemies getting this funding. One of them has obviously tipped NASA off." He swept from the room with a cough of disdain.

Walter made as if to follow him, then changed his mind and decided to snipe at Lori instead. He moaned that he was never going to have a good thesis project, and it was all the fault of the physics department, NASA, and most of all, her, who stood in his way and prevented him from doing the work that would make him famous.

Throat too raw from fighting disease all day, Lori said nothing. Eventually, fed up with being ignored, Walter stormed out, emphasizing his snit by shutting off the lights and leaving her in the dark.

A dim reddish light still peeked through the windows, and small LEDs blinked at various points in the lab. The darkness was soothing, and free from pretense at last, Lori grabbed a box of Kimwipes and sneezed, blew her nose, and gave herself up to a ferocious coughing fit that tore out chunks of ick all the way down her respiratory tract.

When she heard a sneeze just behind her left ear, she wondered how she had managed to echo like that. Her curiosity was replaced with outrage when then Lou stuck his head out from behind the velvet curtains.

"Jesus Christ!" Lori yelled. "I thought you were in Clonic! How long have you been here?"

"Just a few minutes. I got off the plane and came straight here. Then I sneaked in after Walter left. You were too busy—" another sneeze "—coughing to notice." He flung open the curtain; on his lap was a Styrofoam box from which a few tendrils of carbon dioxide were swirling. "It's time for the moment of truth. I have some cells here from a famous Hollywood publicist whose eyes and cheeks just happened to glow green under blue fountain lights." He came out from the microscope area and plunked the box onto a benchtop. "Why Mad Claudine would fill her fountain with powerful 470 nm LEDs is anyone's guess, but it was enough to make Abby realize that something scary might be going on here." He looked exhausted, demoralized, and—dare she say it—a little green about the gills.

"You look awful," Lori exclaimed, opening the box to find seven tiny tubes nestled in a powder of dry ice. "Hard to believe you've been at a spa." She walked over to the cryogenic freezer and took out all of their stored samples—blood and nasal cells from herself and Lou, a nose swab from Walter, and cultured cells from their own and Oriol's incubators. Making sure the samples were all clearly labeled, she added them to the dry ice with the new specimens.

"A spa haunted by ghosts and green fluorescent protein," grumbled Lou. He closed the curtains around the microscope area and found his favorite lab stool, then climbed on and raised it to the height of the benchtop. "Do you know who Moe Deet is?"

"Please, Lou, none of your stupid puns right now. I'm just too miserable." Lori could feel mucus filling her face again.

She took off her gloves and dashed into the hallway to take a couple of pills, feeling as if she were shutting the barn door after shooting the horse and eating its brain.

When she returned, Lou had pulled down a new, virgin DNA extraction kit from the supplies Lori had spent all weekend arranging. He was focused intently on the user's manual. "Yeah," he sympathized, "that's how I felt last week. It wasn't a pun, though—Morris Dietrich, who calls himself Moe Deet, is an agent from Malibu. Worse, he's almost my parents' neighbor. Abby goes to their place at least once a week, and I usually do, too. Now his face is full of GFP, and maybe his brain as well. Abby refuses to come back from the spa, and is threatening to move all her stuff out of my place because she's convinced we're contagious. She refused to give me any of her cells, though. I've been sick, you've been sick, Walter's coughing—"

"We've been—" Lori sneezed "—sick, but not with anything consistent with HIV or rabies."

"Kathy asked to use our lab, and less than two weeks later she was dead. There are a few possibilities here. Maybe we've been exposed gradually, and built up a resistance."

"Or it was the mouse bite," Lori suggested, playing along.

"Or maybe she was doing something she wasn't telling us about. Or Oriol did something to her on purpose, with or without her knowledge."

"Seems unlikely," Lori dismissed. "Or it's unrelated!"

Lou didn't look up from the user's manual. His voice was artificially light as he suggested, "Or she was murdered."

Lori decided to ignore that comment, and get back to the point. "You don't need to read that silly manual," she scolded, opening the Styrofoam box to re-count the samples, then reaching for an agarose gel box of the appropriate size. "I've done this a billion times. I'll homogenize the cells and then you run the DNA kit. Got your primers?"

"I have more primers than you can shake a stick at." Lou looked doubtfully at the marbled blue box containing a few transparent bottles, nothing more. "But I'm a theorist. What if I fuck this up?"

"I'll only give you half the sample and freeze the rest." She set to work dutifully, handing Lou each ruptured cell slurry to extract the DNA.

They worked in silence for a while, until she opened the last of Claudine's samples to find something thick, brown, and grassy, which she could smell even through her clogged sinuses. "Phew! What's this?"

Lou marked his spot in the user's manual with a red pen before he dared to look up. "Oh, right. It's poo."

"What kind of poo?"

"Poo that Claudine wants to feed people," he replied with annoying vagueness. "She wants it tested for worms."

"Well, I'm not homogenizing it, then." Lori set the tube aside; there was no reason to keep it frozen. "Dare I ask why she's feeding people poo?"

"Does 'stark, raving mad' answer your question?" His voice cracked and he went back to his pamphlet, making Lori hush so as not to jeopardize the experiment.

It would be a long evening, and it was a relief to have the company. Everything was new and strange to Lou, all of the clear bottles for separating the cells from their membranes and RNA before eluting the pure genomic DNA as a transparent liquid into tiny tubes. They used an even tinier fraction of this solution to set up the PCR reactions, putting the rest of what they hoped was pure DNA back in the freezer in case they needed it later.

The small rack in the PCR machine held ninety-six tubes, and they filled half, both of them pipetting quickly to add the polymerase after the machine had already warmed up. Lori shut the lid, set it to go for 25 cycles, and they both sat back and scrambled for their handkerchiefs.

"Oh, God," Lori sniffed, "my nose. Let's pour a gel and then take a break. We have two and a half hours before the PCR is done. Do you know how to make an agarose gel, or do you want me to show you?"

"Tell me how and I'll do it," he volunteered, scanning the shelves above the bench for the ingredients.

"An agarose gel is just like a Chinese dessert, but without the sugar or lychees," Lori explained, instructing as he measured out 0.4 grams of agarose into a fifty-milliliter flask. Then he put the mixture into the microwave oven by the door, set the timer to one minute, and watched carefully to make sure the flask didn't boil over. Wearing one thick heat-resistant glove, he pulled out the flask, swirled it, and put it in again for another thirty seconds until the solution was bubbling violently. Finally he took it out again, let it cool, and then poured it into the plastic casting tray on the benchtop.

"Mmmm," he mused. "Suddenly I'm hungry for Thai."

Lori's stomach rumbled, and she realized she had had nothing all day besides ginger ale and cold pills. Their agreeing on a restaurant without an argument was something of a miracle, but they both no doubt felt a bit as if they were going for their last meal. As soon as the gel looked as if it would solidify safely, they left the lab and descended nine floors in a hospital-style elevator. A blast of dry, cold air assailed them as they left the glass atrium of the complex and were exposed to actual atmosphere. The new bio building made you feel as though you were outside, fooling you with its climate control and filtered air.

Without speaking, they hurried towards the commercial district, huddled inside their T-shirts. The Thai restaurant was on the corner, with a small, enclosed patio that was completely empty of diners. They took a table there, reveling in the privacy, and Lori recalled with a shudder how the disappearance of the outdoor tables in Montreal marked the beginning of six or seven long, miserable months where any brief incursion into the outdoors was like a mini Everest expedition. The coffee shop by the university sometimes tried to extend the season with outdoor heaters and huge sheets of plastic draped around the terrace, but few things were as unpleasant as having ice chunks blow into your coffee cup as you were slapped repeatedly with wet plastic.

The waiter pulled over the heater now, but Lori told him not to turn it on, preferring a slight chill to the smell of propane. They ordered jasmine tea and sipped it eagerly, cradling the cups.

"What a day," Lori groaned.

"Tell me about it," snorted Lou. "The only sleep I've had was on the plane. I understand from Walter that things didn't go well."

"I thought we were perfect...but then NASA started accusing us of having secret mice."

Lou put down his teacup, grumbling something about murdering Oriol.

Lori was scandalized; it wasn't like him to talk about violence, even metaphorically. "Do you know it's Oriol?" she demanded quickly.

"It has to be, doesn't it?" Lou recollected himself, and took the opportunity to flag down the waitress so they could order. When she had left, he added, "I know I don't have any secret mice, and doubt that you do, either."

"No, of course not. Are you really sure Abby saw GFP in a guy at Claudine's spa?"

"I went up there to verify," Lou insisted, glancing over his shoulder in case someone was spying on them. "I took a blue lamp with me so I could find and sample the green cells myself. There were patches of green between his eyebrows, on his cheeks, and maybe even coming out his eyes—but I couldn't tell for sure. I didn't want to hurt his eyes with the lamp, and Claudine was furious at me for pestering her VIP guest."

Lori gave a semi-hysterical half-cough, half-laugh. "What did Roger have to say about it?"

"He and Claudine had a shouting match. In several different languages."

"Oh, that's nothing," Lori chuckled. "They're all like that. Did Roger have anything good to say?"

"I hope your precious Roger was less of an asshole in life than he is now, because he did nothing but call me an idiot."

Now Lori laughed for real, snot and GFP be damned. "She's got him pegged, anyway. You're much too literal-minded for Roger's taste."

"I'm sure as hell not about to become a Catholic priest, if that's what you mean by literal-minded. I don't believe in ghosts, either."

"Neither does Claudine, I'm sure. She just likes to do voices. How's the spa? Is it nice, or—you know—manically excessive?"

The waitress came back with their food, and Lou waited a good few minutes before he responded, occupied with long slippery noodles. "She's deeply in debt from commissioning bizarre statues and ponds filled with blue light," he said at last, giving up trying to wind the noodles and cutting them up with a knife and fork. "She's sure she's going to strike it rich, but she hired a lunatic chef who makes vegan chicken feet out of pond grass—or else that part's made up, too. I didn't see the alleged chef, or in fact anyone at all except Claudine herself and her two guests, Abby and Moe Deet." He speared a noodle piece and waved it at her. "If I were you, Barrow, I would worry about her."

Lori countered by pointing at him with a broccoli floret. "I really don't care. My parents are dead and I don't want more."

"You don't have to think of her as your parent—just as an old lady who needs your help."

Lori shrugged. "Let Abby do it."

"She's got her own parents. And mine. In fact, she spends more time with mine than I do."

"So she can trick you out of your inheritance, no doubt. Maybe she's even planning to kill you. And your parents."

"Christ, Barrow, sometimes I wonder why you even pretend to be part of society. Why don't you just become a hitman or something?" He sneezed into his dinner.

"Because I'm good at math and my eyes suck." She suddenly found she had no appetite. The cauliflower in her vegetable curry started to look like mouse brains, and the instant she touched the fork to her lips, she wondered if she was leaving HIV-rabies-GFP on the silverware, the tablecloth...

The image vanished as rapidly as it had come, but the food stared back. She managed to eat a bowl of rice, but dumped everything else quickly into a doggy bag before it made her ill. The rice was supposed to have coconut in it, but her impaired senses couldn't tell; she was reduced to slathering it with soy sauce in a vain attempt to reach her soggy tastebuds. Her temples started to pound and she reached for the teapot, hoping caffeine withdrawal was the cause and not a green brain tumor.

Lou, too, picked at his food and kept checking his watch. There was nothing to hurry back to until the PCR was done, so they lingered in awkward, sneezy silence, drinking endless pots of tea and trying to think of something, anything, to take their minds off their latest experiment.

He kept pestering her about Roger, so finally Lori gave in. "Roger was a classmate of ours, that's all. He struggled with manic depression and hardly spoke to anyone."

"Oh." Lou seemed puzzled. "So Abby wasn't close to him in any way?"

Lori tried to snort, but the burning mucus prevented her. "I doubt they exchanged more than ten words the entire time she was there. I didn't know him very well, either. I encouraged him to stay in school when he thought he wasn't doing well, but no more than that."

For reasons Lori couldn't have explained, Lou switched to speaking French. "But you hooked up with him later, in Montreal?"

"If by 'hooked up' you mean shared an apartment, yes. We were friends and he taught me to speak French. But contrary to what you might hear from Buboes, it never went any farther than that. As you mentioned, he was a former Catholic seminarian. Not exactly my type, but he was my only friend in a cold, lonely, foreign city—so when he died, I couldn't face that place anymore."

He opened his mouth, then shut it again, obviously disappointed. "You mean the whole Bubo pool on whether you're gay or straight is based on nothing?"

"That's right. Radhika is the only person I've ever actually slept with, and I'm sure she did it only because the men in the Midwest were sexist Lutheran pigs, like the asshole Abby was betrothed to." She tried to snort again, more carefully this time. "Sorry to let you down, Lou, but my romantic life is even emptier than you imagined."

"Did you ever meet Roger's mother?"

"Only the time she hitchhiked down from Alberta and interrupted us all in class because she figured out Roger wasn't taking his pills. She's ten times crazier than he was." She shrugged. "I have no idea why Abby wants to hang out with Claudine. Maybe it's a symptom of a brain tumor."

Lou put down his cup slowly. Something flashed in his eyes—was it fear?—but all he said was "Sorry I asked."

When they got back to the lab, the gel had hardened into the consistency of an eight-inch gummy bear. Lori slithered it into a tank of salt solution, then stared at the PCR as the cycles counted down. When the machine finally beeped, she opened it up and handed the samples over to Lou to load.

"Load what, where?" he inquired. "I can't see a thing."

"It's hard to see the gel sitting in the tank," Lori explained, illustrating where she would put her face to get just the right angle. "You have to get your sample into the tiny well and not go too deep, or you poke a hole in the gel and your sample leaks out."

"Goddamn it," he agreed, as a swirl of purple emerged from the well he was loading. "There go the secrets of the universe."

"Be gentler with the pipette," Lori advised. "You know, if this screen is negative, it means nothing—we could have missed the green cells, the primers could have been wrong, the PCR could have been done improperly, or you could have spilled too much sample out of the wells."

"But if it's positive..." This time, he shifted the tank a bit to the left and managed to get the sample into a well, where it settled into a perfect little purple square.

"You know something?" Lori thought out loud. "I'm going to order more primers. We shouldn't be testing Moe's cells just for GFP. We should be testing for particular exact sequences in our virus. Then we know for a fact that it came from right here."

He didn't dignify this with a reply, concentrating on the gel until all the samples had settled into their wells. Then he put the pipette down, shook out his fingers, and reached to turn on the gel box.

"Stop!" Lori yelled. "Put the lid on first, or if you touch the solution you'll get a nasty electric shock."

Lou froze in mid-reach, then backed out of the way and let her do it, grumbling about how he should have stayed a theorist.

"There are no more great projects for theorists," said Lori. "Unless you want to try to explain how agarose gel electrophoresis actually separates DNA of different sizes. It's actually quite a mystery."

It was a mistake to try to mention that—next Lou started to ask exactly why and how the size affected the migration and wanted to publish a math paper on it. The answer was that no one really knew: Like so many things in biology, it just worked. But they managed to kill a half hour arguing about it, enough to see the samples edge their way down the gel, where they would tell a story of some kind about what was going on.

"I'll make a deal with you: If no one's green, we can write a math paper." Lori turned off the power to the apparatus and slipped the gel out of the tank, being extra cautious because she had turned up the voltage to speed things along, making the agarose hot and fragile. The gel slid around precariously on its plastic holder, but Lori had done this hundreds and hundreds of times—often in her sleep, sometimes almost as nervous as she was now—and she slithered the glutinous rectangle onto the illumination tray without even thinking about it. The gel lay in a puddle, waiting.

"Is there DNA?" Lou demanded. "Can I see?"

Lori handed him a pair of goggles and a plastic face shield to protect himself from the UV of the illuminator. There wasn't a second shield, so she settled for just the goggles for herself and flipped on the light to excite the red dye.

Fluorescent pink bands sprang up inside the gel, and Lori compared them with the sample order in her notebook. It took her several moments of reflection to be able to answer Lou's inevitable questions. "Each time you see a band, it means there's a piece of DNA there. The pieces migrate according to size, so the ones at the bottom of the gel are the smallest. This one here, see, is about one thousand base pairs."

"How do you know?"

"By comparing it with the standard `ladder,' here on the left."

It had to be some kind of cosmic irony that had turned this shiny new biology floor over to a pair of former theoretical physicists, and it remained to be seen if they could make something coherent out of their project...or if all they could do was spill things and turn people green.

"All right," said Lou, squinting. "It appears to be on a logarithmic scale. And I do see the GFP piece—it's right there."

"Yes. All of the cells from our incubator have a band right around here." Lori indicated one of the red lines, a thin band about a quarter of an inch long. "Between seven and eight hundred base pairs."

"But the first couple have nothing."

"The first two have nothing," Lori agreed, deciding this was a teaching moment. "The first one means our negative control worked fine. The next two are Claudine's cells; she's negative. The next one has a lot of GFP but no rabies, which is good because it came from one of Walter's good experimental dishes—that's the positive control. His dead cells didn't give enough DNA to test, which doesn't surprise me. We don't have a positive control for rabies, but Oriol's incubator cells are full of it."

"Which confirms that he's been lying to the safety committee."

"Lying like a rug. The next four samples come from me and you. We have GFP in our noses but not our blood. The next one is Walter. He has GFP in his nose—we never got his blood. The last two, unfortunately, come from Moe. Not only does he have GFP, he also has rabies, and he has it everywhere."

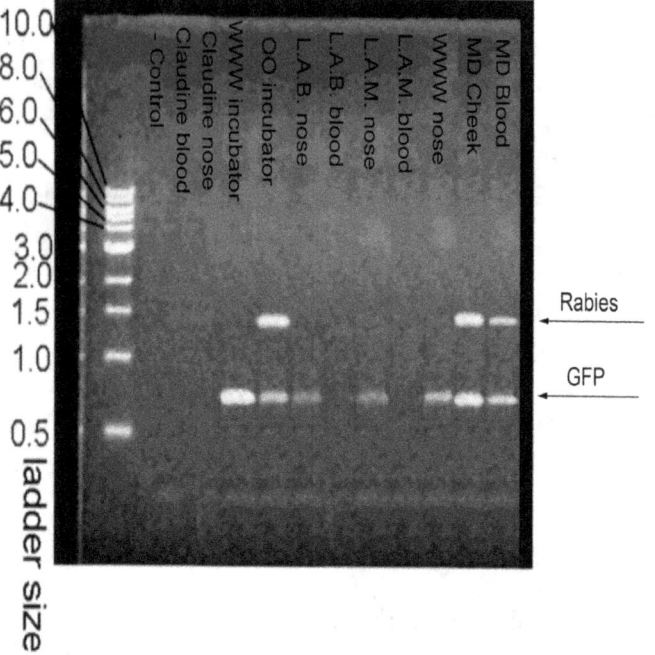

THIRTEEN: SAM'S DIARY, PART 2

From: sjroth@its.sti.edu
To: louism@its.sti.edu, lab@its.sti.edu
Subject: where are the Sqalids of yesteryear?

Hi guys,

Haven't heard from you in a while. Hope things are well down there in the sunshine. After a weekend packing stuff up in Montreal, we finally arrived this afternoon in Sqalid, the capital of Canada's newest province. It was supposed to be just a two-hour layover until we caught the turboprop for Desolute Bay, so we went into the gift shop and I bought a book called *Scurvy* and an egg sandwich of such incredible vileness that merely unwrapping it put me off food for the rest of the day. I was sitting there reading, feeling more and more scurrilous with each passing chapter, when the airline announced that all flights were canceled due to some un-nameable weather condition farther north.

There was a handwritten note with the names of some hotels on the wall, so David and I picked one at random from the high end of the price range (sorry about your travel budget, NOT). It was only half a mile away from the airport, but since we have the three hundred pounds of equipment that they wouldn't let us leave at the airport, we decided to take a taxi. Also it is snowing. Or sleeting, or something equally vile unsuited to October.

I know you like the Quebecois, Lori, so I will give them the benefit of the doubt by assuming that those who end up in Sqalid have been expelled from their home province for major defects of character and morals. All of the taxi drivers had heavy French (excuse me, Quebecois) accents and were beyond a doubt the biggest assholes I have ever met. They got great joy in wresting our suitcases from us and manhandling them while we screamed for mercy for the sake of the equipment. The driver then spent the ten-minute drive to the hotel bragging about how he was gonna take this town by storm, that he came here to be a big frog (pun intended) in a tiny frozen pond.

The hotel is an olive-green-colored box (more on the architecture later!) perched on a little hill. This is clearly the classy part of town, overlooking the beach (their slogan: "In 30,000 years, we'll be Malibu!"). The inside was kind of a letdown, though. The carpet is wet and stinks, and the elevator is broken. Given the drunk/stoned/high looks on the faces of those around me, I didn't want to leave the equipment in the "lockers," so I grunted it bit by bit up two flights of stairs to our room. David didn't help; he was trying to pay an Inuit bellhop to do it, without success. He thinks waving around Canadian dollars will get him someplace, not realizing that despite having flown six hours from Ottawa we have crossed no borders.

Now I'm hungry, but there's only one meal available at the hotel: steak/frites for $75, and the smell is less than appealing. David is down there now, but I am still a bit leery from the egg sandwich, so I'm chewing a piece of dirty gum I found in my pocket (hopefully it hadn't been in the pus lab) and making use of the one modernity of Sqalid: wireless Internet!

My closing thoughts for this letter ranged from "Can a pizza come by FedEx?" to "Help! Get me outta here!" so I'll just skip the sign-off and try to sleep.

Sam

FOURTEEN: SHUTDOWN

IT ONLY TOOK A couple of hours to shut down the BSL-3. Lou and Lori took the surviving cells out of the incubators—there were only a few dishes—and autoclaved them, then disconnected the CO_2 from the incubators, unplugged everything, and got rid of all the trash. After some debate, they decided to leave the −80 degree cryogenic freezer as it was, since most of the samples there dated back to the 70s and they didn't want to destroy them unless they had to.

They wiped everything down with bleach, autoclaved all of the lab coats and hung them on their individual hooks, and changed both the inner and outer door passwords. Finally, they took down the hazard sign outside and replaced it with one that said

BIOHAZARD: CLOSED TO ALL PERSONNEL

Lou was immensely relieved that he'd asked Abby to be with them to document this last step, because just as they were finishing up, along came Oriol.

At first Oriol simply pretended the sign didn't exist, but when he realized it was supposed to apply to him, he started jumping up and down like Rumpelstiltskin. "There are six years' worth of work in there!" he shrieked. "All of my intellectual property! My Nobel Prize is in those cells—you must give me my cells!"

"Too goddamn bad, shithead," Lori screamed back, unable as always to de-escalate a situation. Nearly a foot and a half shorter than Oriol, she ran circles around him like a mean little dog, voice echoing in the low basement corridor. "All of your cells are autoclaved and in the garbage. No one at this school is touching viruses again until I know how Kathy Greenwood died."

Abby stepped between the combatants, holding her arms out but being careful not to touch either Lori's or Oriol's lab coat. She made them remove the coats and hang them up, then escorted all three of them to her office, keeping herself between Lori and Oriol the entire time. Lou followed a short distance behind so that he could get a couple of pictures. He thought they might be useful someday—and if not, they were at least amusing.

Lori couldn't restrain herself, calling Oriol a slob and a liar all the way across campus, leaning across Abby several times as though she were going to reach over to the doctor and punch him. Each time, Abby grabbed Lori's arm and pushed it back where it belonged. "All of your viruses are on plasmids in your own freezer," Lori yelled. "You could recreate any of your experiments in a couple of days. Don't pretend we ruined your life's work."

Oriol was even more bent out of shape than she was, tearing his hair and moaning. "The neurons," he wailed. "The neurons were dividing."

Abby ushered them in to her cool, soundproofed office and shut the door, showing them to a round table with soft leather chairs. She poured herself a glass of ice water and then passed the pitcher around, but no one else was interested. "Coffee?" she offered. "Tea? Valium?"

"This is not a joke!" Oriol pounded his fist on the varnished maple. A droplet of spit flew from the corner of his mouth and landed in the middle of the table, reflecting sunlight.

"If the neurons were dividing, you can make them divide again," Lori scoffed, leaning towards him, smearing the table with fingerprints. "But first you have to convince me that they weren't dividing in Kathy's head."

"You're all hysterical ninnies!" Oriol jumped up, ready to storm from the room until he saw Abby shake her head. He plunked back down, sulking. "Greenwood had been sick for years. You only had to look at her."

The others all exchanged a puzzled glance. "Sorry, Oriol, could you explain?" Lou requested. "I'm not a physician."

"Obviously you're not," Oriol sneered. He had begun to calm down, mopping his face with a tissue and regaining control of his voice. "But I am. The symptoms of lysosomal storage disorders are classic, simply classic. And when I tell you those vectors are safe, you have no business ruining them without my permission."

"Actually, there have been serious concerns," Abby broke in. "We have had a sudden, unexplained death that took place in that lab."

Lou was a little worried that Lori would press that detail, since he had lied to her about where he found Kathy. He needn't have worried, though—Oriol was loud enough to drown out any suspicion. "Only a fool would think that it was because of the experiments!" he bellowed.

"Good." Abby took out a notebook and laid it on the table. "Then why don't you elaborate."

They were at an impasse. No one wanted to say anything about mouse brains, green men, secret clinics, or anything else that might have served to enlighten them all.

Abby appeared unsurprised at the sudden silence. "Fine. There will be a safety committee investigation, but for now, the lab is closed."

Lou and Lori said nothing on their way back to the Physics building, with Oriol less than a step behind. Just before he spun on his heel to return to Biology, he leaned over and whispered, "If you want to know why your noses all express GFP, I'd try asking your own students."

Long before Oriol was out of earshot, Lori started ranting about how full of shit he was, and Lou quickly forgot the exchange. He had other things to worry about. If he was only going to sneeze and not die, he had to make sure that NASA didn't cancel their project in three months' time. This meant hiring at least one more postdoc, preferably a theorist, and stepping up the modeling effort and the work at the South Pole. It was time for this molecular biology nonsense to take the back burner where it belonged, and to focus on the physics side of the grant the way he had wanted all along.

He meant to go home when Lori did, but never quite managed it. It was hardly a surprise, then, when Oriol burst into his office not long after Lori had gone. Unlike Biology, the physics building had no security on its doors.

The mouse-doctor was still wearing his tainted lab coat, the sleeves rolled up past his elbows. Underneath he had only shorts on—or maybe nothing at all, who could tell? There was no furniture in Lou's office apart from the desk, so Oriol sat right down on the edge of it without being invited. Miasmas of ethanol and bleach overpowered his cologne. "Well," he said. "Suppose you tell me what happened."

"I might say the same thing," Lou responded, half hoping Barrow had set up one of her video cameras before she left. "Kathy Greenwood knew a lot more about your secret experiments than she let on."

"I have no 'secret' experiments," Oriol sneered. "The safety committee simply has a ridiculous rule that injected mice cannot return to the Mouse House, so I have to house them elsewhere."

"So, how many of them have green brain tumors?"

"That idiot woman!" Oriol exploded, pounding Lou's desk. "She had no business telling you what I was doing, or stealing my mice..."

"This had nothing to do with Kathy, and I'd thank you not to jostle my hard drive." Lou shut his laptop and stuck it into a drawer, just in case. He'd been expecting the wrath of Oriol, but he hadn't thought to back up his files. "I know about the brain tumors because I *saw* a brain tumor—in a mouse in the BSL-3 lab."

Oriol froze in mid-gesture, fist in the air, and glanced around. He seemed to deflate a little. "One got out," he admitted. "I looked everywhere, but it had escaped. Where did you find it?"

"In a garbage bag. Where it bit Kathy."

Oriol leapt up, threw back his head, and boomed with mirthless laughter. "Is this what all of this hysteria is about?"

"I don't know whether it's hysteria or not. Why do your mice get green brain tumors? Is that what killed Kathy?" Lou lowered his voice. "Is that what killed my Uncle Alex?"

Oriol didn't miss a beat. "The average survival with progressive supranuclear palsy is five years. He lived for six, so technically I gave him an extra year."

This was such a prime example of idiot doctor-math that all Lou could do was shake his head. "Alex died in agony," he reminded Oriol. "In a nursing home, screaming, with a huge brain tumor. If I'd known, I would have asked for an autopsy of his brain. But I had no idea that you were trying to make neurons reproduce inside people's heads. And what about Moe Deet?"

"Patient confidentiality," snapped Oriol, getting up and sweeping around the room as if he intended to leave.

Lou called him back. "You can at least tell me whether you turned him green on purpose or by accident. That will go a long way towards helping us figure out if we have an epidemic on our hands."

Oriol weighed this, expecting a trap. "Nothing you see is by accident," he answered at last, eyes on the doorknob.

Lou was a little bit relieved, but the questions still weren't answered. He turned on his very best condescending professor voice. "I honestly can't imagine any scenario where it's OK for you to be turning patients green."

"Gene therapy is a legitimate protocol!" Oriol squawked.

"Using HIV and rabies? Hmm..." The suddenly tense set of Oriol's mouth said a lot, so Lou persisted, "When we got permission to use this virus for research purposes, we had to promise two things. One, that GFP was the only gene in it. If you're using it for therapy, clearly that isn't the case. I have to wonder just what gene you think it's OK to put into people. Two, we had to convince the safety office that none of our bodily fluids would ever contact the experiment, just in case something we happened to be infected with would recombine with our vector. And here you are injecting it straight into someone's bloodstream."

"Nonsense." His chest swelled with pride. "I inject it only into the most immune-privileged organ of the body."

"Oh, right—straight into the brain. So what makes you think the virus doesn't get into blood vessels in the brain and travel right out?"

"Moe was negative for HIV. I tested him myself."

"OK, fine. Was he negative two months later, too? Who knows how many third-world clinics he's been to. Or what if he had a cold or the flu, and that virus recombined with your gene therapy virus?"

"You're an idiot!" Oriol's hair stood up like the crest on a Muscovy duck. "You have no idea how it works."

"Well, you pretend to—and that's even worse."

"It hardly matters," Oriol scoffed, regaining his composure and preening his crest of hair with one hand. "I'll never have any more patients again anyway, thanks to you."

Lou peeked into Oriol's pupils as if the green of madness would be shining through. "What are you talking about?"

Oriol strode forward and slapped the empty desk. "I'd thank you to stop that series of posts right now."

Lou had never posted to an on-line board in his entire life, but he wasn't about to let Oriol know that. "Why not?" he asked. "They're all true."

Oriol started to froth again, quoting from the alleged "posts" that Lou made a mental note to look up the instant he was alone. Some of the phrases were pretty good: "Untested treatments killed my dad!" was a nice one, but his favorite had to be "Save your money, save your sanity, and wait for a real cure!"

Dr. Ortiz was stupid, Lou decided, the perfect embodiment of why the university should never have betrayed its physical science roots and gone down the path of viruses and mice. "It's really not my concern if you're treating patients legally elsewhere," he explained in what he hoped was a reasonable imitation of Abby's soothing lawyer voice. "It is my concern if you're using viruses that are not properly contained, and that might escape into the environment and infect people or animals."

"Kathy died because she refused my treatment," he declared. "Not because of a mouse bite. I could have cured her, but no—my findings weren't enough for her. Don't *you* want to be cured?" He leaned in closer. "How can you stand to live your life now, compared to what it was?"

"Every night I dream I'm running on the beach, and every morning I wake up screaming," said Lou. "But I'd rather spend sixty years in this chair than have deformed green neurons spilling out of the top of my head."

Oriol swirled his lab coat around him, as if he were going to disappear like a superhero, but finally just turned around and stalked out.

When Lou was sure he was gone, he locked the door, pulled out his computer, and typed in *save your sanity and wait.*

FIFTEEN: SAM'S DIARY, PART 2

From: sjroth@its.sti.edu
To: louism@its.sti.edu, lab@its.sti.edu
Subject: near-death experience

Almost got shot today. I blame you both. If I get a bullet in the neck and end up a C2 quad, guaranteed I will sip-n-puff my way over to you and wreak revenge somehow! (The "somehow" is left as an exercise for the reader—Lou, I hope this gives you bad dreams.)

It all started with hunger. As you know I had had nothing for lunch but a whiff of rotten eggs, and nothing for dinner but BSL-3 gum, so I awoke shaky and ravenous. I also noticed David huddled under his blanket clutching his stomach, and he suggested it would be a great idea if I went for a walk and left him alone, so I figured his steak/frites were fighting back and left quickly before he exploded.

Just down the hill from the hotel there is a big, flat shopping complex called the BoreaMall (ha ha, gag), and I thought it might contain a grocery store of some description. I cut across some icy/muddy hill in its general direction, realizing I was wearing only about half the clothes I should have been. It's harder to judge the seasons here than it is "down South" in Montreal—this is because there are NO TREES of any kind. My California-trained mind doesn't process this well, so I tend to assume barrenness implies warm desert. Nothing could be farther from the truth. It is mid-October, but winter is firmly entrenched. Flurries of something frozen dripped down my back as I slid down the hill towards the store.

Here's the bit on architecture—no trees means no wood, so the buildings are these weird plastic pre-fabs that look exactly like huge Tupperware (crappy cell-phone picture attached, sorry, I lost my good camera in the shooting). The elementary school is a white UFO-shaped thing with windows like airplane windows, the highschool is baby blue with no windows at all, and the BoreaMall is rectangular and flat and covers at least a city block. While I was trying to figure out how to get inside the building, I heard a panicked whisper: "Hey, Southerner! What are you doing? Get down!" I looked around to find two cops (do you still call them Mounties if they aren't on horses?) holding rifles and wearing flak helmets and bulletproof vests. "There's a standoff at the mall," one of them whispered, sounding blasé, as if this were a regular Sunday occurrence. "You should get low and go down by the beach."

I obeyed as quickly as my weakened state would allow, and the sight of the "beach" helped to put me off food again, perhaps permanently. It was a mass of dirty sand, broken floes, and dead animal parts. I saw what I was sure was a severed human foot, but which upon closer inspection had polar bear fur on it. There were many parts of dead Huskies, including a skull from which all meat had been eroded on one side, while the opposite side was still cute and fluffy.

Shivering and retching, I took refuge in the first building I came to, a plastic shack with no windows. Raucous laughter greeted me along with various statements like "This is the place to be!" Looking around, I saw that the walls were covered with guns of every description—rifles, shotguns, handguns, AK-47s. This is CANADA??

"'E can't get us in 'ere, mon 'ostie," chortled some skanky Quebecois. "Grab a rifle and get low."

There were several other scary-looking guys in there, and I tried to press them for details, but none were forthcoming. I decided against telling them I was Jewish and thus not anyone's "hostie" (what *is* it with you Christians and cannibalism?), and just bought a knit hat called a "tuque" and sneaked out.

Breathing shallowly in the rancid beach reek, I walked along the edge of the water towards the other side of town, hoping to be able to cut around the "action" and get back to my hotel. I could see a Mountie or two hiding behind each building I passed for at least a mile, until finally the town had disappeared and I was by a field near the airport. I use the term "field" loosely, as no grass, flowers, cattails, or other earth-like life forms are implied. Just as I thought it might be safe to head up towards town, I heard a cacophony of brain-damaged screeching.

Several teenage boys, wielding bludgeons and walking unsteadily under the influence of something I don't care to think about, came out of the ditch straight towards me. I simply stood there and waited to die, but it seems their target was elsewhere—I hadn't noticed the knot of sleeping Huskies on the beach. So I continued to stand there helplessly while they beat the chained-up dogs to death. There was nothing I could do. I couldn't even puke since I hadn't eaten for an entire day.

I finally got away and onto a small street where there were government buildings. I saw a Mountie without a flak helmet and he assured me this road was safe, and I told him about the dogs. He just shook his head and told me the kids huffed gasoline and destroyed their brains before they were twenty—then he indicated where they went after that: the jail or the neurological hospital.

The jail is the nicest building in town, all pink and purple plastic with big darkened windows. The neuro hospital looks significantly more worn and creepy, though it is a nice shade of mauve, and it was when I went to take a picture of it to scare you guys that I discovered I'd lost my camera. It may be government property, but I have no desire to retrace even one of my steps to find it.

Anyway, this road I was following (unpaved, of course) was all government buildings, since believe it or not, Sqalid is a provincial capital. I was the only pedestrian; even though the roads don't leave town, just about everyone has a car or an ATV, and there are traffic jams. There was a Department of Housing (Why??), a Department of Wildlife Control (Start with the primates!), and a Department of Official Languages and Translation. All the signs everywhere were in four languages—English, French, Inuktitut, and some sort of "Standardized Greenlandic" that all northern peoples are allegedly supposed to understand. Inuktitut, the official language of Sqalid, is written in some bizarre font that looks like Wingdings. I don't understand why they did that; maybe to make jobs for typesetters or something.

Lou, you'd also be happy to know that because this is a government capital, all buildings are fully accessible and have very nice ramps made out of corrugated aluminum. So next time, YOU CAN COME TO THIS HELL-HOLE INSTEAD OF ME.

Right. Ahem. Well, I made it back to my hotel, where several Mounties were stationed out front on plastic chairs, rifles on their laps. They were chewing something, which was a good sign, so I went inside the hotel to the coffee shop. In true Eastern European style, they were open but "had no coffee today," so the only choices were canned sodas ($5 each), some kind of scone-like object, or a ham sandwich. For once the

Mosaic laws seemed reasonable to me, so I took the scone and a Coke and retired to my room to write this.

David was sitting on the bed looking ~~green~~ ill, and when I offered him half my scone he dashed into the bathroom.

There are police helicopters outside, but I pulled my drapes because I don't want to see it.

They say we won't get out of here for at least another two days because of a storm.

I think I have scurvy.

Sam

PART II

SIXTEEN: NEW RECRUITS

A FEW WEEKS PASSED uneventfully, but Lori knew two things: They hadn't heard the end of the story, and she could trust no one. Claudine was nuts, Lou was hiding something, Walter Waddles was sulking, and Oriol was of course Oriol.

She was sure that Lou had lied to her—and the police—about where he found Kathy. When she confronted him, he admitted he'd found her in the BSL-3, but denied ever lying. As for Oriol, he refused to elaborate on his "obvious" diagnosis of Kathy or to specify exactly which of the many lysosomal storage disorders he claimed she suffered from. Lori had done a bunch of reading and learned way more than she ever wanted to know about a large number of gruesome diseases, but had no way of knowing whether he was telling the truth. As far as she could tell, Kathy had no physical problems other than being short. And, most recently, dead.

Her research was at a standstill. During the period of probation for their project, NASA inspectors could—and did—appear at random times, sniffing around the lab, harassing the students, and taking pictures of everyone's experiments. Gone were the days when they could brazenly PCR Moe Deet's cheek cells on the benchtop; everyone but Walter had fled biology and was safely back doing particle physics or engineering.

But she couldn't get the green brains out of her mind. The NASA inspectors were evil, but they weren't necessarily wrong; it was pretty likely that Oriol had a secret mouse stash somewhere. Thanks to old keys and a lock-picking set, she was able to prowl all of the buildings built before 1991. She sniffed and knocked on doors to listen for squeaks, she checked garbage cans and biohazard bins, but she found neither hide nor hair of any illegal mice.

Of course, the new biology complex was a different story, not ready to yield its horrors to prying eyes. It had several layers of security on it, and neither she nor any of the Buboes had managed to defeat them yet. A few students had been stopped by Security trying to break into labs, and one had actually been arrested. The vivisectionists took their privacy seriously.

She still had the DNA samples from everyone, including Moe, so she ordered a whole new set of PCR primers to test. Some were targeted to the ends of their viral genome, so she could see everything contained in the virus, not just the GFP. She also got primers to other viruses that might have been around the lab, such as yellow fever and a slew of cold viruses.

But she never had a chance to try them out. She was too busy teaching and writing grant proposals, reduced to begging for peanuts to keep the lab running. The only student she had left was Walter, and he dragged himself around moping, weeping over each lost day and dish of cells. In just two months, everything she had worked for seemed to have evaporated, all starting from a green mouse brain.

Finally, against all of her better judgment, she decided to recruit a few Buboes to help with the PCR. None of them had ever touched biology before, so she gave them a little test to identify the most coordinated and least impulsive of the lot—she asked interested candidates to draw a little of their own blood and take a picture of the red cells.

Naturally this was against the safety rules, and she had a moment of panic when this year's only female freshman came sobbing into her office, clutching her laptop and weeping that she was "brimming with fluorescence."

Lori took a look at the incriminating evidence, which turned out to be beautiful sections taken with a laser-scanning microscope, and quickly projected them into three dimensions. The flexible disks of the Bubo's blood cells tumbled over each other in a mass of green, and Lori explained hastily that the cells themselves were fluorescent, and that the hapless Bubo had managed to excite them while looking for GFP.

Still, they were really nice pictures, and somehow the student had learned to use the fluorescence microscope above and beyond the call of duty. She also argued, correctly, that the cells couldn't be fluorescent when excited for GFP, because hemoglobin required UV excitation.

"Yeah, I know," Lori admitted. "It's probably hemoglobin breakdown products."

"B-but why are they breaking *down*?" wailed the Bubo.

The only thing that finally reassured her was Lori demonstrating that her own red cells glowed green—which, if the Bubo were in the know, wouldn't have calmed her down one bit.

There were three others, all seniors, who managed to take decent (non-fluorescent) images of their cells, so Lori led all four into the biology lab just as the sun was setting on Halloween night. They trailed along behind her like so many baby ducks down the residential walkway and across campus. It was a clear evening with no moon, so dry that the sounds of traffic and rustling palm trees were magnified as if in a wind tunnel. A faint smell of forest fires arrived periodically on gusts from the hills.

She handed out lab coats and gloves to all—the little she-Bubo got Kathy's old black lab coat—and got them started swabbing their noses and pricking their fingers. She told them that they were "negative controls," but of course she had a real negative control on hand, just in case. The Buboes were more than lab techs, they were experimental subjects; their blood would tell her if the virus had spread, or more specifically, whether she herself had at some point been contagious. They lived in the same House, they ate in the same cafeteria— they even used the same box of Kleenex in the front entryway.

She let one of them prick her own finger with a sterile lancet, because she knew what a thrill he'd get from bleeding his professor. "This is because of that mouse, isn't it?" he wondered cagily.

There were giggles behind him and murmurs of "Have you seen me?"

Lori sighed silently to herself. She never should have tried to hide anything from the Buboes. She tried to explain in a way that wouldn't lend itself to hyperbole. "OK, I think we all know there was a mystery mouse with a green glow. We dissected it and then someone stole it."

The she-Bubo stepped forward, giving Lori a momentary start with her lank black hair and black lab coat. "Why are we testing ourselves?" she wondered. "Shouldn't we be looking at mice? Lab mice and wild mice on campus, not to mention raccoons and chipmunks."

Everyone said professors quickly became useless and that the only good ideas ever came from students, who spent their lives in the lab. When another of the Buboes tossed up his gloved hands and snorted, "Why don't you go collect yourself a bag of road kill!" Lori knew exactly how she would be spending the rest of her Halloween.

SEVENTEEN: DON'T FEED THE TROLL

FROM THE WINDOW AT the east end of his office, Lou could see people dashing about in all sorts of costumes. There was a group dressed as famous scientists gone zombie, a parade of glowing skeletons, and his favorite—someone dressed as the barrel of a GFP molecule. Towards ten o'clock, a bunch of them started pushing crates of pumpkins towards the library, preparing for the annual eleven-story pumpkin drop.

The holiday made him remember Kathy. He had been too preoccupied to think of her since the sad little service they'd had up at what he thought of as the Lonely Atheist Funeral Home. She'd had no one to mourn her, not even any graduate students, and no one responded to announcements of her death or came to claim the few possessions in her apartment or office. She had lived in Postdoc and Visitor Housing right across the street, the ultimate sign of having no life. Lou ought to know—he'd lived there for almost two years after getting out of the hospital, when getting around was a nightmare and it was all he could do to go back and forth across the street every day. He still remembered the stove with only one working burner and the chronic lack of hot water, and the stain in the corner that everyone referred to as "Einstein's barf."

Kathy's place was even worse than his had been. It was as if no one even lived there: no curtains, no dishes, no TV, radio, or phone, nothing but a tube of toothpaste and a plastic basket full of black clothing. The carpet was dotted with purple stains, which for some reason had made Lori sniffle. A thin, aged mattress in the bedroom was covered with a grungy sheet, and a half-empty bag of Cheez Doodles sat at the head—this was apparently Kathy's desk. Lou, Lori, and Walter had removed everything themselves and cleaned the place out for re-rental, silent with embarrassment, not wanting anyone else to see how one of their own had lived.

The late mathematician's office had been a bit livelier, decorated with stuffed snakes and plastic spiders, black streamers and ghost-sheet curtains. Lou and Lori had taken a few decorations in her memory: a lifelike cobra that now curled around the computer monitor in the main office, and a large spider web that hung in front of the projector in the seminar room.

In an irrepressible spasm of curiosity, Lou had also taken her laptop, something he would regret forever. There were no truer words than "A real friend is someone who, after your death, deletes your browser history."

However lonely and anti-social her real life had been, Kathy had made up for it on-line. She was a member of every possible neurological disease forum in English-speaking cyberspace, alternately posting as a patient, a caregiver, a friend, or a fetishist. Sometimes she was a troll, sometimes a counter-troll. One of her favorite pastimes was outing fakers, which always led to site-wide uproar. She'd been the first to jump on "13-year-old girl with pain in stumps," "Help!!! Teen girl with questions, can't ask mom," and the soon-to-be-a-meme MissPoopyPants:

BOWEL WOES
Posted by: MissPoopyPants

I'm a sixteen-year-old girl injured in a freak accident. I was an elite gymnast and I decided to do a backflip off my bed—dumb, I know! My hand slipped on a magazine and I landed on my head. I just got off the ventilator, but I still can't move anything

*below my neck, which means that I can't help at all with... you
know. It's really embarrassing having to have a nurse come and
put her finger up my bum every morning. We usually do it in
bed, with a pad under me. She does digital stimulation for at
least ten minutes. Of course I can't feel it, but I can tell when I'm
"nice and empty" because I get a tingling sensation all over my
face. Anyone else feel this? Then the nurse leaves, and the problem is sometimes I still have poop in me! It can come out at any
time—at meals, in class, even just at the computer. I don't want
my family to know, so I just sit in it until the nurse comes for the
night. Help!!!!*

Disgusted with himself for wasting time with this garbage,
Lou had slammed the computer shut and tossed it in a drawer.
He had no desire to read any more litanies of pus, pain, and
poo, interspersed with the drooling of pervs who got off on
those things. Did the rehab counselors who referred people to
these "support" sites have any idea how much of it was fake?

He'd only taken the laptop out once since, with the wireless
turned off, to look through the math Kathy had been working
on when she died. Most of the science stuff on her computer
was not math-related, strangely enough. There was a bunch of
biology, some pretty electron micrographs in a folder called
Fibroblasts, and all sorts of documentation on the BSL-3.

He finally dug up a nearly completed gauge theory paper
and another that was outlined, so he got inspired to propose
a special issue to the journal he edited: *Quantum Theories and
Cosmology, In Memory of Katherine Greenwood (1978–2008)*.
So far ten people had accepted the invitation to contribute,
which Lou thought was a much nicer tribute than a few hyp-
ocritical tears shed in a scummy hot room in front of a fake
priest.

He quickly forgot about Kathy's on-line life in the scram-
ble to fill the void she'd left behind in meatspace. Math was
doing even worse than Physics in its recruitment efforts, and

her hiring had come after three years of creepy, stupid, lazy, or just plain unqualified candidates. Lou had been on the search committee the whole time, and he thought that they might do better if they searched for graduates of physics departments than traditional math. So he'd added an assistant professor position to their department's list of openings, and made an effort to sign up for conferences and workshops so he could let everyone know that they were hiring.

The CVs poured in, but they were mostly awful. One guy actually said he had taken a year off to "study jihad," and he wasn't even among the worst. Another was a straight-out plagiarist, claiming papers that weren't his own. But most simply had nothing to do with the topic at hand, sending mass *To Whom It May Concern* emails with the contact name and sometimes—but only sometimes—the research subject searched and replaced in a different font throughout the form letter.

In the past two weeks Lou had been to the Westside four times, the East Coast twice, and Europe once. He'd Skyped to Japan, Singapore, and Australia, getting up at odd hours to accommodate worldwide search committees. He lived in that vague haze of not knowing what time zone he was in, which was vaguely pleasant since it helped him forget his cold lonely house. Abby had moved out and taken everything except her piano, which she wanted "disinfected" after Lori had helpfully informed her that piano keys could carry anthrax. Since no one really knew what caused green brains or if it could hide on piano keys, the method of disinfection remained an open question, and the instrument stayed in Lou's living room.

The first pumpkin of the yearly Drop whistled through the air and hit the pavement with a satisfying crunching noise. To Lou's relief, the smashed pumpkin revealed absolutely no green luminescence. At least something at STI wasn't green.

He mustered his courage and pulled out Kathy's computer once more. Somewhere in there, he was sure, was the story of what killed her. He booted it up to the sounds of cheering and splattering pumpkins, imagining the tiny mathematician dressed as zombie Maria Goeppert-Mayer and egging him on in the search. Maybe in some way she was in the room now, and could summon Roger's ghost to call Lou an idiot if he didn't succeed in finding all of Oriol's secrets.

He surfed for nearly an hour without finding anything of substance. Kathy (as "LosingHope") had over 1400 posts on a single neurological-disease site, most of them about suicide and how terrible it would be not to be able to off oneself due to dementia or lack of hand function. A typical one was where she speculated on whether a quadriplegic would be able to commit suicide by chewing a whole pack of gum, then inhaling it—this naturally led to a flame war. She'd also come out in favor of offing Terri Schiavo, but against the growth-stunting "Ashley treatment," mainly because she claimed *Those kids should just be put out of their misery.*

Searching the site for "Mexico," "Oriol Ortiz," "virus," and "GFP" led nowhere. Just when he was about to give up and go vomit, he had the idea to try renewing Kathy's "premium membership" to the site. It was allegedly free but asked for a credit card number, which was suspicious in itself, and he didn't want them to have his name. Fortunately, Kathy's old card number auto-completed and the order went through.

Suddenly there was a whole list of new forums for his perusal: Sexuality (to be avoided as though his life depended on it); Off-Topic Posts (flame wars); and Untested Treatments.

It was all there in the last forum. Right under their GFP-expressing noses for weeks.

Oriol wasn't such a moron after all for accusing Lou for the posts. Kathy's avatar for this forum was a picture of his spare wheelchair in the entryway of the BSL-3, with a lab coat draped over it. Her username was "Cureseeker."

I don't trust this Mexican clinic, she had posted back in May. *What are the side effects? Did any of you try looking at yourselves under a black light after the treatment?*

There was even *OK, I think I'm getting convinced, but I don't want to travel to Mexico alone, and in pain, without talking to the doctor first. How can I get in touch with him?*

That was still before she or Oriol had started working at the university, but after they had both accepted their positions. The plot was thickening faster than a good blancmange, but it still wasn't making sense.

He continued to read and scroll as the STI Halloween proceeded gleefully outside his window. Finally he came across what was very close to what he was looking for.

From someone called Caring_Daughter, now in June:

My father has suffered from progressive supranuclear palsy for almost four years. We tried to take care of him at home, but when he stopped recognizing my mother we had to put him in a nursing home. He's only 48 years old, and I know he'll try anything. He won't last much longer. Is there any treatment available NOW that has a chance of helping him?

Then from Kathy: *I hear that gene therapy is the best, offered by a clinic in Mexico. But I'm trying to find out the details. I especially want to know if I can get the treatment here in California, and not risk my health traveling south of the border. Can anyone give me any information?*

Unfortunately the discussion went to private messages, but less than two months later, Caring_Daughter had changed her tune. By that time, Kathy was working at STI.

Not a miracle!!!
Dad seemed so good for a while... but now he has these splitting headaches, nothing they give him can help. They're so bad in the morning that he screams when the nurse comes to wake him up. He has forgotten who I am and does nothing but moan in

pain. Every day I regret subjecting him to an untested treatment out of desperation.

When Kathy stepped in to defend Oriol, Caring_Daughter became passionate and lost control of her CapsLock key:

UNTESTED CURES KILLED MY DAD

There ARE folks out there working on a cure and they WILL find it, but doesn't logic tell you that it isn't going to surface in some third world country at a price? The scientists who perfect this will be NOBEL PRIZE material, not someone who is making a few thousand bucks selling injections from a clinic in Mexico. We asked ourselves "What harm can it do?" and it's THIS. My dad is GOING TO DIE—maybe sooner than he even would have otherwise, certainly in more pain—and my mom has lost her retirement savings. It's IRRESPONSIBLE if not downright CRIMINAL of you to counsel someone to have something unproven injected into their brain! Everyone—save your money, save your hope, SAVE YOUR SANITY AND WAIT.

There it was—Oriol's phrase. The timing, the disease, everything could have been Lou's uncle Alex, with a few identifying details fudged. But it wasn't.

Caring_Daughter vanished from the boards not long after, but Kathy continued to encourage people to contact "the doctor." Her final set of posts started only two days before she died. They were in response to TooTired, who'd started a thread called "Can't Go On":

I was paralyzed in the same car accident that left my boyfriend blind and with a head injury. I am his primary caretaker even though I have no use of my hands or legs. From the outside, it appears that there's nothing wrong with him (except for his eyes, of course, which are missing and covered over with simple pieces of tape because he refuses prosthetics).

"*Sacrament,*" Lou cried aloud. He stopped for a minute to look out the window, where blue flames leapt from two jack-o'-lanterns on either side of the library steps. This was why he stayed off the Internet. But he'd come here for a purpose, so after a minute he swallowed his revulsion and kept reading.

But he's emotionally labile, has delusions of grandeur, and can't take care of himself. He'll be in the middle of running a bath and forget that he's doing it or why. Last week he flooded the bathroom, which destroyed the floor; he also hadn't had a bath in more than two weeks. I had to call a social worker to force him to wash, but she didn't believe me when I said he was head-injured, and he denied everything and claimed he was taking care of me. He may believe this on some level, I don't know.

I have a primary caretaker for my bowel care and other routines, but she is not reliable. Last week I caught her stealing money and had to let her go. Unfortunately, now I have to rely on my boyfriend to get me out of bed in the morning. If he forgets halfway through, or refuses because Jesus told him it's wrong, then I don't go to work and we don't have money for food.

I'm not sure how long I can go on this way. I have already developed a pressure sore and a chronic cough. If I go into a nursing home, what will happen to him?

We had a perfect life together until the drunk driver took everything. I was a personal trainer, and he was a retired professional athlete teaching at a business college. I can't believe that the smart, funny, hot guy I fell in love with has turned into this. Sometimes pieces of the "old Mike" shine through and I fall in love with him all over again. But mostly I'm just exhausted, and scared, and cry myself to sleep every night. Someone please help, I don't know what to do.

Kathy had responded to this heartbreaking post with instructions to Oriol's clinic in Mexico, claiming he had the "only real cure." And forty-two hours later, she was dead.

Ever since *alt.tasteless* invaded *rec.pets.cats*, nerds had been breaking hearts, corrupting minds, and sometimes destroying lives in cyberspace. Lou had sworn never to get involved, but it was time to lose that virginity. He considered using Kathy's account, but she had left too long a Trail of Troll, so he logged out and created a new identity.

As a first post, it was pretty simple: *Want_Answers: Dear TooTired, please send me a private message.*

EIGHTEEN: SAM'S DIARY, PART 4

From: sjroth@its.sti.edu

From: sjroth@its.sti.edu
To: louism@its.sti.edu, lab@its.sti.edu
cc: wwwaddles4@its.sti.edu
Subject: helllooooo out there

Hey,

How come you guys don't email me back? Lori, I thought you prided yourself on having answered every email promptly since 1991. Don't make me nervous, here.

Walter, if they're both dead or in prison, let me know so I can quit and move to Hawaii. Actually, I might do that anyway. Any faith I had in the human race has been destroyed by seeing the depths to which Canada can sink.

Finally got out of Sqalid, but now we've been stuck for over two weeks in a place so much worse that my feeble efforts will not describe it. When we first left, I was so relieved to escape the squalor that I didn't notice the encroaching desolation. Not a tree, not a flower, not a blade of grass, not even much snow—just bare brown tundra all the way to Desolute.

It was foggy and windy when we landed, and when I asked about the metal carcasses littering the ground, the pilot informed me casually that they were crashed airplanes. Suddenly those three days in Sqalid didn't seem so bad after all, and I thanked him effusively for waiting until the weather was "good" to get us up here.

Yes, it was a nice day in Desolute. Only single digits below zero, winds barely in excess of 100 km/hr, and a fine precipitation falling that I don't believe is anywhere on our known phase diagram of water. Lori, you'd be intrigued to know that this is where Canada's weather comes from. They pack it up and send it on down straight from the Pole.

After three days, we saw the sun set forever... well, anyway, at least until next April. This final sunset wasn't much of an event, though, given that a heavy dense overcast has a tendency to obscure the alleged movement of this formerly so-familiar celestial body. Never mind scurvy—I'm working on rickets next.

All the flags are in tatters here, a testimony either to the north wind or the state of patriotism. Desolute is the farthest north permanently inhabited community in Canada—basically the government rounded up 200 Inuit and pays them to sit here and be Canadian. This is in case the evil Danish army decides to try to claim the frozen north for its own (What's the difference between the Danish Army and Ted Kennedy? Kennedy actually killed someone...). These poor souls live about 3 miles from where we landed, which was just beside a hangar set up for the scientists and their gear and experiments.

Besides paying for signs in four languages and living quarters for token Canadians, your (meaning *their*) taxes also pay for the upkeep of this hangar, all its communication gear, and the lodgings for the researchers to study the all-important Great White North. The "hotel" of sorts is a flat blue-and-red building with a double entryway in which you leave your boots and your extreme-weather orange suit. They told us because it was "warm out" we didn't get an orange suit unless we were going out on the pack ice in a snowmobile (fat chance). You then pass through a gray, dark common area and are assigned a bed in a double room, sheet and pillow provided but you furnish the sleeping bag.

After Sqalid, it all seemed very clean and peaceful, and it took me several hours to figure out there was nothing to do. The first order of business was, of course, food. They feed us well here in Desolute—every day at 7, at 12, and at 5:30 a bell rings and we make our slavering Pavlovian way to the cafeteria, where we are fattened like spring lambs and cured of our scurvy. There's salad! Fruit! Fresh bread! The kitchen also remains open for raiding at all times. This is in fact quite dangerous, as the boredom forces you to try the baked goods one by one. Canadians eat something called a "Nanaimo bar," which is fat and sugar compressed into the density of a neutron star. This I couldn't finish, but I did enjoy my brownie-ice cream sundae, a few peanut butter cookies, and piece of frozen mocha cheesecake (oh yeah!) unearthed in the freezer.

All of this was washed down with orange juice, of course, not only because of my scurvy but because Desolute is a dry town. Everyone is so close to suicide and/or homicide at all times that alcohol would cause the place to self-destruct in a week.

I wanted to take a walk to work off some of the desserts, but was informed that it was dangerous to go alone because of polar bears. This was a very scary thought, especially because the white-out would make them extremely hard to see until the cute black nose and gaping pink mouth were upon you.

None of this bothered David, who from the very first evening went full native. He borrowed some kind of reeking fur coat that probably still contained entrails, and went off in a group with people looking for "homestyle" cooking (seal meat? Salt pork?) and "souvenirs."

I can't even look at the stuff he brings back, and he continues—no surprise—to be tormented by his bowels.

As for me, I haven't left the scientist "hotel." After a few days I grew accustomed to the idleness, and spend most of my waking hours as a vegetable in the common area. This seems to be the universal reaction to Desolute. We're all here until our pilots and project managers decide it's a good time to fly us to our field sites; until then we just sit, eat ourselves into a sugar coma, and wait for the cry of

"Party to Eureka, one hour!"

The same weather that stranded David and me in Sqalid stranded quite a few people here, and it shows. A week of this regime will turn anyone into a motionless humanoid lump who doesn't even bother to turn the lights on. I was once so brave as to suggest Scrabble, but this was met by slow head-turnings and lugubrious sighs, after which a geologist informed me that all the "E"s in the set were missing.

"Don't bother to read any of the books, either," added someone else, "especially the murder mysteries. Key pages are torn out of each one." He then lapsed back into an un-rousable stupor.

The hot showers are wonderful, but I am a bit nervous by now at the resemblance to *Une pure formalité*. If I get a sight of Gérard Depardieu with no clothes on, I will run screaming.

Write back to me. Now. I don't care how green your brains are!! I will be incommunicado once we get on the plane for Eureka.

Sam

NINETEEN: I SEE EVERYTHING GREEN

CLAUDINE WAS A SUCCESS. The only problem was, the spa was not hers any more.

One thing could be said for Oriol: He had good taste. He had hired a horde of workmen to transform the place from a rattletrap into a spa for the stars, all faster than Claudine could blink. She sat in her office and watched as walls came down, fences went up, plants and trees sprang full-grown in place, and wood turned from dirty gray to natural oak to shiny varnish.

There was even a real French chef from a Michelin three-star restaurant—one who proceeded to slaughter all of Claudine's spring lambs and serve them up, bloody and dripping, to the Hollywood VIPs who began to arrive in ever-increasing numbers.

Then the mad doctor convinced her it was unfair not to provide parking for "the handicapped." He paved her future tropical garden with several inches of concrete, and all of his spry, marathon-running patients came pouring in, driving their Beemers, Lexuses, and Humvees adorned with placards prescribed to them by Oriol. One of them ran over Claudine's prized goat and then demanded *she* apologize for letting animals wander into the street. The incident ended with the removal of the 10 mph speed limit sign and the building of yet more parking. A cloud of smog hung over the entrance, permanently aroar with engines gunned by arriving guests.

The goat cart driver became a valet, allowing guests to check in without walking a single foot.

Whenever Claudine tried to object, Oriol and his team of handpicked European architects made her swallow her gall. Carrara marble floors in the Roman bath area, recovered brick from a torn-down Mediterranean palace for the exterior walls, and the frescoes! There were only a few artists in the world schooled in real fresco technique, which involved painting with fast-drying plaster.

Apparently not scared off by his mad-scientist treatment, Moe Deet came back every weekend. Contrary to Abby's and her deranged Frenchman's wild predictions, his head did not explode, he didn't begin to stagger or scream in agony, and he remained quite stubbornly alive. He conferred with the doctor now and then, but came out looking no greener than when he went in.

A little melancholy, perhaps, and clearly blind as a bat, but no greener. To cheer him up on Halloween night, Claudine prepared a picnic of all of her own recipes just for the two of them. No leg of lamb or stuffed wild swan, just tofu salad sandwiches, lentil soup, and an array of fresh fall fruits.

It was a perfect October evening—mild and dry, the apples and pears heavy on the trees. Far enough away from the parking lot and the manicured lawn, the resort thrilled with all the late-night noises of the country: croaking bullfrogs, the occasional sleepy quack or chirp from a dreaming bird, the rustle of busy insects and nocturnal mammals. Claudine led Moe out to the meadow, where all the sheep and goats had been banished so they wouldn't scare the city-slicker guests.

Roger floated nearby, thicker on this night when the dead walked. "Do you see him?" Claudine prodded, opening the thermos and pouring soup into two mugs.

Moe turned his head sideways. "I see very little," he admitted at last.

She hushed; the words had the weight of a confession. For a long time, though, he said nothing, sipping his soup and reaching for a sandwich. The sun reddened behind the trees, then vanished, leaving them both in the darkness of a moonless night.

"Retinitis pigmentosa," he informed her. "A genetic disorder."

Claudine paused, a fresh carrot halfway to her mouth. "Is this why you're receiving treatment from Oriol?"

He nodded, posture hunched as if ashamed. "I was diagnosed when I was ten years old, and was told that I would be completely blind by the time I reached age thirty. So my mission since that tender age has been to retard the effects of aging, which seems to delay the onset. But last year I noticed that the deterioration was starting to accelerate. I went looking for a miracle."

"And all this time you haven't told anyone?" she marveled. "Not even your wife?"

"My ex isn't the sympathetic type," he said wryly. "And I didn't want the word to get out about my condition because my career was just starting to take off. The irony is that I was able to make a great living out of being an anti-aging guru, but the Hollywood folks will only listen to me if they think I am as vain and shallow as they are. If they knew I had a medical reason for what I was doing they would have stopped listening to me long ago. People are strange."

Moe spoke quietly into the darkness, and Claudine, sitting next to him on the blanket by the pond, reflected that darkness became the great equalizer between the sighted and the blind—or actually it gave the blind one the advantage. A sheep and the donkey grazed closer to the two while Moe talked quietly and Claudine listened. Moe leaned over and fed them apple slices and carrot sticks.

"There is no miracle," he said at last. "I was convinced at first that the treatment was working, but now I realize that what I thought I was seeing was just—well...a field of green, if that makes any sense to you."

Claudine began to hyperventilate. She could see Roger dancing with glee in front of the pines. Against her will, Abby's words came out of her mouth. "Do you have any other symptoms? Headaches?"

Moe shook his head. "No more so than usual. Relax, Claudine...I don't think Oriol has murdered me. He has just failed to halt an inexorable process."

Claudine shook her head, trying to banish the memory of Abby's crippled Frenchman ranting to her on the phone. She had wondered at first what on earth Abby could see in an imperfect physical specimen who was also the craziest person she'd ever encountered—and considering her family, that was saying something.

But on the phone, Lou was the reincarnation of Roger, Parisian accent and all. *"He's been injecting people with a virus made of rabies and HIV,"* came back to her now. "Are you sure?" she gasped. "Did Oriol inject you with his—?"

"He calls it gene therapy," Moe affirmed. "We knew the chances for success were slim, and now I just have to learn to accept."

They continued their meal in peaceful silence. Suddenly the thought of being blind didn't seem so terrible, compared with rabid green brain tumors, but Claudine was not about to alarm him further. She pulled out thick slices of French apple cake and almond whipped cream, enjoying Moe's sniffs of delight as she fought against the echoes of Lou's voice in her mind, and the cackles from Roger right in front of her.

"Every day is like a discovery," Moe explained. "I am building a vocabulary of sounds and smells. Along with your plastic wrap, I can hear the male swan, the cob, breathing behind us—don't be alarmed, Claudine," Moe reached out and patted her hand, "he's only keeping an eye on us, just doing his job. Anyway, so there are these marvelous orchestrations of sound going on all around me, but there's so much more. The odors, the glory of the smells! For example, I can smell how the sweat popped out on your skin when I told you about the cob, and I can smell the wine bottle in your backpack. Merlot?"

"Wow, that's really good, Moe. I haven't even opened it yet."

"If I keep going the way I am I'll be able to tell you the vineyard and the year. I was talking to your chef about it one day and now she's all excited to have me as a gastronomy student. She says I am the only person who has a better nose than hers. She's been giving me cooking lessons, beginning with simple one and two-note odors and gradually working up to complex dishes, then it will be on to sauces, and wines of course are last. She thinks I have nosmic talent."

"Gnostic, do you mean?"

"No, she thinks I have a talented nose, right up there with the best. It's all about smells, you know. At least if you're a French chef."

Claudine dug into her backpack and brought out the wine bottle. "Good, you can educate me. When it comes to wine I am a real novice." She handed the bottle and the opener to Moe, who handled the process of opening, pouring, and sniffing with admirable savoir-faire. If it weren't for the way he stuck his nose so far into the glass you'd never know he was blind, unless that was how the chef had taught him to inhale aromas? Claudine had seen the evil lamb-killing Frenchwoman stick her nose so far in little drops hung from her tip like an anemic nosebleed, and here was Moe doing the same thing. Maybe geniuses just got away with more, but golly was she getting tired of indulging otherworldly types who couldn't cross the street by themselves. That was how Pierre Curie, supposedly one of the St.- Pierres' distant relations, was killed—so lost in a world of arcane calculations that he didn't notice the horse cart until it was on top of him.

"Hey, wait a minute, since when did my chef start giving you lessons? I thought you were shunning all human contact."

Moe was startled by this, and then queried, "Does it seem that way? It is not of my own accord, I can assure you. The sheep seem to have decided to shield me from your other employees and guests. They surround me if I try to approach anyone—they are not hostile, but they are quite firm."

"That makes perfect sense!" Claudine exclaimed in delight. "The sheep must think you have something contagious. They'd be happy to see you consort with the chef, since they hate her for obvious reasons. They'd love to see her brain turn green and shoot out her ears." She realized suddenly that Moe was less likely to be thrilled by this theory than she was. "Oh, god I'm sorry, Moe. I didn't mean that the way it sounded. Like she's going to drop dead from being in your company. Damn it, I have no couth."

Moe chuckled. "It's okay, Claudine. I'm over it. I doubt sheep are that smart, and for some strange reason, I don't think I'm going to die. At least not yet, and not from this green virus hooha. Besides, the scientists haven't been ragging on you to shut down the spa lately, have they?"

Claudine sipped at her wine. "Hmm, smooth, that's part of the vinous vocabulary, isn't it? Not too original though. To answer your question, Lou and Lori still insist that we have a serious problem, and Abby left me a lamp that's supposed to help check for green. I have to admit that some of your pals from Hollywood sometimes come up a little speckled, but it doesn't seem to be hurting them any, so I haven't bothered to pass on the information."

Moe sighed. "I suppose I should do something to make sure others know the futility of the treatment, but I hate to confront Dr. Ortiz."

Claudine nodded dumbly. If even this famous man couldn't stand up to the doctor, she wouldn't feel so bad about her own doormat tendencies. But, suddenly, she found herself angry. "Why are we so afraid of him? He's done nothing for us. He brought me pollution and asshole guests, and he made you go blind."

"It was the disease that did that, I'm afraid," Moe corrected her. "What Ortiz *is* doing, though, is trying to exploit me as a cure. I might need your help in putting a stop to this." He reached for the wine bottle, taking a deep breath. "But no more of this. Let me wish you a Happy Halloween, and say hi to your puppy dog here." Moe reached out for Roy, the smooth collie, who'd come up from behind them.

Claudine dropped her wineglass and the blanket, reaching out in alarm for her dog. His gait was crooked, and he tripped on the low grass with a glazed look in his eye as if he no longer recognized her. When he reached their little picnic he collapsed, tongue lolling from his mouth as he struggled to draw breath.

TWENTY: CAPTAIN ROADKILL

Little rabbit Frou-Frou
Hopping through the forest
Scooping up the field mice
And homogenizing their brains

LORI COULDN'T GET THE idiotic refrain out of her head since hearing the Buboes sing it softly as they traipsed across campus in the dead of night, searching for animals that might be vectors of the virus. There were animals all over their subtropical paradise. All of the undergraduate Houses allowed cats, for one thing. Outside the dorms, it was not unusual to spot opossums, skunks, raccoons, rats, bats, and the occasional deer and even jaguarundi.

All the Buboes wanted to take part, not just her chosen four. They started in the dorms with the cats. The Buboes got good at swiftly drawing a little blood from their pets' ears with a diabetes test kit, or getting them to slobber into centrifuge tubes. When it was well and truly dark, they ventured outside, hunting through bushes and ponds for warm-blooded fauna. One brave soul managed to get a sample from a massive raccoon, and another bled a fawn until its mother came thundering after him.

Mice and rats they just scooped up, live or dead, and gave them to Lori in a bag or cage. Squirrels and skunks could be found run over in the road, so the slower or more morbid of the Buboes were put on Road Kill Patrol, armed with blue lamps to check for obvious GFP.

As soon as they delivered their vile burdens, she chased them away and hid herself deep in the bowels of the new lab. She wanted to do everything herself, because she suspected that a lot of their strange results were because none of them—not even Walter—was a real biologist. Molecular biology had a way of tricking you when you least expected it, so she was determined to do everything right and to do it herself.

The first step was to extract the DNA from all of the tissues and freeze it for safekeeping. First she noticed that her tissue homogenizing kit had been dipped into—but she didn't care, because she had plenty of other tricks up her sleeve.

Then there was organ removal. This turned out to be such a mammoth and disgusting task that she was semi-gratified to find extra Buboes lurking in the hallway after she exited the lab, eager to help. At first she ignored them, running next door for the hand-held sonicator that would pulverize brains, livers, and bone marrow into a lovely DNA-containing mush—but when she returned they were still there.

"What did I tell you guys about being up here?" she whispered.

They cackled. "You said *Oh you evil Bubo, I don't wanna see you, scooping up the field mice and homogenizing their brains.*"

"Shh. Have you guys ever used a whole-blood DNA extraction kit?"

Her original plan of doing it all alone—with Plan B being using only her trained students—fell by the wayside as a full dozen undergraduates trooped after her into the wet lab. She ignored her misgivings; they could at least follow instructions in a kit, couldn't they?

"OK, everyone, listen up." Lori was still absurdly trying to whisper, but this didn't last long. "This doesn't have to be gross. We need less than a hundred microliters of blood from each of the data animals, and a similar amount of homogenized tissue from each organ."

They tested blood, brain, liver, and lymph nodes from three rats, eight adult mice plus a nest of babies, one squirrel, and one raccoon. She and the Buboes processed blood from one deer, twelve cats, two professors (Lori and Lou), three graduate students (Walter and a couple first-years from Oriol's lab), and for good measure, four Buboes—who couldn't stand the thought of being left out of their own experiment. The rows of PCR machines on the benches stood ready to accept their samples: Seventy-eight organs with four primers each, plus four positive controls from dishes of Oriol's neurons, made three hundred and twenty-eight tiny tubes.

The Buboes dutifully pipetted A, C, G, and T into tube after tube after tube. They did the PCR as a "hot start"—putting the tubes in the machine and heating them up before adding the polymerase. The enzyme, one-half of one one thousandth of a milliliter into each tube, was too precious for Buboes to touch, so Lori did that part herself.

They were all a bit disappointed that the PCR reaction would take over three hours to run, but it seemed like a good excuse to have some dinner and a nap. The Buboes left in search of a late dinner from food service, but Lori took advantage of the situation to get herself a nice meal for a change. She couldn't find Lou, so she deliberately went to the Indian restaurant that he hated with a passion, claiming that "even the water was bad."

One mango lassi and cauliflower curry later, she went back to Pasteur House and curled up in her nice soft bed. She would have slept all night if the Buboes hadn't pounded on the door, eager to get started. She could hardly banish them after that; besides, she was so tired she didn't trust her own skills. In pajamas and rubber slippers, she stumbled over the olives on the path to the lab, willing her cerebellum awake.

A Bubo could make an agarose gel, right? she tried to convince herself. After all, it wasn't any harder than Jell-O. Sitting at a desk and still fighting to keep her eyes open, she gave her students instructions. "Do *not* try to make more than one gel at a time," she commanded, "or you will get a boiling sticky mess. And for the love of god, stop singing that wretched song."

There were five of them, and twenty gels to be made. They only had four microwave ovens, so Lori supervised as the Buboes nuked and swirled. Their first sticky mess came when someone poured the agarose while it was still hot, so it melted through the tape supposed to hold it in its rectangle and spread out all over the benchtop.

A minor detail—all they had to do was wait for it to cool, scoop it up, and throw it into the trash. The real disaster came after all of the gels had cooled and her four select Buboes grew bored with their limited roles. They wanted to load the samples themselves, and have a real set of data to look forward to analyzing in an hour.

Lori was so busy passing out micropipettes and making sure everyone knew how to use them that she completely failed to notice that no one had a lab notebook or even a scrap of paper. Once all of her dozens of samples had been painstakingly dyed, pipetted up, and loaded into the wells, she casually asked the students which sample was where...and was met by a quartet of blank looks.

Each of them had grabbed a rack with anywhere between fifteen and twenty samples, jumbled them up randomly, and loaded them into the gel without any note of what order they had been in.

"It doesn't really matter, does it?" someone mumbled. "I mean, if we see green..."

"Doesn't matter?" Lori whimpered, clutching her head which was making a valiant effort to explode. She turned to the short round student she'd dubbed Captain Roadkill. "You took the pink rack." She pointedly opened her lab notebook and showed them all her careful notes. "That means you have the `squirrel run over on Colorado Ave.,' the `torbie named

Muffin,' and *my* blood. I think I'd like to know which of us has GFP—or rabies or HIV or FIV or influenza or yellow fever."

"If they're all negative, it's OK," Captain Roadkill reassured hopefully. "...Do you need more animals?"

"No! There's a lifetime supply of DNA. I just need..." she sank into a plastic chair. "I guess I need to re-do all of the PCR. But I can't start it now, because it's almost dawn, and—and this isn't my day job." She glowered at them as they snickered. "I know it's no good swearing you guys to secrecy, but can you at least not say anything to anyone in a suit?"

They nodded with unusual solemnity. With the possible exception of Captain Roadkill, they knew they had fucked up. "If you need a nap, I'll tell the people in the common room to be quiet," offered the she-Bubo, flicking on the power to each of the gel boxes one by one. They may have been futile gels, but run them they must.

"That's a good idea, actually," Lori yawned, "Otherwise I'll be incoherent for class. Aren't some of you supposed to be in my Classical Mechanics class?" They all got cagey looks. Getting Buboes to go to lectures was a vain task, although she couldn't help but think that with all the classes they signed up for, they'd go to at least one. Buboes always told their biology and chemistry professors that they were so busy with physics they couldn't do anything else; what did they tell their physics professors, besides "I was up all night shining lamps on dead animals"?

Everyone was strangely silent as the gel boxes hummed and the room gradually grew brighter with the dawn. There was no point in letting them run a full hour, since they were essentially meaningless anyway, so after just twenty minutes Lori shut the boxes off and took the gels to the UV transilluminator.

As she had feared, the gels were a random assortment of positive bands and a good deal of blanks. There were too many positives to be only the positive controls, but she had no way of knowing if Muffin had FIV or if the deer was rabid or if she herself was coming down with yellow fever. She'd have to spend another sleepless night doing everything over again.

Before the official day started, she shooed them all way and cleaned up the mess. It wasn't all that surprising that they'd botched things—they were undergrads, and what they imagined doing far surpassed what they were capable of. It was also a good lesson for her, and reinforced her suspicion that bad molecular biology was at the heart of most of their problems.

With that thought, she tossed out her gloves, removed her lab coat, ran down the stairs, and sprinted down the brick path under the olive trees to the Bubo dorm. She knew she would be the only one to drag herself across campus less than three hours from now for a physics lecture, facing a classroom empty of everything but a few miniature recording devices. But the lectures would be posted, edited, critiqued and mocked for years to come, so she did her best every day, leaving the Buboes in their jammies to dream of Stockholm.

TWENTY-ONE: A MESSAGE ON THE CELL

THE BED WAS LARGE and empty without Abby in it, and Lou awoke with the sheet twisted around his head, still in the throes of an exhausting dream where was walking across a cold desert in a windstorm. The sand was deep and clingy, and the long robe he was wearing to protect himself from the sun and wind had tripped him and obscured his vision of the rapidly disappearing arrows drawn to guide visitors towards the oasis.

Not particularly difficult to interpret, maybe, but it left him feeling as if he'd run a marathon in his sleep. Lately he'd been having more dreams where he didn't walk or run fluidly, but was obstructed by viscous substances or monsters or invisible forces. His thoughts were not much better, still whirling and sandy, obscuring the answers that he knew were there. Listening in the inky darkness for what could have awakened him, he was treated to a shrill of the alarm reminding him of his rendezvous with Lori at nine-fifteen this morning, right after her Classical Mechanics class.

He was tempted to send her an email and then roll over and go back to sleep. The only thing that kept his eyes open was the vivid memory of Lori and the Buboes running all across campus last night with huge black garbage bags, on some mysterious quest that no doubt involved the mouse brain. She had promised to tell him everything today and to show him an experiment that she claimed would answer all their questions.

The other thing that made him able to face the day was one of Lori's little gadgets. She had hooked a remote control up to the timer on the coffee machine, so all he had to do was push a button from his cozy spot in the bedroom, and from all the way down the hall came the hiss of heating water followed quickly by the sharp tang of French Roast. The aroma penetrated through the sand in his brain, and thoughts slowly began to coalesce.

He wanted to get his NASA money back, he wanted to prevent an epidemic—but most of all, right at this moment, he wanted to figure out what was in the green tumors. He wanted the world to know that even though he was a theorist who six months ago had never even heard of PCR, he had managed to pull the mystery out of a drop of blood and figure out exactly what Oriol had done that had caused them all this grief and green.

The alarm beeped again and Lou sighed aloud, tossing the killer sheet onto the floor and reaching for his clothes, his pee supplies, and his wheelchair. It was a good thing he was an insomniac, since getting ready took at least an hour even if he'd showered the night before. He had to set up a mini-operating room just to pee, not to mention the incredible effort of getting out of bed. The whole thing was such a colossal waste of time and energy.

He knew he was lucky. Luckier than just about everyone else he'd seen at the rehab hospital, at least. He had a job that took only his brain, colleagues who were trained to think that anything was possible with the right gadget, and enough money to get all the gadgets he wanted. Every now and then he'd give in to a good cry, but most of the time he refused to let himself complain. Every second he spent being miserable was another second stolen from his life.

But the posts by TooTired had brought back all of the horrible memories—people set loose from rehab unprepared, doomed to lives of recurrent infections and unspeakable pain, death an ever-elusive friend held off by antibiotics. Was it fair to ask anyone to live that way for decades?

The only thing that had let him sleep at all last night was the hope that TooTired was a fake, just another one of those sickos with Munchausen's by Internet who enjoyed the sympathy and attention they got by suffering and dying over and over. But if she was real...well, if she was real he had to get hold of her and tell her the truth about Oriol.

He couldn't face the struggle of pants and shoes without coffee first. He went into the kitchen in nothing but a T-shirt and boxers—and of course thick wool fuzzy socks, since no matter how hot it got in the house, his feet were always icy cold. He drank the first cup with the lights off, then slowly inched up the rheostat as he started to wake up at last. Although he wasn't hungry, he made some toast with peanut butter and swallowed a few handfuls of blackberries from the bowl on the table. Once in the biology lab you couldn't eat, drink, pee, or even scratch your nose, and he didn't know how long they would be locked away in there before they got answers.

Crunching his third slice of sourdough, he reached for a pencil and tried to make sure he understood what they were trying to accomplish this morning. He had a printout of the long email Lori had sent him last night, detailing everything she'd done with the Buboes and the roadkill. Into all of the purified DNA samples, Lori had added primers that bound to a number of different targets: the flanking ends of HIV, called long terminal repeats; different parts of the rabies genome; a few different envelope proteins from different viruses, including rabies, FIV, and something called vesicular stomatitis virus, or VSV—an envelope that could infect any cell at all. She had also included cold viruses for good measure, though he wasn't sure how that came in. If they sneezed into an experiment, could a cold virus grow in their cells? He didn't think so, but biology always had a way of surprising him.

The feline immunodeficiency virus, too, had come out of nowhere, but he thought he understood her reasoning—if an infected mouse got eaten by an FIV-positive cat, and the FIV recombined with the green virus, terrible things could happen. It was the same principle as an HIV-positive researcher bleeding into the experiment, but more likely; there were FIV-positive cats everywhere. He wasn't sure if there were any FIV sequences in their virus, though, or if recombination could occur between FIV and HIV. Those were questions for later.

Lori had done the PCR last night and run the gel to see what was there. They didn't expect all of these primers to give products. If Oriol's virus didn't contain the sequence targeted by a particular primer, that well of the gel would be empty. The problem was the positive pieces. Running an agarose gel would only tell you that a piece was there and was of a certain size—it couldn't tell you exactly what was inside the piece. The primers aimed at the ends of HIV should amplify everything Oriol had put into the virus, including the GFP—but they wouldn't be able to guess what it was from the size. They needed to have it sequenced, and even though the actual sequencing wasn't done in their lab, it would be the most complex molecular biology he had ever done.

Any pieces isolated by the PCR they would have to be cut out of the gel and purified. Lou had asked Barrow about this, and she'd told him that "cut out" meant eactly that—using a plastic kitchen knife to separate out the piece of agarose that glowed with DNA. Then they would run that agarose piece through a purification kit much like the one for the mouse brain, getting at the end the usual transparent liquid that looked like nothing at all.

Then came the tricky part. They'd have to stick this piece of mystery DNA into another piece of DNA, a special type called a cloning vector. Lou imagined this cloning vector as a sort of DNA suitcase, holding their piece and keeping it safe to carry around. Once that was done, the piece inside the vector could be grown up into large amounts and sent off to the campus facility to be sequenced. In just a few days, they would get a file telling them the nucleic acid sequence—the exact order of A, G, C, and T in the innards of the virus. Then they could match it with on-line databases to figure out what gene or genes it was, and even if there were any mutations stuck into those genes by accident (or by Oriol).

Excited now, Lou was ready to get started and was about to go get dressed when the doorbell rang. Sure it was Abby, he opened the door still in his underwear.

Lori's head appeared almost at the height of Abby's, but that's because she was wearing in-line skates. She stumbled into his kitchen and collapsed on a chair, hair and eyes wild under her helmet. "I didn't want to put it in an email," she whispered, still breathing hard from the three-mile climb.

"Hm? Barrow, it's kind of early." He glanced at the clock—not quite nine. She must have let class out early and done three-minute miles up the hill. "Would you like a cup of coffee? I have almond milk."

She shook her head miserably, and Lou put his own cup down, knowing that anything that made Barrow refuse a caffeinated beverage would be scary enough to make him drop things.

"Sam just called on an iridium phone," Lori continued, speaking so low he had to bend in close. "He says David is all speckled with GFP."

The buzz of hummingbirds punctuated their silence. The garden smelled of honeysuckle. It was a beautiful day.

Lou fought to remember who David even was. "You mean the postdoc we just hired? He was only here for two days. He never had a chance to—"

"Get bitten or fucked by anyone," Lori finished. "This means the virus is spread by casual contact."

Lou suddenly thought of something even worse. "Sam's at the North Pole with a green man! We have to get him out."

"I know." Lori put her elbows on the table and put her face in her hands. "But the planes don't run after November 1. I don't want to cause an international incident."

"Well, we just need to start making phone calls. We'll charter a plane if we need to."

Lori got to her feet, clutching the table for balance. "Good, I was hoping you'd say that. What I need right now is someone who can be an asshole on the phone, sometimes in French."

Lou gulped what remained of his coffee, which had gone stone cold. "What about the molecular biology?"

"That's on. I'll do that first thing, and fuck the NASA inspectors. I want to know what's in that virus."

TWENTY-TWO: ALL THE RAGE

JUST AS SHE GOT back to campus, Lori remembered that the bag of mutilated road kill was still in the biology lab. Skates on her feet, she clambered up the flights of stairs as fast as she could, clutching at the handrail. There were still only a few people in the hallway at this hour, but she heard a voice from the lab saying, "*Clearly* searching for GFP" in a tone of scorn.

It was a familiar voice, so Lori opened the door cautiously and peeked in. Walter Waddles was holding a decapitated field mouse by the tail over the UV illuminator, swiveling it this way and that as he talked to himself. He hadn't put it close enough to the light to find the GFP if there were any, Lori noted with disgust, bursting into the room.

"Gimme that," she commanded. "It's mine."

Walter continued swirling the mouse. He was wearing his *This is Walter's* lab coat and two pairs of gloves. "Finders keepers," he giggled.

"I was tired, I forgot, now give me the bag," Lori muttered. "...The Buboes were helping me. We were doing some PCR."

"Funny how you don't seem to worry about NASA inspectors when you want to do something frivolous," he accused, "yet my thesis research comes to a standstill."

Lori stopped in the doorway, realizing that her student was in the middle of a major hissy-fit. She tried to head it off at the pass with a bluff. "The hell it does. I know you've put the virus in a rabies coat."

As she expected, he looked taken aback, but didn't appear to be trying to hide anything. "Well, yes, actually. I wanted to show you the results—I have some beautiful pictures of infected neurons."

"But there is no mention of rabies on the Biosafety protocol."

"Well, no, not on ours." Walter tittered nervously. "But our lab is shut down, and I didn't have to do any cloning at all...I just got some rabies from Dr. Ortiz."

"I'm sure you did," Lori replied dryly. "Do you know if all of Oriol's viruses happen to be in rabies coats?"

"They might be," Walter mused, still with an air of perfect openness. Could it be that he had no idea how wrong what he was doing actually was? "Why?"

"Well," Lori admitted after a pause, "we're afraid that David might have been exposed to a GFP-carrying virus somehow. Sam is certain that David has patches of green fluorescence on his face and in his eyes. And we're even more afraid that this implies the virus is reproducing."

"That's impossible," Walter declared confidently. "I test it every time for replication incompetence."

"You do?" Lori wondered. "How?"

"Like this!" Walter put the mouse down on the UV transilluminator, where it seeped. Then he removed his outer pair of gloves and went to the whiteboard, scrawling wildly, his back turned so she couldn't see his expression.

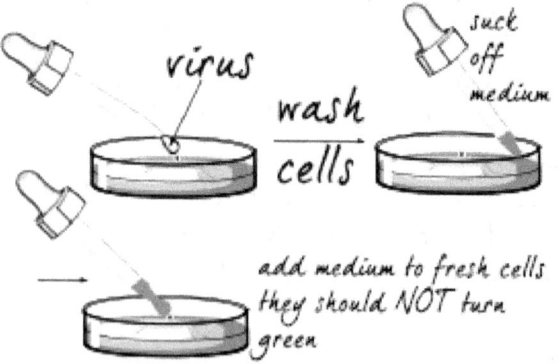

virus

suck off medium

wash cells

add medium to fresh cells they should NOT turn green

"See, if no new virus particles are being made, the medium from the infected cells should not be able to turn any new cells green," Walter explained. "I keep the infected cells for weeks and test them every few days."

"Sure," Lori mused, "but Sam once described this vector as a `biohazardous hermit crab.' What if your viruses in a dish are safe, but the virus got out and recombined with something in the environment? There could be a replicating strain somewhere on campus, in mice, or cats, or people...and it could have any kind of coat, and be spreading in ways related to that coat. Did you show off Oriol's mice to David, and one bit him? Or take him to Pasteur House, where he was bitten by a cat? Anything?"

Walter was starting to look worried. "I don't think so. You can't ask him these questions?"

Lori groaned. She didn't want to have to explain how remote Eureka was, or how impossible it was proving to relay any information. "All we know is what Sam is telling us," she admitted. "He got one minute on the iridium phone."

"Well..." Walter clenched his jaw, and a rosy blush invaded his cheeks. "I did catch David snogging the mathematician."

Lori literally almost fell over, one foot sliding out in front of her as she grabbed the wall. She sat on the floor to remove her skates, heart pounding. This changed everything. "WHAT?" she yelled, then narrowed her eyes at her student. "Are you sure you're not just making this up?"

He protested with pearly-toothed innocence. "They knew each other from way back. They went to grad school together. She's probably the reason he came here."

"But then..." Lori fought with her laces, which seemed determined to resist her. "He must have gotten it from her. I just can't figure out how she could have died so quickly, unless the mouse bite got the virus straight into her bloodstream..."

Walter approached Lori with a slight look of scorn, and waved his hand in front of her face. "Dr. Barrow? Are you OK?"

Lori had finally gotten one skate off, and started on the second. "What do you mean, am I OK? Do you think I'm insane? I'm not. Kathy got bitten by a mouse with a green brain tumor and died less than a week later. If David got it from snogging her, the virus must have been reproducing in her."

"I know," Walter dismissed. "But Dr. Greenwood didn't have a brain tumor. There was an autopsy. She died because she tripped and fell in the parking lot and hit her head."

Lori leapt up, the lab tiles feeling cold through her racing socks. "Who told you that? Never mind, I think I know. The same person who gave you the rabies coats. What else has Oriol been putting in a rabies coat, dare I ask?"

"It's just GFP," Walter protested.

"Bullshit. If it's GFP, why does it cause brain tumors?"

Walter seemed stymied by this, and changed the subject. "Does David have cancer?"

"I don't know. I told you—he and Sam are incommunicado. Does the virus cause cancer every time?"

"We don't think so," said Walter, turning not pink this time, but slate white. "About half the time, I think. And sometimes the neurons really do reproduce as what appear to be healthy neurons."

Lori spoke slowly and patronizingly, being sure to piss him off. "If it's just GFP, why should it make neurons reproduce?"

He was indeed irritated, but couldn't find an answer. The only thing that could really cause him shame was a bad experiment. After trying a few worthless theories, he was forced to concede that Lori wasn't crazy, and picked up a pipette to join her in the sequencing effort.

TWENTY-THREE: I'LL HAVE NUNAVUT

LIKE A FOOL, LOU had thought his task would be easy. It was just a matter of a plane ticket, after all. But after an hour on the phone to absolutely no avail, he had developed a new slogan—"There is no hope in Sqalid"—and a series of puns about Canada's newest province that ran obsessively though his head as he talked to one languid, browbeaten, morose bureaucrat after another. *What part of your province is nice? Nunavut!* and so ad infinitum.

Unlike Alaska, where people lived off the grid and could do anything with a single-engine plane, a moose jaw, and a roll of duct tape, Nunavut was a study of French bureaucracy crossed with Arctic desolation. There was apparently no Avgas anywhere in the province, meaning no bush pilots, so everyone was held in thrall to the single commercial airline serving the various villages—and it was completely inflexible, impervious even to the massive bribes that NASA potentially could offer. It did not fly between November 1 and April 15, period, and absolutely never landed on Ellesmere. Sam and David were not going to get out of Eureka on the airline.

Lou hesitated to play the "medical emergency" card, afraid the two students would end up quarantined in Sqalid or worse. He finally managed to call Sam on the iridium phone, but Sam wasn't able to tell whether David was healthy (albeit green) or whether he was acting funny. He said something about staggering, but Lou was unimpressed. A small part of him also suspected Sam was doing this because he was bored out of his wits in the Land of the Midday Moon.

Finally he gave up. If David was green, he would just have to be green until spring.

He considered joining Lori in the bio lab, but decided to call Abby instead, just in case she could think of a brilliant way to get their students out of Nunavut.

It was a mistake. She didn't care about David and started yelling immediately; it took him a good while to even understand what she was shouting about.

"Say that again," he prompted. "Claudine's dog...?"

"Died of a brain tumor!"

That's what he thought she had said, and he had only one question. "A green one?"

There was a contemptuous pause. "How would I know?" Abby began, then continued immediately, "Oh no. Not a chance I'm going to ask Claudine to harvest cells from her dead dog."

"We have to know," Lou insisted. "It's starting to make sense."

Saliva, he thought. The virus was spread in saliva, like rabies—only it appeared to be much more contagious than rabies, or at least to act more quickly.

Then he had a realization so horrible that Abby's next words went right past him, a hum of babble in the sinking realization that all of a sudden was painfully obvious: *he* was the link to Moe Deet.

Lou's parents had a dog who often licked him. The dog regularly visited Moe Deet's yard and, who knew, no doubt licked him too. If there was anything their sociable, web-footed Newfie had plenty of, it was saliva.

Were animals more susceptible than people? So far, a mouse and a dog had died, but only one person—even though many people had turned up green.

"...and been keeping things from me, besides," Abby finished with a hiss of exasperation.

"That's terrible," Lou sympathized. "...Er, you needed to know, right?"

"Of course I needed to know—and so did you. You're the one who brought the lamp up there."

Suddenly he was all ears. "The lamp?"

"Right! That battery-powered LED you brought to the spa. I've asked Claudine to inspect her guests with it, and she's found green all over the place, especially from people from L.A. She told herself they `seemed fine' so she didn't even bother to tell me—and didn't even write down who these people were!"

Lou put down the phone, oblivious to its incessant buzzing as Abby continued to expostulate. If this was as big as he was beginning to suspect it might be, then they were endangering everyone by just shutting down the virus lab and running some silly PCR reactions. They needed to do more—but the whole idea was so outside his experience that he couldn't even imagine what. Call the CDC and quarantine themselves? How did that work?

Lori would know, of course. When the phone finally stopped buzzing he shut it off and hurried next door to the biology building, hoping Lori would still be there.

She was hard at work, along with Walter Waddles, who was wielding a butter knife over a very large agarose gel. Lou waited until they had capped all their tubes and shut off the UV transilluminator before he explained, slowly and carefully, that he was Patient Zero. "I used a cell phone in the BSL-3," he moaned, "and took the lids of the cells, and now we're all going to die."

Walter and Lori exchanged a knowing look, but didn't seem particularly alarmed.

"Aha," Walter exclaimed. "So it *is* the drool!"

"And I got sick first, and I think I was the sickest," Lou persisted. "Could I have HIV?"

Lori finally looked nervous. "I don't know. Could you?"

Lou lowered his voice. "I still worry about what god-awful disease I'm going to get from all the blood they gave me. They didn't expect me to survive, so I think at the end they were using Kool-Aid and giving homeless guys a dollar for a donation."

"Oh!" Lori looked scandalized in that ridiculous politically correct way that even she fell prey to sometimes. "Did you ever have any mysterious fevers?"

"All the goddamn time," said Lou. "But I got tested more than once, just not recently. Remember when you talked about bleeding into the experiment? We've all bled into the experiment, with our constant nosebleeds. God only knows what's in those dishes."

"So why doesn't Abby have it?" Walter wanted to know.

"How do we know she doesn't?" Lori snapped. "She refused to give us any cells."

"She never had that terrible cold," Lou reminded her. "I stayed away when I was sick, and maybe it takes a *lot* of drool, like Newfie-level drool."

"Or broken skin!" Walter was listening avidly and interrupted with glee. "David had that moustache full of scabs, that's probably all it took."

"Now you *are* making shit up!" Lori accused. "`Full of scabs'? But seriously, when you say he `snogged' Kathy, are we talking a peck on the lips or full-on tongue-in-throat action?"

Blood suffused Walter's translucent cheeks. "I don't know! I didn't look closely. I think it's safe to assume all viruses were juicily exchanged."

"Hm," Lori mused. "So does any of this tie in to Kathy's alleged lysosomal storage disease?"

There was a silence of deep and profound confusion. "Huh?" Walter blurted at last.

"Oriol told us that Kathy was dying of a genetic storage disorder," Lori pursued.

"He did? Well, of course that's not true!" Walter's face twitched as if his mouth were fighting his brain over whether he was going to say more. His eyes were troubled, almost tearful. "It's possible that he believed that...once. But he shouldn't have told you—I mean..."

Lou watched him, paying closer attention to the emotions than the words. "It seemed important to Oriol for us to think that Kathy was dying," he said carefully, emphasizing each word.

The implications were not lost on Walter. "Oh!" he exclaimed, eyes growing even more watery. "But no...I mean, he had to be wrong. I know he had some of her cells—"

Lori perked up. "Cells? As in fibroblasts? You use cultured fibroblasts to diagnose lysosomal storage disorders. Can you get me some of her cells?"

Fibroblasts, Lou thought, *somehow that rings a bell.*

"No, of course not!" Walter howled. "He's her physician—that would be so unethical."

"More unethical than pretending she was ‘dying anyway’ rather than admit that something in our mutual lab killed her within days?" Lori shot back.

Walter sagged. "I don't think it's true," he protested feebly. "I mean, look at these gels. Look at all these negatives."

Lou came closer to see the gels, which Lori and Walter had stained for GFP in fresh samples from themselves, and from a huge array of wild and pet animals from all over campus.

"Fine," Lou conceded. "So then why is Kathy dead, David green, and Claudine's spa totally infected?"

They looked blank for a moment, but Lori stepped in quickly. "We need to answer these questions one at a time. I'm starting to suspect that something is going on at the spa."

"We need to do something," Lou insisted. "Something real—not just talking and running these stupid PCR reactions. Abby moved out of my place because she thought I was contagious, and went straight into the plague zone. She still refuses to give me cells. She's not behaving rationally."

"Maybe *she's* Patient Zero," Lori suggested hopefully. "Didn't I say she was acting as if she had a brain tumor?"

"It could be true!" Lou cried. "Whether she gave it to me or I gave it to her, we both have it—and maybe she's been innocently spreading it all around the spa."

"She's not snogging Claudine," Lori objected.

"No, but she's probably weeping on her shoulder, getting licked by her dogs, and sharing dishes. Not to mention getting facials—I'm sure Claudine has touched Abby's snot."

"I would agree that none of us should be having intimate contact with anyone," Walter admitted. "At least until we're sure. Of course," he tittered, "for most of us this isn't a big problem."

"Seriously?" Lou had thought Walter was one of the better-socialized ones. "Don't you kiss your grandma?"

"Not since the last major holiday."

"Lori, what about you? Have you kissed anyone or petted any dogs since we started making this virus?"

She considered this carefully. "I don't think so. I do share a house with a bunch of undergraduates, but I have my own kitchen. They use my Kleenex on a regular basis. Anyway, they're negative. I screened four of them and none of them have any viral sequences anywhere."

"It's too early to panic," Walter insisted in a slow, soothing voice. "Dr. Lou, you should definitely get an HIV test, and don't kss anyone until we finish the last round of sequencing."

"And I'll make sure we get cells from Claudine's dog," Lori added. "And try to get some from Abby, too."

Lou wasn't sure what to make of their cavalier attitude, but there was one thing he did pick up on. "You managed to get something that needs to go to sequencing?"

"Right." Lori looked more serious than she had before. "The insert in Oriol's virus is more than twice the size of GFP, so there is something else in there—and we're about to figure out what it is."

TWENTY-FOUR: JE SUIS MAUDITE

"LOOKS LIKE YOU WERE right." Claudine raised her glass in a toast to a spot on the laboratory wall that glowed a bit more brightly than the rest of the flat surface. "Good for you. There's an epidemic of what will come to be known as the Green Plague and everybody is going to die." She sidled up to the wood, adopting a confiding tone. "Just think, I'll be famous because it started right here at the Whey of the Goat—assuming anyone remains alive to tell the tale, of course."

She looked around at her office *cum* lab, benches lined with state-of-the-art laboratory equipment competing for space with aquariums swarming with aquatic life and terrariums filled with exotic plant species whose pharmacological effects no one had even gotten around to studying yet, at least as far as she knew. She blinked back tears. "This is NOT the way it was supposed to turn out, you know. I have worked my whole life to make something of myself, and it was finally starting to happen."

Unsteadily Claudine walked over to the corner of the room where the sumptuously fitted-out snail tanks were housed. Usually spending time with her gastropods did for her what yoga or meditation did for other people; contemplating the mollusks' funny hermaphroditic habits or admiring their subtle, phosphorescent hues was very soothing. It never failed to humble her that creation's largesse allowed as much *lebensraum* for the quaint, the slow, and the faintly ridiculous as for the swift and the beautiful. There was a message in that, if only people cared to look.

"Hello, my pretties," she crooned, and then stopped. Was it her imagination, or were the *Helix aspera* looking sluggish? Rather than sliming all over their trees they were huddled at the bottom of the tank. A few of them were lying on their sides, their formerly perky horns pitifully limp. She'd recently changed their diet to a super-iguana food on the advice of a mollusk-master, but perhaps it wasn't agreeing with them. Or maybe she should stop fighting the truth that everybody continually tried to force down her throat. She was doomed. Cursed. Maudite. Choking back a sob, she reached into the tank and pulled out an inert snail. Purple, now motionless between her fingers, had been one of her best producers. The other snails tickled her hand with their funny little protuberances, maybe signaling affection, or maybe they were trying to tap out feeble messages of distress, who knew? All she could say for certain was that everything was turning to *merde* all around her.

Suddenly she was filled with a white-hot rage. "Go ahead, smite me some more, you sadistic motherfuckers. I won't give up until you kill me! As for you, *mon fils* of my heart, STOP LAUGHING!" She hurled Purple against the glowing spot, where the mollusk shattered and trickled slime all the way down the wall. "Purple Haze!" Claudine yelled, laughing hysterically before finally collapsing in a heap at the foot of the snail tank.

A skinny arm wrapped around her shoulders. Gentle fingers coaxed her to her feet, settled her down into a stuffed armchair, and pressed something hard and cold into her hand.

"Drink this," Abby commanded.

Claudine took a swallow, then coughed from the fire. Next she sipped more carefully, realizing that the glass held cognac. She had stashed the fine brandy under the snail tank, after confiscating it from the chef who had threatened to give the ortolan treatment to the local songbirds.

"Calm down, calm down," Abby soothed. "I'm sorry Roy died, but we'll give him a nice funeral—"

"And then take his brain out, if I'm not mistaken?" Claudine threw her glass to the ground, but it merely bounced. "What is that in your purse? A bone saw?" She made a grab, but Abby sidled out of the way, shushing and stroking her as if she were a pet who'd just had its shots.

"It's okay, Claudine, take it easy, there now, that's a good uh..." She opened her purse and pulled out, not a bone saw, but one of those horrible fancy phones that did everything besides make calls. "I'd like to get Lou on the line so he can help explain what's going on."

"Why should I listen to that fool?" demanded Claudine in a peculiar basso voice.

Abby looked startled, glancing at the wall to the spot where Roger had been. He wasn't there any more, though; he was hovering overhead, cackling.

"Please, Claudine," Abby pleaded, "we're trying to help. No one is thinking about anything as drastic as..."

"Shutting down the spa and killing all the sheep?" Claudine finished for her. "Maybe we should hang Moe while we're at it."

"Abby, Abby?" Lou shouted from the speaker phone. "What's going on over there?"

Abby left Lou in suspense while she refilled the glass and put it into Claudine's hand. This time she gulped the spirits, heedless of the burn. Waves of warmth spread all the way down to her stomach, where she could feel the drink dancing around the edges of her ulcer.

"Claudine is a little upset," Abby explained, with her law-yerly tendency to understatement. "I came up here to help her send off her dog—"

"And steal his brain!" Claudine yelled.

"—and I wasn't the only one here," Abby finished. "Oriol Ortiz got here first—and he *does* have all his dissecting tools with him."

"Why would he be up there?" Lou demanded. "Unless he is investigating an epidemic of green, and somehow the spa is involved. Or unless he *caused* said epidemic."

"He said he was here because Moe is his patient," objected Claudine, feeling a strange sense of detachment from her fury at the direction the conversation was taking, but wanting to keep the record straight.

"It's even worse than that," Abby continued. "Oriol is being shadowed by a private investigator, and it's the same guy I see all the time at the LEPERLab. I'm sure he was hired by NASA."

There was a long silence. Then all Lou said was, "Hm."

"What do you think?" Abby wondered, her nerves beginning to peek through her studied calm.

There was another pause. "I really don't know," Lou admitted. "I'm taking some notes here. Because there is some sort of plot to take my project. And I'm not sure at this point if Oriol is a plant, a shill, or just a tool. And if you say you saw other green people, well...try asking them if they've had any contact with Oriol. But also ask them, if you can, if they might be HIV positive. We can't rule out contagion yet."

Claudine murmured her assent, and Abby finally closed her horrible device and put it away. Claudine waited, the walls fuzzy in different places, not sure if this was the cognac speaking or her dead son. "Roger always loved dogs," she mused. "Do you suppose Roy will come back and they can play together?" She started to blubber, her whole body racked with violent sobs.

Abby clearly decided that more cognac would ill serve Claudine or the situation. She left the room for a few minutes, returning with a peanut butter sandwich and an aspirin instead. After a few minutes of choking on tears, then snot, and finally on multigrain bread, Claudine was finally ready to go outside and bid goodbye to her beloved collie.

It was a strange procession out to the gravesite. The sheep formed a woolly barrier between Moe and Oriol, escorting each of them to separate sides of the gathering. When Claudine tried to get close to Moe, an old horned ewe gently nosed her away. To Claudine's expert shepherd's eye it looked as if the sheep were taking over Roy's function, only in this case the sheep were herding the humans. She appreciated sheep more than most people, and knew better than to underestimate them. Especially Bracegirdle. In fact, shepherding duties had been shared out between Bracegirdle and Roy, because Roy, no dummy, knew who was really keeping the sheep in line. Something was going on, and the sheep were trying to tell her something.

Claudine positioned herself next to Bracegirdle, and during the short service she hissed at him: "Bracegirdle, what's up?"

The sheep looked at Claudine, then gazed meaningfully in Oriol's direction. Claudine cleared her mind and allowed the images to form. A story of ovine-style love and betrayal gradually emerged. The sheep loved Claudine, had come to love Moe, their two shepherds, and profoundly distrusted the Bird-Man. It didn't take a rocket-sheep to deduce that it was only when the Bird-Man showed up that things began to go wrong. Now Roy was dead and Moe was sick and the Bird-Man was still hanging around. What was he doing here, and what more destruction did he have up his sleeve?

A vivid image of Oriol flapping the wings of a black wizard-cloak popped into her head, and as she watched the wizard turned into a huge black bird. It flew over the spa, sprinkling the fields, meadows and cottages with a glow-in-the-dark green dust, all the while cawing in triumph. Bending down, Claudine curled her hand into Bracegirdle's wool and brought her face close to his ear, pretending to be comforting him while she whispered, "Thanks, BG, I get it. We're not going to let the Bird-Man or any of the rest of these crazy scientists get away with destroying us and the spa. I have had it with them. We'll get Moe to help. And no need to keep me away from him—he's not sick. At least not the kind of sick that will make me sick." Picking up a handful of earth to throw down on Roy's pitifully small coffin, she felt a resurgence of feelings long suppressed: self-confidence, strength, hope. She was through being pushed around by mad scientists, dead or alive. It was time to start fighting back.

"I hope you are feeling better, Claudine," said Abby sympathetically, as they walked to the dining room for dinner. At least she was trying to sound sympathetic, but Claudine thought she saw the iceberg underneath the ice floe that Roger had warned her about. If her plan was going to work, she was going to have to ramp up all her instincts as she played one mad scientist against the other. Of course your standard mad scientist à la Oriol was so obsessed you could set a bomb off in front of him and he wouldn't notice, but Abby didn't quite fit the profile.

"*Écoute*, Abby, there is something I want to discuss with you. I know you are up here to get Roy's brain." She silenced the young woman's protest with a wave of her hand. "Please. Let's sit, eat, discuss. We can make this work for all of us. I am not the enemy, you know."

The food came, and Claudine laid out the elements of the plan. "We'll go out once it's fully dark and dig up the grave. After we put Roy in a canvas bag, you can take him back to the lab down south and autopsy him there. That means you won't have to do any dirty work. Except for a spot of dirt shoveling."

Because she was squeamish, Abby wanted to take the coffin and all, but Claudine explained that she wanted to leave the empty coffin for Oriol to find. "We'll rebury it and wait for Oriol to show up. Once I catch him in the act of grave robbery, I'll be able to ban him from the spa forever. And we'll prevent him from getting his claws on Roy's brain. We'll kill one bird with two stones." She ducked her head to hide the mad gleam in her eye.

Abby didn't seem too reassured, but she was able to swallow a few bites of her pasta primavera as Claudine continued to explain how she'd tried but failed to keep Oriol from coming up to the spa. "He's charismatic, you know. He manages to convince Moe that he needs 'treatments,' but can't quite get Moe to go down to see him, so he comes up here. He has destroyed my beautiful spa with his spoiled rich guests and their motor vehicles. The whole place stinks, and it's noisy all the time—even the frogs are dying. I can't take it anymore, Abby."

Abby listened carefully, taking notes on a napkin and saying little. By the time they had finished their sheep-milk coconut crème brulée and were strolling back to Abby's cottage, it was fully dark, with no trace of the waning moon.

"I'll see you in about an hour, then," said Claudine, patting Abby on the back. For a moment she felt sorry for her. Competitiveness was okay, but only up to a point. Combined with vainglory it just didn't work. Abby was so used to being the smartest person in the room, she didn't know when she was being duped. What she didn't realize was that, as smart as she was, there was always going to be someone somewhere who was smarter.

An hour later the two women made their way to Roy's grave, armed with flashlight, shovel, and other equipment. Abby ended up doing all the shoveling, of course, but to Claudine's credit, she did the hard part of putting her dead dog in a canvas bag and carrying it back to her place. The plan was to put the corpse in the freezer, then in the morning Abby would pick it up before she headed back home. They returned to the grave again for more shoveling, covering it so it looked as it did right after the funeral. Abby hung around for a while with Claudine, prepared to be a witness to act two. But the cold and the late hour were finally too much for her, and she trudged back to the cottage, leaving Claudine to her lonely vigil.

Morning came, and the coffin stayed buried, with no signs of the doctor. Not even Moe had come to comfort Claudine in her grief, or to bring a blanket. Somehow she had expected him to guess that she was there, and she felt cold and abandoned, sniffling a bit as she wandered down to the main office.

After checking the guest list and the outgoing delivery roster, she knew why no one had visited her. Despite her wobbly legs from cold and lack of sleep, she ran to Abby's doorstep, pounding on the door with both hands.

Abby answered in her bathrobe, hair piled on her head in some kind of old-fashioned net. "What happened?"

"Oriol's gone," Claudine announced.

"Well, that's good, right?" Abby asked, bleary-eyed. She ushered the distraught woman inside. "So all went according to plan? You caught him and barred him from the property and he left?"

Claudine looked at her with reddened eyes. "No, not exactly. I mean he's gone but so is Moe. Oriol has kidnapped Moe."

Abby looked puzzled. "But, Claudine, Moe is his patient. Oriol wanted him to go to his clinic in Mexico to finish his treatment. Moe probably went with him."

Claudine tried to fill Abby in on part of the story, to explain why Moe distrusted Oriol and would never voluntarily go with him. Abby looked skeptical, the way the scientists always did, giving Claudine the look you give grandparents reminiscing about their old hippie days.

Finally Claudine threw up her hands and stomped away, shouting over her shoulder. "He's been kidnapped. And I am going to Mexico to find him. You can come or not, it's up to you. Now please come and get Roy from the freezer so you can do your horrible experiments."

TWENTY-FIVE: SAM'S DIARY, PART 5

From: prisonerofcanada@yahoo.ca
To: grandmechant@gmail.com, geek_en_patins@yahoo.ca
Subject: <no subject>

Lou and Lori,

Do you know anything about a helicopter, an Air Canada jet spray-painted black, and a gang of guys in Hazmat suits?

If so, FUCK YOU for not telling me, and I want answers, NOW.

If not, prepare to panic.

They got David and me out of the North Pole, but they're treating us with BSL-4 gloves. I don't know where we're going. Clearly it's south, and I'm afraid they're going to hand us over to the Americans at the border.

We just left Desolute on the jet. There's no one on the plane but us, the pilots, and two guards swathed in space suits. We're being forced to wear masks and gloves and unable to eat or drink.

Help!!! (or Stop helping!!! as the case may be)

Sam

Sent from my iPhone

PART III

TWENTY-SIX: FIGHT OR FLIGHT

IT APPEARED THAT DAVID Snavel had been expelled from no fewer than eight previous schools since the age of thirteen, mostly for practical jokes that were not even worthy of a Bubo. Once he had hacked into some professor's Facebook profile and posted a Photoshopped picture of the teacher smoking a joint. Another time he had earned his living writing term papers for other students, and somehow been busted.

Any other time she would have found the file hilarious, but Lori was not in the mood to be amused, and was mostly infuriated at all of the administrators who had brought down the force of their wrath on harmless exploits. She was just killing time, waiting for experiments to run. Abby had delivered the dead collie, which Lori had dissected to remove the brain—but now the brain had to sit in fixative for a few days before it could be sliced and inspected. Even sooner than that, they should know what was in Oriol's virus.

The sequencing facility had promised to deliver the results from their cut-out piece of DNA sometime that day. So Lori watched her inbox, clicking "get mail" every few seconds.

"Just a minute, Walter," she grumbled impatiently as a thin blond figure appeared in her doorway.

The figure harrumphed and entered without being invited, making her look up in surprise to find what could have been a computer-rendered image of her student a half century from now. The Dean of Students looked around futilely for a chair, then stood glaring down at her.

"Er, sorry about that, Dr. Waddles," Lori corrected herself.

He gave a curt nod. "I do indeed come about my grandson. We are all concerned."

She didn't know, nor did she have any idea who "we all" were. "Is something wrong with Walter?"

"With his project, yes." Dean Waddles folded his hands over his heart. "Our family goes back many generations here, you know. All of us have received our degrees in physics. I like to think that we all made significant contributions to the field. But now my grandson's project has been stalled, over concerns related to animals—I know you have newfangled ideas," he chuckled with paternal condescension, "but honestly, *is that physics?*"

Lori found herself cringing at those three words, which were the worst insult a physicist could deliver next to "not even wrong." "He's working on models of neuronal networks," she justified, trying to keep her voice from becoming defensive. "The only way to get the neurons is to kill mice, so that's where our problem is. I'm sure we'll get it worked out."

Dean Waddles grumbled and didn't go away, rambling on even as Lori saw the email from the sequencing facility loading into her inbox. "Could he not focus on the theoretical aspects? I seem to recall that a year ago, you yourself were a theorist with impeccable credentials."

He was calling her a traitor, but Lori was too anxious about the email to care. "He certainly can, Dr. Waddles," she promised hastily, throwing in a few sentences of description with some partial differential equations for good measure. She could see that Grandpa Waddles was weakening, and at last, clutching a few papers on mathematical neuronal modeling, he turned for the door.

"Keep me updated on Walter's progress," he ordered before leaving. "I do not want to see anything slow him down—I certainly will not tolerate anything that might get him into trouble."

Lori shivered a little as if the threat were for her, but she had other things to worry about, and immediately forgot the Waddleses in a massive scroll of As, Cs, Gs, and Ts. It meant nothing to her like this, of course. All she could tell that the sequencing had gone well, because it was a clean array of base pairs without unknowns. But it would take her only a minute to copy the sequence and paste it into a search engine that would match it to known genes.

The last 822 base pairs of Oriol's virus matched up perfectly to GFP, as they should have. The other 1200 were something Lori had never heard of, and she had to check the match several times and read a few papers before she started to get the picture. There actually was a gene called *Evil*, and it was an oncogene—something that made cells reproduce uncontrollably.

She wasn't sure exactly what it meant, but it was certainly interesting, and might explain what they'd seen in that first ill-fated mouse brain. Prepared for a long discussion, she paused to eat a banana, then went across the walkway to the physics building and knocked on Lou's door.

His office door was unlocked and everything was a shambles. For a second she thought he'd had a tantrum and smashed things—books were on the floor, the paper he'd been working on was crumpled and scattered, the drawers were open and his carefully organized supplies of every type were jumbled on the desk.

But it only took a moment to realize this was much more a ransacking than a smashing, and she could hear scraping noises from her own office next door. Realizing how lucky she was to have escaped unseen, she ran out, back down the stairs, and took refuge in the building's only secret room.

There was no one in the basement hallway, so she stopped in the bathroom to pee and fill a water bottle in case she ended up hiding in the BSL-3 for a long time. Once through the first set of doors she breathed a little easier, and paused in the vestibule to put on booties and a lab coat, and to listen for suspicious noises from inside the lab. When there was nothing, she slipped inside and locked the door behind her.

But it appeared that the unthinkable had happened. The computer for the microscope was open and its hard drive had been removed. She ran to the incubators to see if they had been tampered with, and nearly screamed when Lou stuck his head out from behind the tissue culture hood. "Barrow," he whispered, pulling aside a makeshift curtain of lab coats. The hard drive was in his hand. "Thank God it's you. The DEA came to arrest us."

"The who?" Lori wondered. "The DEA? That doesn't make any sense at all."

"I know." Lou peeked warily around the cryogenic freezer, then went back to his place at the microscope and resumed installing the drive. Or tried to—his hands were shaking so badly he quickly gave up and set the screwdriver down on the benchtop. "It has to be over the green virus somehow, but I don't know any details. I was at the computer store when one of the grad students called and said that Sam and David had been taken away by the CDC, and that three men in black were destroying my office. They promised to find you and warn you."

"No one did—you don't suppose they got detained, too? It would make sense if the CDC came for us, but the DEA I can't explain. Do we know if Sam is green?"

"We don't know anything!" said Lou, and to Lori's dismay, he burst into tears. He didn't dare to wipe them away with his vile lab gloves, so just sat there with the hard drive in his hand and two streams running down his face.

"Well, look," Lori attempted, "I blame Oriol."

Lou didn't take the bait, but continued weeping that Sam was his only reason for living, and that if he didn't get a PhD then he (Lou) was the world's greatest failure and might as well hide down here eating yellow fever virus until he died.

"He was already traumatized enough! How could they quarantine him? It's Waddles they should put in the BSL-4 slammer, and he's *your* treacherous grad student," was the gist of what he was trying to say, which wasn't all that helpful.

Admittedly, Lori had felt the same way about her first PhD student, also named Sam. Her first had also been her best, and every time something went wrong or he was discouraged, she would stay awake all night and worry. She wondered if the grad students ever appreciated that their advisors considered them as their own children, and in many cases cared more about their futures than about those of their genetic offspring.

After her Sam she'd had a series of losers, so now she was jaded. Two of them had spent time in the nuthouse—one just because he wanted to get out of the qualifying exam—and one she'd fired for falsifying data. In fact, none of the students after her first had been any good at all until Walter Waddles.

She considered telling Lou all of this, but was impatient to find out what was going on. There was also limited comfort she could offer in their absurd surroundings. The lab was noisy with the ventilation that maintained the negative pressure, the rumble of the freezer, and the occasional beeps from the incubator. It stank of dust and mold and autoclaved plastic. And of course they were afraid to touch each other with their officially contaminated rubber gloves.

Lori changed her gloves, pulled a giant Kimwipe out of its box, and handed it to Lou. "My life has no meaning," he sniffled. "I'd rather stay down here until I starve than get arrested."

"You're not going to be arrested," she insisted. "Oriol has been putting an oncogene called *Evil* into HIV in a rabies coat. We need to sneak out of here and find Abby, and then she can confront Oriol and come back here to save us."

This appeared to be wrong, too. "Abby can't help," Lou wept. "I'm… I'm really worried about her, Barrow."

Lori's first instinct was to laugh, but when she looked into his eyes she could feel goosebumps prickle under her lab coat. Still, she wasn't going to leap to conclusions; she was going to make him say it. "What do you mean?" she whispered.

"I thought you were just being an asshole when you suggested she had the virus, but then I realized that she really was not making sense. She's been hearing voices—claims the spa is full of ghosts. Yet for some reason she keeps going back there, and every time I speak to her, she sounds more...addled." He shook his head miserably. "You know me—Denial Man. I've been trying to pretend it's not happening."

"Maybe it's just Claudine's influence," Lori suggested, trying not to let on that her knees were going weak. She pressed one hand against the cryogenic freezer to steady herself.

"You told me Claudine was dotty, not that she was hopelessly demented." Now that he'd gotten started, Lou was spilling his guts. "It sounds as if she can't even take care of herself any more. And there are...there are a few things I haven't told you. I thought it wasn't important. I had almost convinced myself that Oriol was injecting viruses into his patients, and that there was no contagion, but then with David Snavel...and now Abby..." He turned his face away, trained well enough not to put it into his gloved hands. "There's no way on God's green Earth that Abby would let Oriol inject something into her."

Lori tried to grasp at logical straws. "Why won't she give you her cells?"

"I don't know. It all started there. She said she wanted nothing to do with our experiments. Then she moved out, but instead of going somewhere safe, like Minnesota, she went straight up to Clonic and the dead dog. She keeps talking about how she and Roger were going to get married."

Lori gave a diseased whoop, not sure if she was laughing or

crying. "I can't even imagine the size of the brain tumor that would make her think that."

"I know. I kept telling myself that brain tumors should cause headaches and seizures, not just..."

"...Believing weird shit? We can't say. We have no idea what Oriol is putting where in the brain. Maybe he's practicing with implanting false memories."

Lou gazed at her seriously. "Is that possible?"

"Not that I know, but what do I know? Maybe Abby's hippocampus is full of GFP. Now not only are we contagious, but the DEA is after us and we don't even have a lawyer."

"And we could develop brain tumors any minute."

"That, too. Though strangely enough, I feel fine." Lori thought fast. "Is it possible that the GFP-cold we both had managed to protect us from the tumors?"

Lou gave a strange laugh. "You're the biologist, not me. What—you think Oriol might have vaccinated us or something?"

"I don't know. All of us who worked in the lab were sick, but none of us appears to be dying of brain tumors. Abby didn't have the cold—you said it yourself—and neither did Kathy or David."

"That we know of," he reminded her.

"You would know if David had blown bloody snot—Sam would have logged it in detail. As for Kathy, she died too fast even for a cold to have time to incubate. Somehow we're resistant. If Oriol didn't vaccinate us, maybe we were just exposed a little bit at a time with our..."

"—With our execrable lab technique? Admit it. None of us had any business fooling with that virus to begin with."

Now he was sounding like Dean Waddles. "Oriol had no business putting *Evil* into anything. Adding an oncogene raises the biosafety containment level, and none of us on the safety committee knew about it." Lori hesitated, still searching for answers. "Another possibility is that only people who got the virus with *Evil* in it got the tumors. Maybe the rest of us just turned a little green."

"Well, I'm not doing any more stupid PCR. I've lost my mathematician, my postdoc, and now my girlfriend. I've had it."

"You don't know that yet," Lori tried to reassure him. "If we can't get Abby to help, we'll have to sneak out of here and confront Oriol ourselves."

"According to Abby, Oriol is on his way to Mexico."

"Mexico?" Lori was bewildered. "Is his office being ransacked, too?"

Lou sighed and blinked a few times hard. "Well, Barrow, this is part of the few things I haven't told you," he explained finally. "Oriol has a clinic in Mexico. I didn't think it was important because I couldn't imagine how it could relate to our GFP problem, but now, well—I'm not sure."

It was a strange confession, delivered with contrition, as if Lori would care. She couldn't imagine a connection, either; but if Oriol was hiding out there, that's where she was going to go to track him down. Lou was less than enthusiastic, muttering about amoebic dysentery, but Lori didn't even have to say anything—she just gestured round the room to show him what his choice was. When he finally seemed to accept the necessity of becoming a fugitive, she climbed onto a lab chair and tried to stand on it.

It slid out from under her and she scrambled for balance, clutching the cold metal tissue-culture hood that hadn't been turned on since October.

"Watch it!" Lou yelled. "That's the chair I found—I mean, be careful! What are you trying to do—chew your way through the ceiling like the mouse?"

"Pretty close," she agreed, finally unearthing an old step-stool and trying again. She had to poke the tile up with a broom, but then was able to grab the edges and pull herself up into the hole. "The tunnels go all the way to the admin building, just behind Pasteur House," she elaborated, peeking down at him. "I'll run and get the Bubo wagon, and you go out and meet me—or no," she decided, "wait here and I'll come get you. That way if I disappear, well…you could probably live for weeks on nutrient agar and saline. Just don't drink the pink medium, it's full of Phenol Red."

She pulled her head inside the tunnel, sneezing at the close, stuffy air that reeked of rodents. It was dark, and she crawled along until her head hit something unexpectedly hard—and she was greeted by a chorus of squeaks.

There they were, Oriol's secret mice, shoved into the steam tunnels, sick and neglected and kept in the dark. She wanted to barf, but instead just crawled back the way she came and asked Lou for a pair of scissors and a Ziploc baggie.

He didn't need to know that she used his good scissors to break the neck of one of the secret mice. Then she sealed it in the baggie, stuck in into her pocket, and realized she couldn't go any further until she got rid of the mouse cage, which completely blocked the passageway. Crawling backwards, she tugged it along until she reached the hole, then dangled it down while she quickly swapped sides with it. Fortunately, Lou did not appear to be paying attention—he was making computer-repair noises.

Having traded places with the mice, Lori resumed crawling, this time on the far side of the cage. She'd have to go a few meters in the open before she got to Pasteur, so she prayed that the agents would still be in her office as she emerged quickly from the tunnel and dashed towards the residential parking lot.

The key to the Bubo wagon was in her pocket. Gas was in the tank. All she needed to do was sneak Lou out to the loading dock, and they'd be on their way to the border. But first she had to hide the mouse. It wouldn't be safe in her apartment if the DEA was after her, so she dashed around to the back of the overpriced snotty café, the H-bar and Grill.

The rear entrance to the H-bar was unlocked, and the single employee was busy grilling panini. Within a second, the rabid green mouse was nestled into the café freezer in between the chocolate gelato and a bag of peas.

TWENTY-SEVEN: ANOTHER DAY IN PARADISE

MEXICO REMINDED CLAUDINE OF Quebec, only turned up a notch. She was from the United States' northern little brother, where non-Anglos suffered from poverty and discrimination, and the Europeans sneered at the way they spoke French. But while their Big Brother in the middle was merely condescending and bossy towards them, he was clearly downright arrogant and vicious towards their southern brother. Nothing had prepared her for the barbed wire fences and sheer nastiness of the border guards when Abby drove their rented mini-van through the frontier crossing.

Once over the border, the landscape immediately turned bleak and depressing. A chain-link fence clogged with colossal amounts of trash, from take-out cartons to used diapers, lined the roadway leading towards their destination and obscured the view of the endless sand-and-scrub plains. Here and there were scattered one- and two-room roofless adobe structures, choked with weeds where windows and doors were supposed to be. The horizon was as flatlined as a newly expired heart attack victim, the sky lowered with oppressive menace, and the occasional cactus seemed to signal a warning to stay away.

"I see vultures," said Claudine. "They're circling."

"Remind me why we're doing this again." Abby fumbled with the A/C knobs, sending a blast of cold air onto Claudine's feet.

"Because he kidnapped Moe!"

"Is Moe going to agree with that? Or do we need evidence that Oriol is doing something illegal so that we can confront him?" Abby wondered with exaggerated patience. "Injecting people in California, for example?"

"I don't have any evidence of anything," Claudine admitted. "But if he was somehow funneling NASA money to the clinic..."

"Impossible," Abby declared. "Lou or Lori has to sign all the expense reports for the NASA fund, and I read them *very* carefully before they do so."

"Well, I'm not sure how coherent a story Moe will be able to tell if he has a green brain tumor," Claudine responded dryly, and that ended the conversation for the moment. They drove on, the bushes becoming a bit bigger and lusher as they neared the coast, but still dominated by thorny desert scrub.

At last, Abby carefully maneuvered the van onto a small dirt road bearing a sign welcoming them in six languages to Cuernavaca-By-The-Sea, "A Paradise of Health and Beauty for Men, Women, and Children."

Fortunately, the place appeared to live up to the promise. It really was by a sparkling sea—and, even better, it was off the beaten track enough that it had escaped the tourist plague. As soon as they arrived, a team of assistants came to carry their luggage, show them to their room—Abby requested that they both be put together in a suite—and issue them thatched sandals for walking around the property. Shortly after they had settled in, two young women with perfect teeth and nearly perfect English took them on a propaganda tour.

The arrival of Dr. Oriol's clinic had done little to alter the villagers' traditional lifestyle, they explained, which was to augment their home-grown beans, corn and red-and-green pepper diet with freshly caught fish. Indeed, life had improved since the clinic had come into their midst. It now employed about half of the local population, and young people were choosing to stay rather than move away to the big cities or to the *maquiladoras* to find work as soon as they reached age 14, as was the case in most other subsistence hamlets throughout Mexico. Dr. Oriol had even set up an educational fund for the town's children who wished to pursue careers in medicine, his only proviso being that they work in a small rural clinic—it didn't even have to be his—for a year after they finished their studies. The clinic had just welcomed its first batch of trained nurses, three of them, all from the local area.

It was over two hours later and nearing sunset before they were finally left alone to confer in their room. The suite was roomy, airy, and spotless, and the surf whispered up the sands on its back-and-forth forays.

"I don't ever want to leave," Abby announced, pulling back an embroidered curtain to reveal the sun sinking into the Pacific. "Lou would love it here. Just listen to the water. So soothing."

Claudine looked up from her notebook where she'd been making a long list. "Have you forgotten the order of business? Moe has been locked up by this fiend and we certainly aren't going to get any help from the locals. They all think Oriol is a saint."

"Well, you heard Señora Garcia. Look at all he's done for the town," Abby pointed out. "Maybe he's not as bad as you think. And besides, you still don't know that Oriol has him locked up. The real question is, is he really giving Moe the same virus that he's putting into mice at STI? Do the patients know it's made out of HIV and rabies? And then—"

His sandals were nearly silent, but Oriol's squawk betrayed him as he stopped at the door to their room and knocked briskly three times.

Claudine's heart pounded a bit with trepidation, and she staggered back as Oriol tried to envelop her in what he must have imagined was a warm, welcoming hug. It might indeed have been, had she not been so suspicious—and had he not been wearing a lab coat with a few infectious-looking stains.

"How wonderful it is that you all came down to see me!" Oriol exclaimed, giving Abby a jaunty wave (at which Abby turned pale). "Look who's here to greet you." He pushed the door open wider, gesturing for the new guests to come in. "Plenty of room in the suite for the four of you."

Lou and Lori appeared stunned into silence. They were covered with dust, especially Lori, who was also wearing a lab coat even filthier than Oriol's.

When no one spoke, Oriol continued his cheerful welcome. "Are you just here for the scenery, or are you coming to check out my health and beauty treatments? Claudine, I'm sure you'd be thrilled by my new, all-natural Botox!"

"All natural, like a can of puffy peaches," muttered Lori. "Oriol, we know what—"

Abby interrupted quickly. "I'm certainly here for your treatments, Dr. Oriol," she cooed. "I'm looking for anything I can to reverse sun damage. I try to be careful, but when you're Scandinavian living in L.A...." She smiled winningly, showing a nearly complete absence of crow's feet. How she did it, Claudine had no idea.

"Good, good, good." Oriol rubbed his hands delightedly. "Let me personally escort you all to dinner, and then I'll give you a tour of the *entire* facility."

Claudine thought there was something louche in the way he said that, but her paranoia ebbed as he led them through the beautiful old ranch house to the spa dining room, talking about his morning among children at the burn clinic and his free melanoma center.

He found them a table overlooking the sea, then vanished into the kitchen for a few minutes, returning with special anti-oxidant smoothies for each of them. After a dinner of fish so fresh it melted in the mouth, and a pepper and dandelion salad that perfectly blended hot, crunchy, and bitter, Claudine could feel all her free radicals being scavenged on the spot.

The prandial delights were so distracting, it didn't even occur to anyone to inquire about Moe. Their after-dinner conference was less of an intrigue and more of a siesta.

"Didn't you love the food?" Abby asked rhetorically, flopping onto her bed.

"He seems to be doing the community a lot of good," Claudine acknowledged, relegating her notes to the bottom of her duffel bag. "It can't be easy to run a hospital and a spa as well as do research at America's best science university."

"What?" Lori shrieked. "Is that all it takes to make you forget what he's done?" She lowered her voice. "We could all be dying of green brain tumors at this very moment."

"Pish and tosh," Abby snorted, lying on her back with her hands folded behind her head, staring at the thatched ceiling.

Lou and Lori exchanged a conspiratorial glance. Lou was clutching a water bottle—the only thing he'd dared to ingest at the resort, muttering throughout the meal about Shigella and red tides. No wonder he was still suspicious.

"And what does Roger have to say?" he asked in French. "Did he accompany you?"

"Of course not," Claudine replied calmly. "Roger is not allowed to travel. Now, just stop it with that eye-rolling right now, young man. I know what you're thinking."

"Don't make fun of Roger!" Abby wailed, sitting straight up in bed like a vampire in its coffin.

Lori edged closer to Lou but refrained from meeting his eye. "Look, euh...we're just worried. About both of you. I know Oriol is charismatic, but we came down here to confront him for something terrible he did at the university."

"Really? We came down here because he kidnapped Moe Deet," Claudine explained.

"We don't know that for sure," Abby corrected. "That's why I'm here. It could all just be a misunderstanding."

"Misunderstanding, my ass," Lori snorted. "Oriol made an illegal virus containing a gene that causes cancer." She reached into the scummy-looking pocket of her lab coat and extracted something long and thin.

Lou cleared his throat, squeezing his bottle so hard it crumpled. He continued speaking French, maybe so as not to be overheard. "Please, Abby and Claudine, tell me...is there any chance that you have taken any of Oriol's medicines, or allowed him to inject you with something...anything...?"

"Of course not," Abby exclaimed. "We've never been here before, and Oriol is not licensed in the States. I can't imagine that someone of his reputation would risk everything to practice illegally, when he has this beautiful clinic here."

"I know for a fact that he would and he did," said Lou, but with lassitude in his voice as if he knew he were fighting a losing battle against the full tummies and the warm sea breeze.

"And he's risking everything by using unapproved viruses in the lab," Lori attempted. She pressed a button on the long thin gadget, and a blue light flashed.

"Nothing you wouldn't do if the grant inspectors were coming," Abby retorted, flopping back down. She glared at Lori. "You keep away from me with that lamp."

"I just need to see—" Lori began.

"No." Abby put the pillow over her face. "You aren't giving me wrinkles with your stupid lamp. You're completely insane."

"At least tell me if either of you has had a terrible bloody cold within the past six months," Lou urged, as Lori gave up on Abby and turned towards Claudine, waving the lamp.

"No," Abby retorted, as if this were an old argument. "That's why I won't give you my nasal cells. I think both of you are nuttier than fruitcakes, and jealous of Oriol. For once there's someone smarter than you at that university. I'm starting to think he's a hero."

"If that's not a sign of a brain tumor, I don't know what is," Lori snapped. She gave Claudine a cursory inspection, seeming disappointed at the lack of green. "Fine. Lou, why don't we just go home?"

Claudine didn't wait to find out if that was a bluff. "Stop! What about Moe?"

Lori turned around slowly. "Yes. What about Moe? You say he was kidnapped? Good. I have a plan."

"Oh, good," said Claudine.

"Oh, God," said the only non-atheist among them.

TWENTY-EIGHT: EVIDENCE

IT WAS STILL PITCH dark when Lou's eyes snapped open. He wasn't sure what had awakened him, but he didn't have to wait long to find out. The clamor of thumping footsteps, clanking porcelain, and violent hurling reverberated through the door of the single shared bathroom.

He knew it. He had tried to warn them. Now he had to find out where Oriol was and confront him before the supply of bottled water and PowerBars ran out.

By the time he'd put on clothes and got out of bed, more footsteps had joined the first, and there was a whispered, clench-jawed argument over who had to discharge her intestinal tract into the bathtub. It was time to get out of there.

Lou was looking forward to this. Or at least he would have been had he known where the culprit was hiding.

The rapid tropical sunrise lightened the sky just as he entered the large open walkway between the guesthouses. A warm breeze illustrated why nothing but the thatched roof was ever needed. Oriol's "campus" appeared to stretch mainly to the southeast. Towards the west there was nothing but boats and water. He looked for buildings that looked more like labs or hospitals, but it was hard to tell—they all had the same faux-Spanish stucco appearance.

He went down to the courtyard, where the pretty ocotillo and scent of jasmine couldn't conceal the sight of the woman on the wooden bench. She was cooing and smiling at a baby whose face ended with horrifying abruptness just above the eyebrows.

Lou's vision grayed, and he told himself over and over not to try to look inside its head. *Reason 1,564,781 not to have kids,* he thought. "Er, excuse me?" he asked politely.

The woman looked irritated, as if her full, uninterrupted concentration was the only thing that could make the creature grow a brain. "Yeah?"

"Er, I'm trying to find Dr. Ortiz's surgery," Lou tried. "He told me to be there first thing in the morning."

The woman suddenly looked pitying and gave Lou a searching look, clearly curious about what horrible condition he had and no doubt hoping it was worse than her baby's, as if that were possible. She tried to steer him by the shoulder, but he shook her off in repulsion, feeling tainted by the same hand that had just touched the monster's smooth, glossy skull. Confused by his inexplicable distress, she withdrew her hand and instead pointed to a pinkish building under a canopy of palo verde. Murmuring condescendingly, she asked if he needed help getting there.

I don't look that bad, do I? Lou wondered, as he rolled his eyes and shook his head. *At least I'm not throwing up.*

The building was gapingly, eerily empty and pink, like the baby's head. Lou went round and round its corridors twice, before he gave up on manners and started poking his face into any unlocked room. Hearing heaving and groaning behind one door, he thought at last he'd found something alive; but it turned out to be some kind of machine, dripping clear liquids into an array of glass tubes. Suspended above a basin nearby was a huge, fleshy pink expanse. When he looked a little closer, he saw it had a bellybutton in it. Next to the basin was a jar containing something brown and white, floating in liquid—the head of Claudine's collie.

He backed out of the room as fast as he could, and crashed into something metallic that emitted a shriek. After struggling to turn around, he found himself looking into the shocked face of a woman in an electric wheelchair who said all the things Lou was going to say— "Oh my God, I'm so sorry, are you OK?"

Yet another one who thinks I'm more afflicted than they are, Lou thought, and decided to play it up. "I'm not sure!" he exclaimed, twitching a little. "I was supposed to meet with Dr. Ortiz, but he—"

"—ran away," the woman agreed. "He was in the middle of examining my husband when he suddenly leapt up and dashed from the room."

"Do you know where he went?"

The woman shrugged helplessly. "My husband said he forced an old lady onto a boat, but..." she gestured with a clawed hand towards her temple and laughed harshly.

With a pang of nausea Lou realized this woman must be TooTired, the caretaker of the brain-damaged man who'd lost her perfect life to a drunk driver. It was a strange feeling to meet someone whose sob story you'd read on the Internet. He wondered if TooTired was trying to match him to that same horrible site—was he MotoCrash? WantToLive? Or perhaps merely CaringSon or LoyalBrother, in which case he wouldn't deserve any pity.

A little white lie was fitting at the moment, he figured. "That old lady was my mom," he confided. "She's trying to convince my dad not to have the Oriol Treatment, since he's just going blind and not going to die."

TooTired nodded sagely, as if she knew the whole story. "He can't really have put her on a boat," she declared firmly. "Why would he do that? Have you looked in all these rooms?"

They poked around the molecular biology lab for a bit, then went back to the reception area, but there was still no sign of Oriol—or the brain-damaged husband, who had apparently also wandered off. Finally they were so bold as to take the keys from the front desk and try them on the doors to the small rooms.

In the very last room at the end of the hall, a man was lying on a gurney with pins sticking into his face. A cloth drape covered everything but his mouth, exposing a strange, bristly moustache that had been half shaved or electrolyzed. On the bald part, the lips had been slit open and the upper one was pinned to the side like a piece of cloth waiting to be added to a sewing pattern. Lou had no idea whether this was a legitimate procedure or some sort of hideous punishment meted out to spies.

As grotesque as the mouth was, it was hauntingly familiar. "David?" he yelled.

"Eeeh uhhhh," squeaked David Snavel.

"Did Oriol do this to you? No, don't try to talk—can you nod your head?" Lou gently pulled back the cloth so he could see David's eyes.

David nodded feebly.

"OK, the real question," Lou persisted, ignoring TooTired's look of intense curiosity. "Did you *want* Oriol to do that to you?"

David nodded again and flapped with his hands, which were strapped to the gurney.

"Oh." Lou was incredulous. "Really? Are you nuts? No, don't answer that. I suppose Oriol ran out in the middle of vivisecting you?" He turned away from David to shut the door. "We'll just wait for him, then. I mean, he can't leave you here *too* long, or you're going to be in agony from those pins sticking your lips to the sides of your face."

David squealed pathetically, and TooTired opened her mouth as if to say something, but changed her mind.

Lou knew that silence was probably the best course at that point, but he somehow found himself telling TooTired the truth, or at least parts of it. He said that he'd come to rescue not only his "parents" (that wasn't so much of a lie, was it?)

but also to confront Oriol for misappropriation of university funds.

TooTired stared uncomfortably at the floor. "You might think I'm here for myself," she stammered, "but actually I'm not that desperate."

"Good!" Lou declared. "So you can help me tell Oriol that he needs to stop doing this."

TooTired continued to look awkward and uncomfortable. "Maybe you'll think this is wrong, but I *want* my husband to try the treatment. He has a head injury that has changed his whole personality."

"Yes, I know," Lou found himself saying, still unable to activate the censor. "I mean, I think I know. That is...I was pretty sure I recognized you from on-line. Except I thought he had no eyes?"

TooTired inspected Lou's face carefully, clearly trying to guess who he was on the wretched site and annoyed at being unable to. "I, er, made up that part," she admitted, turning pink. "I didn't want to be recognized and, well, I guess I got a bit carried away."

Lou was immensely impressed that even those with the most squalid lives imaginable still exaggerated on the Internet. They bared their made-up pain, and people like Kathy sucked it up like emotional mosquitoes. *Do you know that one of our math professors was a troll?* he wanted to ask, wondering if TooTired would froth with rage the way those sites always did at the unmasking of a fraud.

TooTired was spared this squalid tale, for at that moment Oriol swung open the door. As if he hadn't even seen them, he went to a cabinet, pulled out some supplies, then snapped on a pair of gloves and injected something into David's lips.

Only then did he turn around. "I need you to leave the room now," he said evenly. "This is a surgery. I'll come find you folks right after," he told TooTired.

"Oh, no you don't," Lou announced. "You can dice up postdocs later; right now I need you to listen to me."

The mad scientist, looking as calm and respectable as possible, merely narrowed his eyes slightly. "He's not your postdoc. This is an important patient of mine."

"That's my postdoc, David Snavel."

David squealed pathetically, and a small crease of suspicion appeared between Oriol's eyebrows. "Someone here must be mistaken. This man told me he was a Valley porn star called `The Nozzle.'"

"Why would you be doing surgery on David?" Lou persisted as though he had not even heard what Oriol said. "Don't you know that he's infected?"

TWENTY-NINE: LE BATEAU IVRE

THANKS TO HER FRENCH constitution and spa diet, Claudine was fine while everyone else tossed up their guts.

She did, however, badly need to pee. When it sounded as if there would be no breaks in the bathroom, she sneaked out of the suite and down the wooden stairs to find a nice spot behind an ocotillo bush.

She was just hiking up her PJs with a sigh of relief when someone grabbed her elbow. *"Tabar—"* she shrieked, loudly enough to wake any guests who weren't already up puking.

"Shh," murmured Oriol. "It is a beautiful morning here, is it not? Let us go see the sunrise together."

Somehow they ended up down by the beach, even though the water was on the west side, where the sun doesn't usually rise. Hearing the lapping waves started Claudine's heart pounding a little, especially since it was still dark and she couldn't see exactly where the water was. "Dr. Oriol," she quavered, "I don't really...euh...like the water."

Without a word, he steered her away from the surf and towards a small thatched structure. She hoped it was a tea shop, but her hopes were dashed when Oriol flicked on the lights to reveal a wall hung with an assortment of the most rickety, untrustworthy boats imaginable. There were open canoes that could dump you, kayaks that could trap you upside down as you gulped water, and even more dilapidated vessels she couldn't identify.

Of course, Oriol used the only enticement that would work with her. "I need your help, Claudine," he urged in his oily way, in the meantime strapping her into an orange life vest as if her agreeing to get in a boat with this lunatic were a done deal. As if reading her mind, he added, "Moe is doing fine. He's wonderful, in fact." Her senses were in a whirl as Oriol continued in the same vein—visual acuity numbers off the charts...people impressed with his miraculous recovery...how lucky he was to be treated by the Louis Pasteur of his day.

In the midst of all this braggadocio, the faux Louis Pasteur was dragging a dented canoe out the door, a vehicle the real French genius would have better sense than to go anywhere near, she was pretty sure. Hurrying towards the beach with his canoe, the Iberian madman called over his shoulder, "But he keeps saying he wants to leave. And it just wouldn't be a good time. It might impede his full recovery."

There was no explicit violence, but Claudine knew she had no choice in what happened next. Oriol's powerful arms gripped her shoulders and propelled her across the beach, chattering loudly to interrupt her attempts at protest. "I am taking you to him so you can persuade him to stay. Just for a few more days. A week at the most."

The trip in treacherous water, its rocking horrors compounded by Oriol's incessant chatter, was worse than anything she could have imagined. All Claudine could do was cling to the sides, shut her eyes and quiver. She'd rather eat a plateful of roasted cowpats. She'd rather take a mud bath filled with snakes. She'd rather drive an SUV on the freeway in L.A....

The canoe shuddered to an abrupt stop. Claudine screamed, then opened her eyes. It was finally light enough that she could see they were in an alcove of some sort, a secluded bay with a white sand beach fringed by coconut trees. The beach stretched up to a two-story rose-colored villa that appeared to have a tropical jungle complete with scarlet macaws and toucans flitting from tree to tree as its backyard. It was idyllic. Oriol helped her from the canoe and removed her life vest before dragging the boat onto shore. Her feet got wet, but she forgot about that as she saw her darling Moe run down the steps of the villa, dart across the beach and into her waiting arms. They cleaved together for a long time.

Finally she noticed the silence. The mad doctor was gone—with her life jacket, of course. She could just see the tiny dot of the canoe receding over the horizon.

"Moe!" Claudine gasped. "He's kidnapped me the way he kidnapped you! Now we're both stuck on this, this—where the hell are we, anyway? I have to admit, it's beautiful, if you like the beach. Anyway, we're in the middle of nowhere, without a canoe or a paddle, not that I'd ever get into one of those contraptions again. We'd make a great rowing team: you're blind, and I'm afraid of the..."

"I'm not exactly blind," Moe objected mildly. "But, admittedly, I am not the miracle cure Oriol claims I am. I'm happy the way I am, Clo, even if Oriol isn't. Right now I just want to go home to the spa and be with you, and the sheep and...I am so glad you came to find me. I thought you were under his spell completely."

Moe blubbered into Claudine's neck for a few moments while she patted him and surveyed their surroundings.

"The first thing is breakfast, and then we'll figure out what's what. The villa, *chéri*—it's yours?"

Moe's villa had everything one could wish for, if one were looking for a hideaway to escape detection forever. "It's Dr. Ortiz's special getaway retreat," he explained. "Very luxe. Swimming pool and an orchard in the back yard, dripping with tropical fruit. All kinds of exotic birds, too—and no snakes. Usually the gardeners, the pool boy, and the cook would be here by now, but instead I got you." He beamed fondly in her general direction.

In the absence of the regular cook, Claudine did the honors, finding enough food in the well-stocked kitchen to last them several months. She just hoped that it wasn't part of Oriol's plan to leave them stranded that long. They took their avocado omelets and toast spread with guava preserves out to the veranda, overlooking the sea.

The magnificent view, which included a pod of orcas leaping joyously in the sparkling waves, was unfortunately wasted on them. Claudine resolutely kept her back to the water while Moe described some broccoli-shaped blobs pulsing in a sea of lime gelatin that sounded distressingly like his descriptions of the sheep back home.

After a decent meal Claudine was never quite so responsive to a call to action. "I must say," she pointed out, "for a kidnap victim you're being treated pretty well. Why don't you just stick it out for the rest of the week, and then we'll go home? As long as we have enough sunscreen we can tough it out."

Moe sighed. "You just don't realize what he's like, Clo. He drags me to these `seminars' of his, where I have to fake-read eye charts to wow prospective patients. He's sure I am his path to the Nobel Prize. Eventually he's going to figure out I've memorized all the eye charts and really don't see much besides green blobs."

Claudine eyed him dubiously. "You have to see them to memorize them," she objected.

"Sure, if I am an inch away and can look at them sideways I can see them. Sort of. I am afraid Oriol will try even more drastic treatments on me once he knows the extent of my blindness. He's never going to let me go, Claudine. He's a fanatic—you think he's going to give up his Nobel Prize?"

"Right, well. Okay then. So we leave. Is there a way to get out of this secluded paradise that does not involve canoes?"

Moe smiled. "Umm, actually, yes. There's an idea I've been toying with and now that you are here...You saw the movie *Papillon,* right?"

"I read the book," said Claudine coldly, sure she didn't like the direction of his gaze, which was pointed towards a stand of coconut trees. She began to wonder if she liked Moe that much after all. Did she like anyone enough to lash coconuts together into a raft to embark upon the dreaded sea?

THIRTY: THE NOZZLE

"D AVID IS FULL OF GFP!" Lou insisted, as Oriol held the scalpel over the hapless postdoc's face. "Did you infect him, or did he get it from the lab?"

Oriol's hand shook. He tried a couple of times to steady it, but was unsuccessful. Finally he shuffled over to the corner, pulled out a folding plastic chair, and sat down. Little noises came from behind his surgical mask, and to Lou's horror, he saw the doctor had tears in his eyes.

Suddenly Oriol ripped the mask off, clutched his chest, and screamed in hysterical, gasping laughter.

"Oh!" he wheezed, stomping his feet and wiping his eyes. "Oh! Oh!" He babbled something in Spanish, followed by more howling.

"What the fuck?" said Lou.

"Ah ha ha ha...." Oriol took several deep breaths, giggling. "Oh my. Oh *dios mio*. I guess my physics friends don't know too many people at the CDC."

"Spit it out, Oriol," Lou snapped. "You are in a lot of trouble."

Oriol's eyes widened in mock innocence. "Me? I haven't done a thing. If this man is your postdoc David Snavel, he has just been taking you all for a ride. He doused himself in fluorescein knowing you were all sensitive to the subject, and got a free plane ticket out of Canada." When he had recovered sufficiently from his attack of mirth, Oriol reclaimed his dignity and spoke in a patronizing tone. "I have done nothing wrong, and my medical practice is none of your business," he lectured. "The CDC has kept me informed throughout this ridiculous episode—it is nothing but a prank by your own trainees. I would thank you to pack up your spies and leave me alone."

"Not done anything wrong?" Lou responded coolly. "I know what happened to Kathy Greenwood."

To his credit, Oriol could not be bluffed very easily, forcing Lou to admit that he had been with her in the BSL-3 the night she died. Oriol pretended to be indifferent, but Lou could see him grow pale and slightly unsteady.

"She was fragile," he murmured.

"Uh huh. Like my Uncle Alex?"

Oriol swiped the sleeve of his lab coat across his forehead. "What do you want?" he said in a near-whisper, turning away from David and TooTired.

"Oh, very little," Lou responded. "I just want my NASA money back."

Oriol looked incredulously from TooTired to Lou and back again. Then he laughed his condescending chuckle that made all the students hate him. "You are a fool, Louis," he sneered, pronouncing it *Luis,* which always drove Lou insane. "What I'm doing is so much more important than any NASA project."

"I'll show you who's a fool," growled Lou. "You can't add two numbers. What you do is no more scientific than bird-watching, and then you dare to make our students carry around your mice and use rabies virus—"

"Watch how proud you are that he's your student when he goes to Stockholm," crowed Oriol.

"WALTER IS GREEN, TOO!" Lou bellowed.

"If Walter has green nostrils, that is not my problem!" Oriol shouted back. "I told him not to—anyway, it's not your affair! If you're so smart, how many people have you saved?"

"None at all. That's not the point."

"Of course it's the point," cried TooTired, motoring over to them so close that Lou could see the tracheostomy mark on her neck and two deep, round scars on her forehead from being in a halo. "Are you really claiming to be smarter than Dr. Ortiz?"

"Dr. Ortiz is injecting people with a virus made out of HIV and rabies that is supposed to make neurons reproduce, but half the time it causes cancer." Lou felt faint looking at her scars and her thin, paddle-like hands.

"But the other half the time, it can help," TooTired protested. "I've seen the results. I've met people here."

"It's not worth it—" Lou tried, but was interrupted by a scream that wasn't really a scream because TooTired's breathing muscles didn't work right.

"What do you know?" TooTired breathed, gasping a little. "What's your injury level—T12?"

"T10," he answered with reluctance.

"If I were a T10, my life would be perfect." She punctuated the statement with a weak, wheezy cackle as if to demonstrate her lack of intercostal muscles.

"You have got to be fucking kidding." Lou gave a bark of dry laughter.

"You have fingers, don't you?" TooTired wheezed. "You can use a keyboard. You can drive a car. Besides, I'm not even here for myself. Do you know what my husband is like? He has *zero* quality of life. His personality is gone. Who are you to say it's wrong to try everything?"

"Who am I to say?" Lou echoed. "Look—what is your real name, anyway?—I *work* with Oriol. I've seen the tumors."

"I've seen the cures," retorted TooTired.

"Luis, Agatha," Oriol interrupted, all poise returned, "I'd thank you to take this into the hallway. Luis, I will speak with you afterwards in my office. You can even have your postdoc back—just as soon as I am finished with him."

As the door closed behind them, TooTired muttered, "Agatha? Where'd he come up with Agatha? It's Margie."

"He doesn't care what your name is—he's a selfish, egotistical..."

"Shh. Not here. Do you know where his office is?"

Lou didn't, so Margie took the lead, clearly familiar with the campus. The doctor's main office turned out not to be in the building, which was a blessing of sorts, since the waiting room was now filled with an assortment of freaks. The empty-head-baby woman was there, along with worse cases. He felt as though the short bus had discharged its contents as he followed Margie through the gasping, demented throng. *If only I had my GFP lamp*, he thought.

Oriol's office was a distance away, down a sandy path lined with desert plants. Margie explained that this put the doctor halfway between the "unviewables" and his attractive celebrity patients, the ones come for Botox or nose jobs. "Or tummy tucks," she added. "That's what we saw hanging in that research room."

"You mean someone parted with that much flesh voluntarily?" Lou was relieved she had told him, so he hadn't betrayed his ignorance by accusing Oriol of grave-robbing or worse. But that collie head—it had to be Claudine's dog, and one of them had to grab it.

TooTired (Margie) turned off abruptly into one of the stucco huts. Unlike the guest rooms, which were open to the breeze, this building had air conditioning. Potted plants—miniature palms, cacti, calamondin oranges—decorated the waiting room, but their domesticated scent paled in comparison to the outdoors.

They were the only people in the hut. Lou was nervous at first about talking in what was apparently a public space—and he was more than a bit confused at Margie's sudden interest in what he had to say—but everything was so quiet and deserted, and Margie's eyes so eager, that he finally began his story.

"Oriol started working at our university at the beginning of the summer," said Lou, taking a moment to try to remember what month it was now. Almost Thanksgiving—the tropics had a way of throwing a person off balance. "He looked me up right away. He knew what had happened to me, and other things too…He knew I was vulnerable." He hated this, wished it was dark so she couldn't see his face. "I think you know what I mean."

"You mean how, for the first couple of years, you always think there will be a miracle?"

This wasn't so hard. He was glad he didn't have to explain. "Right. And your memories are so vivid, you think that it wouldn't take much at all to make you spring up and run…" *Damn it*, he thought as his voice shook. "Anyway. Oriol also knew that I had a distant relative with dementia. He called him my Uncle Alex, but he's not my uncle, really; more like my dad's third cousin or something. I had never met him, but I was his closest living relative. He was in a nursing home and no one else knew or cared whether he lived or died. I had sent him some money once, and my girlfriend, who's a lawyer, had helped him with some paperwork. Somehow, Oriol knew all of this the first time we met. He managed to convince me to get the old man to 'accept' Oriol's experimental treatment, with the stated promise that if it worked, well—we'd all be cured within the year." He finally managed to look her in the eye. Her eyes were pale gray and red-rimmed, her skin dry; she looked as if she needed to sleep for a week.

She huffed noncommittally. "I'm not sure he really promised that."

"He sure did a good job implying." Lou glanced up at the windows to make sure Oriol wasn't coming down the walk. "Meanwhile, Oriol started working at the university. For strange historical reasons, the biosafety containment lab is in the physics building, and mostly overseen by physicists. This means that none of us who run it are really experts—we didn't know when Oriol was just being a bit lax with the rules, or when he was being downright dangerous. Still, it was clear that he was violating every safety rule in the book. He brought unapproved viruses into the lab, he did unsanctioned animal experiments, he lied about what he was working on. But I tried to protect him, the same way I promised to keep what he had done to my Uncle Alex secret. I believed in him, and I didn't make the connection between Uncle Alex's treatment and the scary viruses that Oriol was cooking up in our lab."

"This is that rabies thing?" Margie sounded doubtful.

"Yes. The outer coat is made from rabies virus so it goes straight into neurons, the way the disease does. The inner part of the virus is made of HIV, so that it can integrate into a cell's genome, so the cell and all its descendants will express the delivered genes forever. All the viruses contain a green protein so that you can see where they go. But worst of all, Oriol's special virus contains an oncogene—a cancer-causing gene. He was trying to use this to make neurons reproduce in people who needed a few extra."

"But wouldn't that just cause—?"

"Cancer? Yes. I started to wonder about Oriol when it looked as if the virus was getting out. First there was a mouse with a green brain tumor. Then a bunch of us got a terrible cold, and our noses expressed green protein. And so when Uncle Alex died of a brain tumor, well—it was pretty obvious that what Oriol was doing in the lab and what he was doing in people were one and the same, and that they both were highly unethical. Not to mention risky. Also, because I had been protecting Oriol, everyone thought that random green people had to be the lab's fault, and there was a huge panic. Especially when we learned that our newest trainee was infected—though if we believe what Oriol told us just now, he was faking it. We still might lose our funding over the whole business, but I don't want to admit..." He swallowed. "...to admit how much I was taken in by his snake oil. You told me you've seen 'cures.' What did you see?"

Lou was determined not to say any more until Margie had spilled her share of the beans. But she had almost nothing to reveal—she'd seen poor old Moe forced to read from an eye chart, and heard a lot of references to the Nobel Prize. The crippled didn't walk, the demented didn't think—yet, to Margie, green-pupilled Moe was the miracle cure that convinced her Oriol was the real deal.

Lou wanted to remain rational, but he was shaking all over with wrath. "Can't you see it's all a lie!" he shouted at the top of his voice, hoping Oriol could hear.

When Margie just looked startled, and then afraid, Lou fought to get his voice under control to explain. He didn't even know where to start. "Moe is not a miracle cure," he attempted. "He may have a few new neurons in his retina—but does he really see anything besides green? Look, Margie...I have spent the last six months with Oriol's experiments literally under my nose every day. I see those so-called cures in a dish, and I see the papers that he publishes in top journals. It is bullshit science. He throws random genes and viruses into neurons he's pulled out of a mouse, and then tries to extrapolate to curing people of complex central nervous system diseases. It can't be done. Even in the dishes, things go wrong—the cells often die or start dividing like crazy, turning into what looks like cancer. None of this gets in the journals. He picks his very best cell on his very best day and announces to the world that he has a miracle."

She looked irritated. "Oh, now I know who you are. You must be Want_Answers. I started hiding your messages from my feed because I was sure you were a phony."

Never again will I post to any message board, Lou told himself. *I was right when I wrote that shit off in 1991.* "I want the cure as much as you do."

"No you don't," she insisted. "Or you'd be willing to try anything."

"Not after I saw Uncle Alex die screaming with a brain tumor, and Oriol claim a cure with poor blind Moe, who's probably only seeing the cancer growing in the back of his eyeball."

Margie was unconvinced. "Are you calling Dr. Ortiz a fraud?"

"Yes!" shouted Lou, then tried to be logical again. "But no more so than ninety-nine percent of the so-called scientists who publish in the biomedical literature. That's why the vast majority of drugs that companies license from academics don't work. There's an enormous gulf between a dish of cells and a person—but professors rely on publications to survive, so most of what's out there is just someone's most perfect experiment, with no bearing on anything that will ever help anyone."

"Do you only publish your most perfect results, too?" Margie wondered.

"No, but I'm a physicist. No one really cares what the result is; it just has to be right. That's why it took me so long to figure out that Oriol was a moron."

"Don't use that word!" she chided. "That's why I wouldn't answer your messages. I was sure you were a troll. No matter what you think of his work, no one can call Dr. Ortiz stupid."

It's like talking to the fucking wall, Lou thought. All of the things he had been afraid to say to Barrow, thinking she wouldn't get it—but at least she would understand that the one unforgiveable crime Oriol had committed was scientific inaccuracy. "Let me put it this way. For every one Moe, how many of Oriol's patients have died of cancer?"

"But at least there's a chance. Maybe a small one, but it's a chance."

If she'd been his student, he would have failed her on the spot. As it was, he needed to just shut up. Too late, he realized that he had said too much and that she was probably not on their side, at least not yet. His story did sound pretty fantastic, and she was still caught in the clutches of hope—if it was the thing with feathers, it also had talons and a beak, and tore chunks from the soul while perching there.

Fortunately, managed to stop talking before he told Margie about the others or what they wanted to do. If he were lucky, he could get Oriol under his power before she found out.

THIRTY-ONE:
ECHAPPER BELLE

M ERDE," MUTTERED CLAUDINE. THE chain-link fence with the strands of lethal-looking barbs strung along the top wasn't insurmountable, probably, but what stretched beyond it was desert. And really deserted desert at that, of the sub-Saharan type where plants were restricted to tiny shrubs and animals were all of the burrowing sort.

"It figures, Clo," said Moe coming up from behind, yards of pith helmet veil muffling his words. "The jungle garden is all planted and carefully tended but it's only about an acre altogether. Beyond it is..." he waved his hand vaguely, not sure exactly what was out there.

Claudine helped him out. "Cruel desert," she offered. "Stretching as far as the eye can see. Endless flat plains hold no terrors for the Canadian, as long as they are covered with snow. But this—the sun makes it all so unnatural. Don't look, it's too hideous."

Moe peered over the fence and reported back. "It looks like a very closely shaven golf course to me. Kind of like an infinite putting green. Without the little flags. But I told you we couldn't escape by an overland route. Let's go back to the beach."

The two castaways headed towards the beach and the coconut stand, continuing the argument that had kept them talking with their mouths full through a delicious lunch of fish and corn soup, crab salad, and papaya and passionfruit crumble for dessert. Claudine had hoped that sufficient nutrition would fortify her for the ordeal ahead, but staring at the waves gave her a familiar sinking feeling. *Ha ha,* she thought, *there's a reason they call it a sinking feeling.* Breathing water instead of air had to be absolutely the worst way to go.

"Are the waves always this big?" she asked Moe, hoping he'd miss the shrill note in her voice.

"Actually, they look bigger than usual, but I must be imagining it."

"You're not, Moe. The sea knows me. It knows when I am around. It is after me. There has got to be another way. You say the service boat comes twice a day. What if we force the boatswain to take us aboard and deposit us on the mainland?"

"The boatswain? Force him? Clo—you're not making sense. And I know I'm like the last person to say this, but you're looking a little green. Here, sit down."

Moe led her to a little hillock of grass where they could sit and watch the tide ripple across the sand.

"Claudine, the sea is not out to get you," he said firmly. "You have a phobia. An unreasonable fear. Why don't we sit here awhile and just look and listen. Waves lapping gently on the shore is a very soothing sound. Once you realize that the sea is not out to get you, we can work out some sort of escape plan. Just relax."

Claudine could hardly believe it, but she did feel herself falling under the sway of the waves' rhythms, and before long Moe's soft voice was lulling her to sleep. Heaven knew she was terribly sleep-deprived at this point, what with the anxiety of searching for Moe, and then everyone with their putrid gastric problems thumping back and forth to the bathroom all night, and to top it off the terrifying trip in a leaky canoe with the demented doctor. It didn't look as if Moe was in immediate danger, so there was no need to rush into some lunatic escape plan that would land them at the bottom of the sea. Maybe she could talk him into taking a few days to explore their surroundings further.

There had to be a way out of here, she was sure, though Moe insisted he'd only seen people come and go by boat. What was it with people and boats, anyway? Being on the water doubled one's risk of sunburn, because of the glare, but people didn't seem to care. In a semi-doze she watched the waves advance and retreat, advance and retreat. *It must be low tide*, she thought idly as the water pulled further back, exposing a sparkling expanse of beach littered with small, shelled creatures.

She was about to suggest that they go gather the pretty shells when suddenly Moe shrieked, "Claudine, wake up! Run! RUN!" Then he was pulling on her, dragging her out of her cozy nap in the most annoying way, and she was about to snap at him to let her sleep for once in her life when she looked up to see the great wall of water headed towards them.

So this was the end. Somehow she must have had a presentiment that this was how it was to be, which explained why she had always been so afraid of the water. But now that it was here she felt no longer afraid, but on the contrary filled with peace. She batted Moe off like a pesky fly and waited serenely for the sea to come for her.

Come it did, towing her under and along the bottom, pushing sand, shells, and water into her mouth. She didn't resist, lying limply as the wave spat her back to the surface.

Then she fought and screamed like a madwoman as fingers gripped her throat. It was *les mains de la mer*, she was sure, especially when they began to speak to her in Quebecois. They were taking her to join her son, and they pushed her down once, twice, three times.

"*Du calme, Claudine, tabarnak!*" *Les mains de la mer* rolled her over a hard tube, pushing the water from her stomach. She coughed and lay still. "Are you *maudite*?"

"I most certainly am," Claudine replied, and shut her eyes. But another voice came along right after, and soon Moe was next to her, pounding her on the back. "Spit it out, Claudine, spit it out!"

"Is she OK?" asked *les mains de la mer*, in a surprisingly non-sinister fashion.

Claudine coughed once more, spitting water off the boat. She opened one eye.

"Oh, good." Lori picked up a set of oars. "Let's get out of here. We don't have much time. I pushed the canoe over the land, mounted on my skate wheels, because Oriol's minions were patrolling the shore."

"Here comes another set!" Claudine gasped as Moe's gardener and poolboy—his jailers, really—came running down the beach, looking for their boat.

"We've got a few minutes," Lori explained, breathing hard with the effort of rowing over the waves with the added weight of two more people inside. "I hid their canoe. But just in case—Claudine, can you get off the tank?"

Claudine realized she was sitting astride something long and hard and cylindrical, like a Wile E. Coyote rocket ship. She didn't want to give up her secure perch, but Moe coaxed her down, where she sat trembling in his lap.

Lori rowed, but the waves kept pushing them back towards shore. Their jailers were coming now, and Claudine regretted not having gone straight to the bottom with Roger. Now Lori was giving up, dropping the oars and crawling towards the tank.

"Hold onto your hats!" she cackled. Then she turned a valve, there was a hiss, and they were rocketing towards the opposite shore. "Helium!" Lori yelled over the noise. "It was in the hut with the boats."

They were still off shore when the tank sputtered to a stop, but at least their pursuers were long gone. So, unfortunately, were the oars.

Lori leapt from the boat. The water only came to her waist. "Come on, guys—we made it!" Getting no response from her stunned passengers, she got behind the canoe and started shoving it towards the beach.

Finally Moe got out to help, too, and soon they had delivered the completely overwhelmed Claudine to dry land. She fell on her knees, kissing the rocks and praising them in all the languages she knew, until Lori grabbed her by the elbows and jerked her upright.

"They're coming," she hissed. "Run."

THIRTY-TWO:
J'ACCUSE

ORIOL DREW ALL THE shades in the office building, banished TooTired, and locked himself and Lou in a back room, where a window-mounted air conditioner would screen them from eavesdroppers.

Lou shivered, either from the blast of A/C or the thought that he was alone with a murderer. "There's nothing you can do to scare me, Oriol," he announced bravely.

Oriol settled himself in behind the desk, right in the path of the blast of cold air that made his lab coat billow. He leaned forward and spoke in a low voice. "What do you want?"

"As I said, I want my project restarted."

Now the doctor settled back, hands behind his head, laughing. "If NASA thinks you are involved in my work, you have only yourselves to blame. You stole my mice, you traveled all the way to Central California to biopsy my patient, and now you're down here. Obviously you're all involved."

"We wouldn't have been involved if people hadn't been turning green and dying," Lou objected.

"No one has died green," scoffed Oriol. "Those of you who transiently expressed some GFP never got very sick, and I had nothing to do with that. I have offered several times to train your students in proper sterile technique, but you refused."

Lou had not come here to listen to Oriol's ridiculous sermons about lab procedures. "OK," he said at last, thinking how proud his parents would be to hear him deliver a line straight out of a cheesy screenplay. "So if Kathy Greenwood didn't die green, the only logical conclusion is that you murdered her."

A muscle twitched at the corner of Oriol's eye, but other than that he remained perfectly still. "She was delicate," he said at last. "I'm sure you didn't know this, but many of her family members have died of a lysosomal storage disease, very common with her Ashkenazi heritage—"

Lou cut him off with a rude guffaw. He had to do it twice before Oriol stopped blathering. "Uh huh. Is this what she told you?"

Oriol looked hurt, much more so than when he was accused of murder. "What do you mean?"

"I mean that was only one of at least thirteen deadly diseases that she claimed to know all about on various sites on the Internet." He went on to provide lurid details, ignoring the doctor's snorts of disbelief. "Also," he concluded, "I know that she was one hundred percent Scots-Irish."

"That does not mean she couldn't have the disease." Oriol's certainty seemed to waver just a little. "I saw her cells. Her fibroblasts. It's classic."

"Uh huh," Lou snorted. "Well, it just so happens I saw your pictures of her fibroblasts, which she left on her computer. There was nothing wrong with them—except maybe some artifacts from being grown at the wrong pH."

"What do you know about electron microscopy?" Oriol shouted.

"Kind of a lot, actually. How do you think I managed to win a five-hundred-million-dollar astrobiology proposal?"

Oriol looked ready to object, but finally it seemed to sink in that Lou was one person he couldn't pseudo-science into submission. "But then why..." He pressed his fingers to his temples. "Why did she come to me? For years she had been coming, asking questions, promising to refer patients to me." When he looked up, he was angry. "Why did she steal my mice?"

Lou shrugged. "I don't have the slightest clue."

"But you were there that night!" Oriol pounded his desk. "You borrowed a cryo-cup from my student, and never gave it back, and I found it in that lab."

Lou gave what he hoped was an incredulous laugh. "Please forgive me for being distracted from returning your cup by *Kathy's sudden death*. I was there because she said she had something to show me. But then I went out for a few minutes, and when I came back, she was unconscious and the mouse was gone."

Their eyes locked for a moment, then Oriol looked away, pretending to adjust the A/C. "It was an accident."

"Good," Lou prompted. "Do go on."

"She wouldn't give me my mouse." Oriol fiddled with the settings on the device, still not looking in Lou's direction. "Each one is precious—I cannot report statistics unless I have at least four from each group. I tried to take the cage, and she held on to it. She was sitting in that horrible chair down there, that rickety broken one, and when I pulled...well, I guess she fell backwards and hit her head."

"You 'guess'? She wasn't lying backwards when I found her. She was face down in the tissue culture hood."

Oriol finally turned forwards, some of his confidence returning. "I am a physician. I checked her pulse, I cleared her airway. I didn't believe she was seriously injured...but I did not wish to be discovered in that lab."

Lou was skeptical. "I can't imagine you'd think it was OK to put someone face down on that hideous surface."

"No, no, no!" he objected. "She was conscious when I left—I swear it. She had even taken up her pipette again. I was certain that she was fine."

"She did have a pipette in her hand when I found her," Lou agreed.

Oriol shook his head back and forth, like a troubled elephant. "That's why I didn't have trouble believing she had some bad genes somewhere. She was so tiny, so wasted—and then this trivial injury..." He switched abruptly back to a whisper. "Why did you protect me, if you were so sure I was such a monster? You didn't say anything to anyone, not even your colleagues."

"No. I believed in your research." He scowled. "Call it the thin green line of silence. It took me a while to figure out you were a fraud. If there's ever a cure, it won't come from you, because you're too stupid and self-centered to do anything but stroke your own ego and surround yourself with shallow worshipers. And yes—" he interrupted as Oriol was about to speak—"you should quote me in the press release when you get your Nobel Prize. Because even if you do win the Nobel Prize, your science is still wrong."

Oriol seemed genuinely hurt by this. "I do my best. You cannot hate me because there are no miracles."

"Then maybe you should stop advertising them as miracles," Lou grumbled.

"It's the nature of the business," Oriol shrugged, smiling again. "I think you yourself know what it's like to have people hate you for your work."

Lou was outraged; he had to clamp his mouth shut to keep it from falling open like a carp's. "There is no evidence that what happened to me was anything but a random act of street violence," he hissed. "I was in the wrong place at the wrong time. It certainly didn't have to do with my science."

Oriol wasn't listening. "I have had three attempts on my life," he mused dreamily. "Can you believe that?"

"Truthfully? I think I can."

Oriol ignored this. "At my former school, I was forced to hire a personal security guard. A few nosy students discovered I was using cats in my pain experiments..."

"Stop it now!" Lou shouted. "I came here trying to believe you were not a monster. You're not helping."

"I understand," Oriol purred. "We're all so vulnerable to the lunatics out there."

Lou regretted having started this conversation. He was terrible about confronting students over minor cheating; what made him think he could negotiate with someone as smooth and persuasive as the magnificent Dr. Ortiz? "Even if Kathy's death was an accident, are you still convinced you've done nothing wrong?" he persisted. "Uncle Alex *did* die green."

"An unfortunate first-generation virus," Oriol confided with mock sadness.

"And Claudine's guests? What about them?"

"Oh!" Oriol waved a hand; now he was chuckling. "That's nothing. I probably shouldn't have linked GFP to the Botox that I was making in *E. coli*, but it made it so much easier to purify." He snickered at Lou's shock. "No virus. Just cheaper, cleaner Botox— `variant Botox,' I call it. Perhaps next time I will use a protein of a different color, one that's more difficult to detect by random busybodies..."

"And Moe?"

To Lou's astonishment, Oriol beamed with warmth, as if he were receiving an Oscar. "This man Moe Deet is my Nobel Prize."

"He does have the virus? The second-generation one?"

"Third," Oriol boasted. "How long has it been since the University has had a Nobel Prize in Physiology or Medicine? Thirty years. Moe was blind, his retina was black and empty in the middle." He gestured with his finger as he spoke, drawing neurons in the air. "And now he has neurons, fresh new cells!"

"Green ones!"

"So he sees things green—at least he sees!"

"Maybe all he's seeing is lumps of tumor." When Oriol seemed to cringe at that, Lou rubbed it in. "Ever think of that? He's just seeing GFP. Besides, Claudine thinks that Moe is here against his will."

"Oh, Claudine," sighed Oriol, with an attempt at light amusement that sounded somehow cruel. "She could do with a few more cells, if you know what I mean." He tapped his forehead. Seeing Lou glare at him, he went on, "One week. I need only one more week. It will not hurt him—I just need to take pictures of his retinas. You will see me in your office with the Nobel Prize!"

"Egas Moniz won the Nobel Prize, too," Lou reminded him. "For inventing the lobotomy."

"Perhaps he deserved it." Oriol smiled benignly. "You know, none of this would have happened if you had just let dead mice lie."

Somehow, even though he'd got Oriol to confess to manslaughter and botched human experimentation, it was Lou who ended up feeling guilty. "We're physicists," he tried to justify. "We're nosy about everything."

"Good," said Oriol. "You will get your project back. Have Absinthe draw up a contract. I will sign anything. And while you're at it, I suggest you turn your curiosity to Greenwood. There was something in that story that I still don't like."

And just like that, Lou was dismissed. He no longer knew what to think. The only certain fact was that, indeed, no one besides Alex had died green. It should have been a massive relief—he could stop worrying about Claudine and Abby, at least.

But then he remembered the collie. He lingered outside Oriol's office building until he saw TooTired go in, leading a confused and staggering man by the hand. Then he sneaked back to the surgery building, borrowed the keys once more, and checked in on David Snavel and the dog head.

David was gone, but the head was still there. There was no time to find a bag big enough to hide it, but the people in the waiting room were such freaks that his theft would no doubt go unnoticed. At least he remained un-detained as he headed slowly back to the guest rooms balancing the head on his lap.

There was no one in the suite. They all must have recovered from their stomachaches and gone off somewhere, and Lou's phone had no connection. He placed the dog head on the bedside table, ate an energy bar, and waited. And he waited some more.

Then his early morning got to him, and he climbed into bed and was immediately fast asleep.

Screams awoke him—how much later, he didn't know. Claudine, soaking wet, was cradling the dog head, trying to show it to Moe. Lori stood dripping next to her, in her bathing suit, legs coated with sand.

"We escaped," Lori explained succinctly. "Now we're leaving. Let's go. And why do we need a *second* dog head?"

THIRTY-THREE: THE MISSIVE OF DAVID SNAVEL

THE BUBO WAGON WAS emptied out, but apparently there was nothing sinister about this—Lori had used her devices to rig up a boat to save Moe and Claudine. The only thing that seemed to surprise her was a wad of papers stuffed under the windshield wiper, which she took, glanced at, then handed to Lou with a derisive *Ha!* Then she helped the still-sodden older couple into their van, and since neither of them could drive, Abby took the wheel.

Lou and Lori lagged a few minutes behind, pausing while Lori carefully sorted her human-powered vehicle paraphernalia. She even oiled the bearings in her skate wheels and stacked them up in a special holder.

Lou looked over his shoulder nervously. "Aren't we fleeing?"

"Oh, no," she yawned. "Claudine and Moe are fleeing. There's nothing Oriol can do to us."

He wasn't so sure, but nothing could make her hurry. Finally installed in the driver's seat, it took her another full minute to figure out how the ignition worked, and another to find reverse. As she roared out of the sandy lot with a rattle and struggled to control the alien vehicle, Lou tried to keep his mind off their impending ditch-plunging death by glancing through the papers.

Barrow drove the way you might expect—like someone only comfortable with speed if it was in a peloton of in-line skaters clinging to each other's buttocks, and who encountered freeways no more than a half-dozen times a year and then only if you put a gun to her head. Sometimes she was too cautious, sometimes too aggressive, and she constantly followed too close as if she were trying to get into someone's draft. They hadn't gotten far before he made a noise that inspired Lori to offer him the Kaopectate.

"I'm not barfing," he corrected. "I'm trying to choose between outrage and laughter. Would you like to like to hear *The Last Missive of David Snavel*?"

"Is that his own title?" Lori sounded annoyed, and started in on a full-out rant about loser postdocs and how much she hated them. It went on for a solid ten minutes—she didn't even seem to breathe—before she admitted that yes, of course, she did want to hear the missive.

Holding the sea-stained papers up to the window to gather the last of the evening light, Lou began reading aloud.

"*Honestly, who* wouldn't *do anything to get out of Eureka? Ponder this a moment before you continue. I am in hiding now, but if you want to find me—either to kill me or to hire me back—I'm sure you will be able to. After all, it was no more than 24 hours after I fled to Mexico that you all came pouring down here after me.* Ha! He thinks we were after him. Isn't that cute?"

Lou turned to the next page, shifting it towards the rapidly sinking sun. "*So far, life in science has been nothing at all what I expected. When I was a little boy, mixing baking soda and vinegar rockets and playing with my chemistry set, I dreamed of the day I could be in a lab all day long without anyone nagging at me to clean up my mess and come and eat.*

"*The adult experience has been a series of bizarre disappointments. I did my PhD at NYU and won the American Physical Society thesis award, but only because everyone else in my year was a bunch of idiots. Everyone, of course, except Kathy Greenwood, who transferred into Math after the first year because she couldn't stand any of us. So rather than have a ray of light to look at in the rest of my classes, I had only stinky guys who would go nowhere.*

"I, too, thought I would go nowhere, but the award and Kathy's help got me an interview with the legendary Lou Maupertuis—Legendary! I like that—but from the moment I arrived at STI, things became increasingly strange. I went in on the morning of the interview prepared to re-do all my derivations on the board, and all that Lou cared about was whether I could spend a year at the Pole without murdering someone."

"Oh, for god's sake," Lori grouched. "Get over yourself. Your thesis is just *not* that interesting."

"Actually, I did mean to ask him about his derivations—but never mind. He keeps going for pages, it looks like." Lou riffled through the lined notebook paper, hoping he could finish reading before darkness settled in definitively.

"At first I was insulted—until I found out that not killing people at the Pole was a much harder task than I had imagined. I know that you sent Sam along to test me, but did you ever realize that a more urbanized cry-baby could not possibly exist? All that man did, from the instant we got on the Air Canada flight, was complain about how it wasn't Manhattan. 'Oh, poor me! I can't get a pumpernickel bagel! You expect me to sleep WHERE? What is this backwater—my favorite Broadway show will NEVER come here.' Oh, dear." Lou felt a pang of guilt. "Poor Sam. I didn't realize he was so unsuited to fieldwork."

Lori gave a little cough that sounded like "Whiner." "I knew," she admitted. "But he can suck it up. Who else is going to go to these places? Not me. I paid my dues."

Lou didn't argue, because he wanted to get through the letter before the sun set. *"Believe it or not, I loved the Arctic. I got to eat whale blubber, and got a whole bunch of amazing souvenirs from Desolute that Sam wouldn't even look at because they 'smelled like fish.' I'd go back there in a heartbeat. I thank you so much for this enriching experience.* Bleah. Now he's just sucking up.

"*The station at Eureka, though, I admit, is lacking in culture. It's nothing but a bunch of broken equipment hidden under dusty tarps, poorly heated by a propane stove. Dressed in parkas and mittens, we all tugged pieces out from under the plastic and tried to put them together. I was useless, relegated to the role of the clumsy theorist not even allowed to dust for fear I'd drop things. Sam is a theorist too, but he has the saving grace of outstanding spatial skills—he could tell everyone just how and where to rotate something to make it fit where it belonged. He could barely use a screwdriver, but at least he had a function. I did nothing but sit there and get laughed at by Canadians.*

"*Three times a day we were fed bland, institutional meals that we didn't really want, but eating was something to do, so we shoveled down the noodle soup and shepherd's pie like monkeys in the zoo.*

"*Once a week we were treated to one hour of a painfully slow Internet connection. It was just enough to remind everyone that the real world was still out there, waiting, and it made me feel even more worthless than ever. One week I sent Lou an idea for a paper. The next week Lou wrote back, 'Not bad, see what you think' and mailed me a complete manuscript that I couldn't add to in any way.* Honestly!"

"Is there a story here, or just this egotistical rambling?" Lori demanded.

"It gets better, I promise. *While waiting for this evidence of my humiliation to download, I happened to notice that Sam was being cagey with his laptop. He was either looking at porn or reading secret messages, I decided, so I poked around a little bit on the university web site to see if I could get into Sam's account.*

"*The first thing I learned was that Kathy had DIED and that no one had told me. The only woman I had ever adored— idolized even—and I couldn't even pay her my last respects because I was stuck in Canada. I was determined to get out and teach you all a lesson.*

"It was pretty gratifying to find that I could guess Sam's password in only two tries. ROTH314, what a bonehead. So that's how I learned about the green brains, and that you all might have been responsible for Kathy's death. It took me a few days to come up with a plan. There were packets of fluorescein in the first-aid center, and I ripped a few open and let the stuff dribble over my face. Then all it took was a strategic black light and I was GFP Man.

"I'd done such a silly, campy job of it that I was sure Sam was just going to laugh. Instead, he grew deathly silent until the next Internet Hour, and then spewed a stream of hysterical messages into cyberspace.

"Lou wrote back immediately: 'Don't worry, Sam, even if I have to charter a jet, we'll get you out of there.'

"What was I to say? Even when the charter was black and from the government, I was so relieved to get out of that place that a couple of days in the BSL-4 was like Hawaii in comparison. They even had orange juice, so Mr. Whinerhead could shut up about his so-called scurvy.

"But I know I can't go back to STI. At least not until Sam cools off a little bit, and whatever tempest I caused at the university has a chance to burn itself out.

"My first thought in coming down to Mexico was to get a job. Kathy had told me about Oriol's clinic, and said he needed a statistician to deal with his data. Aha! I knew that bastard couldn't add two numbers!

"But I rented a red convertible at the airport, and as I drove it across the border, other ideas started to form in my head. Oriol would be unlikely to recognize me, since I was from physics...I could pretend to be a celebrity, get some plastic surgery, and start a whole new life! Brilliant!

"I couldn't really claim to be a movie star, because then he'd wonder why he didn't recognize me...but then I had it: I'd claim *to be a gay porn actor from the Valley. Even if Oriol did know all the gay porn actors, he'd be too embarrassed to admit it. Also, they all have funny faces, so I'm believable.*

"Of course, this plan was about as ingenious as the GFP idea. If you care, I am easy to recognize now—when Lou interrupted my plastic surgery, Oriol refused to continue. So now half of my mouth is a porn star's, and the other still has that ghastly moustache that no amount of shaving or electrolysis could ever touch.

"If you have hearts, please find it in them to forgive me. If you don't, well—I have a pretty nice paper on the Cosmic Microwave Background that's almost finished. I promise if you take me back I will work hard and stay out of trouble.

Yours sincerely,

David

P.S. I'm sorry about the DEA. I didn't really mean it. They're gone now."

"WHAT?" Lori pounded on the steering wheel and let out a volley of curses, half in English and half in Quebecois. "That little...that bastard...I'm going to pull out every one of his last remaining moustache hairs with green-mouse tweezers!"

"Well..." Lou tried to look on the bright side. "I guess we can skip the Dubya masks once we're over the border, at least."

"I suppose." Lori sounded reluctant, as if the cops would be more likely to recognize them than they would be to suspect two people driving through Southern California in Dubya masks. She finally relaxed, though she was clearly still fuming as she fumbled for her passport. "Maybe we can even stop in San Diego for a burrito. I don't know if Oriol tried to poison us or it was just the food, but I'm better now, and I'm starving."

It was fully night now, so Lou folded David's letter and put it away. The Bubo wagon clanked along for a long while as neither spoke. The secret of Kathy's death weighed on Lou's mind, but he feared discussing it with Lori until he'd had some time to reflect. He deeply wanted to believe that Oriol had picked Kathy up gently from the floor and taken her pulse, reassuring himself she was OK before he fled from the room. There was certainly no evidence that her death had been anything but an accident, so even if Lou did have qualms, it would be futile to try to turn the doctor in.

The irony of it, he reflected, was that the whole thing would have been more comforting if Kathy really had died of a green brain tumor.

"Maybe she had scurvy," Lori suggested, apropos of nothing.

"Who?" Lou couldn't believe she could read his mind like that.

But she always could. "Kathy! That's why she was so pale and bruised-looking, and died from a little bump on the head. All she ever ingested were black coffee and Cheez Doodles."

"Maybe she was a spy for NASA," Lou added. "Stealing the mice to get us into trouble."

But Lori didn't laugh. "Well," she mused after a moment, "I think she was a spy for someone."

THIRTY-FOUR: SAM'S DIARY, PART 6

From: sjroth@its.sti.edu
To: lab@its.sti.edu
Subject: take this green and shove it

Well, I am out of the CDC, no thanks to you. I honestly don't care. I am moving to Santa Cruz and none of you is ever allowed to contact me again in any way.

Who stole the mouse brain? I, Samuel J. Roth, of Brooklyn, NY, and Princeton, NJ, stole the mouse brain. And threw it in the trash. Yes, the *regular* trash. I didn't autoclave it, incinerate it, homogenize it, or bury it twelve feet deep. Somewhere out there in a landfill is a plastic orange tube containing your wretched green mouse brain.

Naturally I spilled the beans when I was hauled off to the CDC, which caused panic visible even through a space suit. I think they would have gone through every landfill in L.A. if the new guy hadn't finally confessed he'd turned himself green as a "prank."

How did I break into the BSL-3? Don't be stupid—you used physics for the passcodes. If you want to be a biologist, be a real one, and use something retarded for the passcodes like the number of base pairs in a mouse brain genome, or something. Oh right, I forgot—there are no numbers in biology. Silly me.

I have only one thing left to say to you guys and it is this: FUCK science! You're all lunatics! It's not an ivory tower— it's a locked ward! You all stay here and shoot and stab and poison each other; I'm getting out before I become one of you.

Sam

THIRTY-FIVE: FEED A COLD

ALL OF THE MYSTERIES were solved, Lori thought, except for one. How had Claudine's dog died—from licking Abby, or from something Oriol had done to him?

The first dog head had clearly been a decoy. Lori had put it in fixative just before the DEA invasion, and although she hadn't had a chance to look at it, it looked essentially normal.

The same could not be said of the brain Lou had nicked from the clinic in Mexico. It was a blown-up version of déjà vu as gloppy green cells spilled out of the skull and onto Lori's dissection tray. This time, unlike with the mouse, she took beautiful pictures onto their new hard drive. Then she took the brain home where it couldn't be stolen and put it on a rocker set up in her bedroom. Maybe Sam had been the culprit with the original mouse brain, but she wasn't taking any chances. The little mouse from the H-Bar freezer then joined the dog brain, rocking in peace in an eternity of GFP.

Because the brain from Oriol's clinic was already in formaldehyde, getting the DNA out for PCR was a bit trickier than usual. There were published protocols for getting DNA from preserved tissue, but Lori had never tried it before and she didn't trust her skill. Just in case, she also ordered fluorescent pieces of DNA that would bind their viral sequences, which she could add directly to the brain slices on a microscope slide, giving them images of where the viral genes were on the level of one cell.

The DNA pieces were a special item and took a while to arrive, and meanwhile they were all distracted by trying to demonstrate some results to get their NASA money restarted. With Sam, David, Kathy, and Oriol all gone, Lori and Lou scrambled to do everything themselves. The days slipped by, with the dog and mouse brain slices waiting patiently in a slide holder, frozen at –20 degrees C.

It wasn't until the Thanksgiving break that they could be assured of enough time to run a series of PCR and labeling experiments without the NASA inspectors rearing their ugly 9-to-5 heads. On Thursday Lori was alone with her probes and stains, but on Friday Lou blew off his parents' Malibu beach party and joined her in the conference room for instant noodles on a hot plate.

"Mmmm," he said, spooning up crunchy ramen. "This is so much better than having family and friends."

Lori couldn't tell if he was being sarcastic or not, so she didn't respond to that. "I have lots of pretty colors for you to look at—none of them green. I made labels that attach to enzymes and other proteins for a few different viruses, and put them on the slices of dog brain—the one Oriol had and the one Abby brought back, just in case."

Lou drained his soup bowl and rubbed his hands in anticipation. "Oh goody. I assume we get to hide in the gnarly pus lab, too?"

The lab was a lot less gnarly since it had been shut down. Most of the incubators were empty, and the smell had all but vanished. They didn't need to even turn on the culture hood, because all of their samples were fixed and on slides, so they could actually hear each other speak without the constant roar of laminar flow. Lori handed slides to Lou and noted his observations in her lab book, not bothering with the camera at first since they were just going through the brain Abby had brought. Neither of them expected to see anything there, and they didn't.

Finally, with great anticipation, Lori brought out the first slice of the brain of the mouse she'd taken from the steam tunnel. "Stained for HIV. Coat protein is red, structural protein is yellow."

"Hm," said Lou, scrolling through the filter sets. "I see the GFP. Oh, wait—is this your yellow?" He projected the image onto the camera.

There might have been something there, but maybe not. It was less than overwhelming, and Lori was regretting her yellow dye; it was too much like GFP. "Humph. Try this one. Rabies: coat is blue, enzymes in red."

Lou switched to a filter that emitted only a faintly visible violet. He scrolled around a long time before concluding, "There's some rabies, but just in this one spot."

They took pictures in each color to overlay later. So far it was all making sense: The rabies and GFP overlapped, and were found only in the goopy, tumorous areas of the brain.

Finally, with great anticipation, they got to Oriol's dog brain. The slices were big, and Lou spent a while scrolling around, taking a few pictures of the GFP. "Would you call this yellow or not?" he wondered, gesturing Lori over to look.

"No. That's green." She flipped the filter to violet. "Besides, there's no rabies. If we see HIV, we should see rabies." Back to blue. "But it is green. I don't know. Maybe it photobleached." She scrolled around some more, then found another slide.

They spent almost an hour going through the dog brain, looking in vain for HIV or rabies. "How can that happen—I thought everyone who died had rabies?" Lou mused.

Because I fucked up, Lori thought. Maybe Oriol's fixative had done something to the tissue. Maybe she hadn't fixed it correctly; she'd never fixed a dog brain. She hated being a fuckup, feeling like a little Bubo in front of the evil professor. "I'm not sure yet. Try this; it's adenovirus. Should be orange."

"Wow!" He didn't even bother to look through the eyepieces, just sent an image straight to the software that showed each green cell with a vivid orange nucleus. "Why's it in the center like this? I thought you said it was the coat protein?" He turned the power down so that they could see the track of orange leading through the pathways of the collie's brain.

"Yes, but the stain is for the DNA," Lori replied impatiently, searching through her box of slides for the front end of the dog brain: the part with the nose in it. Maybe she hadn't screwed up after all.

She watched silently as Lou took pictures of slides from nose to cerebellum, trying to put the pieces together both literally and figuratively. "I guess the good news is that it's no surprise that an adenovirus could be spread by casual contact," she said at last. "It's a cold virus. So if you or Abby had a cold, the poor dog could have just licked you and caught it."

Lou finished saving his images and looked over at her, blinking in the dim light. "And the bad news?"

"The bad news is that this is not Oriol's virus. Either this one appeared spontaneously, or it's something someone made that's completely different from what Oriol is using on his patients."

"Couldn't he be using a whole bunch of things? The guy is making green Botox, for Pete's sake."

"I suppose. But adenovirus is known to be pretty worthless clinically, for the reasons that we saw. It gets into your nose and that's it."

"I suppose we should be grateful—otherwise we might have brain tumors."

"I suppose. But I'm worried that someone else made this, and that I'm responsible for this someone else, who has taken it upon himself to lie to me." She went through her slide box one more time. "Here. Try this."

Lou only spent a few seconds with the slide before delivering his verdict. "Orange. More adenovirus."

"Yeah. Those were some of Walter's dead cells from the incubator. Are you starting to see the picture here?"

"Walter Waddles? His whole family works here! How could he be such a fool?"

"He probably thinks he's untouchable." Lori glanced up at the ceiling tiles, deciding that the villain would probably also take advantage of the holiday to come retrieve his illegal mice. "Let's finish up here," she suggested, "and then I'm going to crawl into the ceiling and wait for him."

"All right. Do you mind if I head to the Westside, then? Do you need anything?"

"I wouldn't mind a sleeping bag," Lori admitted. "And maybe yoga mat, and how about an e-reader—it could get pretty boring up there."

Lou went off in search of her supplies as she settled into the tunnel. The mice were still there, squeaking feebly and smelling unclean. She hoped that Walter, or Oriol, or whoever it was would tend to them pretty soon. It was uncomfortable and hard there, so she was infinitely grateful when Lou arrived with some bedding, handing it up through the hole. He also lent her his personal Kindle Fire, saying it was backlit and could be read in the dark, which sounded great until she saw what was on it.

Introduction to Loop Quantum Gravity. Quantum General Relativity. Several volumes of *Fundamental Theories of Physics.* All of his own homework that he'd put together for his relativity class. The only thing that wasn't a textbook was the biography of Marie Curie written by her daughter, in the original French.

The hours went by, while she paged through the biography and the homework problems without much enthusiasm. It grew chilly in the tunnel and she climbed into her sleeping bag, glancing at the mouse cage. The mice, too, seemed to be settling in for the night.

That is, until one of them approached the cage bars and spoke. Its voice was squeaky but intelligible. "I'm so hungry," it said. "We've been starved for days."

"Oh!" Lori exclaimed. She felt foolish talking to a mouse, but hadn't it spoken first? "What do you eat?"

"Little biscuits," the mouse replied. "And my bottle... please, fill my bottle."

Wracked with guilt, Lori started to crawl through the tunnel—then bumped her head on the cage and woke up. She was twisted into a pretzel and every joint hurt; she had no idea how long she'd been dreaming.

The mice started squeaking, but not because of her. Someone else was approaching with the unmistakable sound of rattling mouse biscuits. Then there came a roar—a scream—of outrage and terror.

Lori nearly screamed herself, but at the last moment recognized the voice and remained stone calm, though her heart still thudded audibly. There were few things in the world less scary than the voice of Walter Waddles.

"You!" howled Walter. "You've been stealing my mice!"

"Your mice?" Lori shot back. "You're not supposed to have mice. You're not ALLOWED to have mice." "Well, OK, they're not my mice," Walter babbled, caught. "But I'm supposed to take care of them, when... while..."

"While your secret illegal advisor is in Mexico turning people green?"

Walter poured a cascade of food into the mouse cage. "Can we *please* not talk in here?"

Lori was glad to oblige, if only because the squeaking of demented mice made it hard to read Walter's tone of voice. "OK—but check their water, too. You can't just treat animals this way."

"The mice are fine," he whined, but got a jug out of his backpack and glugged it into the water bottles one by one.

"Why don't we leave campus and have some dinner?" Lori suggested.

"Dinner?" echoed Walter. "I think you mean breakfast."

It was, indeed, early morning on a beautiful Saturday after Thanksgiving. The mountains glowed pink, and the palm trees rustled peacefully in the traffic-free silence. Birds tweeted, and the sky was a perfect light blue, promising a brief high in the nineties with the dry, crisp air of a desert fall.

As expected, Walter was wary, expecting a trap, but he followed Lori out of the building anyway. "Any restaurant requests?" she inquired.

Walter shook his head with an air of resignation, as if he knew he was about to be taken out into the woods and dispatched with a bullet to the back of the head. Lori led him across the street to the commercial district, hungry and not really caring if her student was terrified. She prolonged the walk a little to give restaurants a chance to open, heading partway up the hill to her favorite waffle place.

She started off with a seemingly innocent topic. "Solomon Rose retired," she mused. "And we haven't managed to replace him, have we?"

Walter tagged a bit behind. "This department has had hiring problems for at least ten years," he mumbled. "It doesn't have anything to do with us."

"Don't you think they've tried to hire people to turn things around?" Lori wondered if Walter was really that naïve, or if he was letting nothing slip.

"Well, they tried to hire a couple of Nobel laureates and other big cheeses, but they turned the position down," said Walter.

"Before that."

"Before that? There's you and Lou..."

"Right." Appetizing smells were already drifting across the sidewalk from the waffle place, even though it wouldn't open for another ten minutes. "So when the department fails to improve, whose fault is it?"

Walter laughed, seemingly relieved to have found the answer. "I suppose that, as junior faculty, it's yours."

"Exact. But it's not a joke." Lori stopped in front of the restaurant and glared into Walter's shifting eyes. "We were hired with impossible expectations, but when we won this project, I was confident that we might actually be able to meet them. But now the project is suspended, and that suspension has something to do with *you*."

Walter still looked blank, but the students were good at that. Lori gave up and pointedly ignored him, leading him into the restaurant where they were the first ones to be seated.

The waitress brought them coffee and orange juice, and Walter seemed to realize finally that this was not a waterboarding session but instead an opportunity for the grad student's greatest dream: free food. The place was much more a romantic hideaway than a spot for a business meeting. There were only a few tables, most of them for two, and all of them draped in ruffly pink and white tablecloths. Potted palms provided privacy in all the corners, and colored pencils and notepads were left out for doodling; each table had a drawer where patrons' comments, sketches, and sometimes other artwork could be found. Once Lori had seen a napkin torn into a perfect depiction of the L.A. skyline.

Since it was the weekend, there would undoubtedly be a line around the block in less than a half hour, and the acoustics in the place would become unbearable. But for now it was only Lori and Walter, glancing nervously at each other like some sort of parody of a terrible first date.

Lori poured herself a glass of orange juice. It was fresh squeezed and thick with pulp, no doubt much better than what Sam and David had been served in the CDC BSL-4 quarantine.

Walter stuffed the complimentary mini-muffins into his mouth with both hands and guzzled juice, water, and coffee from three different mugs. Lori hid a smile in her juice glass, imagining him crawling around in the stinking mouse tunnel. *You haven't even started to suffer, Walter my boy,* she thought.

Knowing that waffles would put her to sleep within an hour, Lori got something called the "veggie protein breakfast" in vain hopes of energy and stamina. Walter couldn't decide between the chocolate chip waffles and the Southwest omelet, so finally ordered both.

"Oriol is trying to help us get our project back," Lori continued, now that she had Walter captive. "But there's a problem. NASA might believe that Lou went to the spa by chance, and that none of us actually experimented on Moe—but their private investigator has seen you running around campus with mice. If you are on our payroll, you are not allowed to work with mice."

Walter gulped. "Well...I mean...since the project is suspended, who's paying me?"

"We paid your full stipend in the beginning of the year."

"Oh." He looked down into his coffee cup. "Couldn't we make it so that Oriol paid half?"

"We could *have*, had we known in time," Lori agreed. "But we had no idea that you were putting illegal mice in the steam tunnels. And worse than that—you've been turning people green."

The food came just as he was starting to blush and titter. He used the interruption as an excuse to busy himself with condiment bottles, carefully dosing out ketchup, sriracha, and maple syrup and ignoring Lori's statement. "I didn't do anything wrong," he protested, attacking the food as if he had been the one locked up in a cage and deprived of mouse biscuits.

Lori leaned over the table. "You've been using adenovirus," she accused.

Walter looked up, munching away innocently. "Well, sure." He speared a lump of waffle and a piece of omelet on his fork and brought the whole thing to his mouth. "But that's BSL-1. I wasn't required to tell you guys."

"It stops being BSL-1 when you put an oncogene into it." Lori looked at her unseasoned tofu steak with distaste. She should have got the macadamia nut waffles and then just gone home to bed.

Walter put on his very best baffled-student look. "Huh? Oncogene?"

"How do you think Oriol's neurons were reproducing?" Sriracha sauce would redeem anything, she decided, dousing it liberally over her plate.

"I don't know," he protested. "That wasn't my project. I just wanted to see if adenovirus would work with my cells. All I put it in was GFP."

"Uh huh. How do you know it was just GFP? Don't tell me. Oriol gave you the DNA. Did you sequence it?" She waited for him to shake his head. "Did you even run it on a gel, and happen to notice it was twice the size of GFP?"

Walter choked, put down his fork, and took a hefty swallow of juice. "I did notice it was bigger," he admitted. "But I thought that was just some cloning junk."

Lori would've banged her head on the table if it wouldn't have meant a faceful of hot sauce. Instead she nibbled at her tofu, willing herself to calm down before she spoke. "Walter— I'm going to lock you in a room and make you write the safety protocol on the blackboard a thousand times. So then what? *Did* the adenovirus work on your cells?"

Walter seemed to lose his eating momentum. He pushed aside his unfinished toast and reached for a glass of water. "No. All it did was kill them."

"Uh huh. I think we saw that. And then?"

"Well...so then I tried to ultraconcentrate it," he admitted.

"Yet another safety violation. I suppose that's when our noses all turned green?"

He looked miserable, pushing all his plates away. "I didn't mean to."

"I'm sure you didn't. But it's easy to make an aerosol and get the stuff all over the place. Fortunately, we all seem to have had intact blood-brain barriers, so the GFP died out and we're all fine."

His face twisted and he looked at her searchingly, as if he couldn't believe how dense she was being. "Except the dog," he said at last. "Because collies have defective blood-brain barriers. And so, apparently, did Kathy Greenwood." He looked around the restaurant, which was starting to fill with diners. "I know it's my fault. That's why I didn't tell you about the virus. But I guess you caught me."

THIRTY-SIX: RESURRECTION

THE MORNING SUN BOUNCED off the metal vase in the corner and right onto the pillow, the way Lou had set it up to do to wake him up for swim practice in high school. Given that it was the last week of November, the sun's angle meant that it was just past seven o'clock, much too late for swim practice. His arm was trapped under Abby's head, and he didn't want to wake her, not sure when she'd come to bed the previous night.

Maybe his parents' guests were interesting for someone trying to learn French, but otherwise they were a crashing bore. He'd left the party early and then gone to bed when he realized Lori wasn't answering emails and so was probably still in the tunnel. Of course she had no phone; he suspected she'd never sent a text message in her entire life.

It had been a long time since he'd slept in this room—or since anyone had, if he could judge by the dust tumbling in the sunbeam. All sorts of rubbish decorated the desk and the walls. Across from the bed, hanging on the wall, was a rubber nose he'd used to play Cyrano de Bergerac. Next to it was a black stain from a failed chemistry experiment. A bunch of swimming and skiing ribbons lay jumbled on the desk next to the few textbooks he hadn't taken along to grad school.

The whole thing made him claustrophobic. Unable to stand another moment without email, he slowly pulled his arm out from around Abby.

Not slowly enough. "What time is it?" she mumbled, raising her head.

"Seven-thirty."

"Ooooh. God." She stretched and yawned, then curled back up with the pillow. "My Broca's region hurts."

"Yeah, I know what it's like trying to speak a foreign language for hours. We should get up and do something before they start force-feeding us again."

"The caterers won't show up until ten."

"I know. I grew up here, remember?"

"Oh, right. Was this your room?"

"Years ago." He really wanted to get out of here. When Abby turned her head towards him, the pillow gave off a cloud of dust, and he sneezed.

"Oh no," Abby worried.

"It's just the dust! I'm free of everything—HIV, GFP, rabies, even adenovirus."

She accepted that, leaning in to kiss him. "Did you really think I had a brain tumor?"

"You had me going for a while," he admitted. "It isn't like you to start babbling about ghosts."

"Oh." Abby tossed her hair, tickling his face. "It's easy to start believing when you're out there in the middle of nowhere with Claudine. You'll see when you actually stay there."

"God forbid." Lou squeezed his eyes shut. "Roger doesn't like me."

"It's nice. I swear. And that's not really Roger."

"I don't think I'm ever going to get over having to stalk Moe with a lancet, a tube, and a bucket of dry ice."

Abby gave a dry laugh. "*You're* not the one who had to convince NASA that this was innocent and unrelated to your project."

"Oops. I make your life interesting, don't I?" He tried to put his arms around her, but she wasn't interested in cuddling all of a sudden; she looked worried.

"So is Moe dying?" she asked after a moment.

"I don't know," Lou admitted. "Oriol apparently put different viruses into people. I have no idea of their relative danger."

"Well, is it safe for Claudine to kiss him? What if he bit her?"

"I think that's OK."

"Really?"

"Really. A few of his neurons divided because there was an oncogene in them, but the virus itself was never reproducing, so it can't go into any of his other cells or into anyone else."

"Are you sure?"

"Well—maybe if Moe got bitten by a bat, and then got a blood transfusion in Zimbabwe..."

"All right, I hear you. So all this time, the problem wasn't that the virus was escaping, it was that it wasn't working the way it should have?"

"Ironic, isn't it? We all worry about a Superbug, and Oriol made just about the scariest one you could think of—and it doesn't do a damn thing besides kill a mouse. He's not even going to get into trouble, is he?"

"I don't think so." She inched away a little, tensing with their ongoing disagreement. "We don't have proof that he's done anything illegal, and you saw how much good his clinic does. I'm still not convinced he's the fool you think he is."

Lou could only respond with a kind of growl. There was no way to explain to those who didn't get it. They wanted magic, not science. "Well, fuck Oriol. Let's take the dog for a walk. Have you seen Moe's canoe-shaped mansion?"

Abby seemed reluctant to get up, but the sunbeam was insistent, dancing over her face as she tried to cover it with a pillow. Finally she tossed the pillow to the floor. "Fine. I'll take a shower."

"Put on your bathing suit afterwards. I turned up the heat in the pool before I went to bed." He threw back the quilt, rousing a cloud of dust. It was nice to be in this corner of the house away from all the guests, but it really did need to be aired out.

He was scooting down the stairs on his butt when Dolphin ran up, panting and woofing. "What is it, puppy? Do you want walkies?"

In reply, the Newfie lowered his huge head and shook it, splattering Lou and the staircase with thick, ropy drool. It was such a relief not to have to shine the blue lamp on everything that Lou grabbed the animal and hugged him tight, praising him effusively for his beautiful slobber.

Dolphin didn't seem all that interested in walkies. When Abby made her appearance, they barely made it to the end of the block to see Moe's place before the dog led them back, barking excitedly.

A thick mist rose over the pool, making it look warm and inviting. Thinking the dog probably just wanted a swim, Lou followed him down the brick path to the poolside.

One of the chaises longues was occupied by a guest. Stretched out, wearing nothing but a towel over her face, the woman bared her skinny freckled body to the winter sun. She was a natural redhead.

Abby tsked disapprovingly. "Hmph. Gingers should not sunbathe."

"I can't see how it would do them any harm," Lou objected, "...when they're *already dead*."

The woman pulled aside the towel. Her short hair was orange, with black at the tips, and her eyes were grey. She wasn't Kathy—but the resemblance was uncanny.

"Oh, here you are at last," she exclaimed, sitting up and putting the towel over her lap, then donning a pair of chic sunglasses. "I guess I missed you last night. I'm Kathy Greenwood. The real one."

"Oh!" It was rare that Abby was at a loss for words, but even she took a few moments to recover. The dog jumped around, pleased with himself. "I see. So...who was the fake one and what was she doing?"

Kathy blushed a little. "She was an investigative journalist, of course."

"Oh, Jesus Christ," grumbled Lou. "No wonder she wouldn't talk about non-abelian gauge theory."

"Yes—I agree there was a little disconnect there, but you have to admit the physical resemblance works pretty well." The woman smiled, showing the braces on her teeth.

"Horrifyingly well," Lou agreed. "Did she really die?"

Kathy's smile vanished. "Sad to say, yes. It kind of scares me about working there."

"Only kind of?" he muttered.

"She had to go on a crash diet to look like me," Kathy continued. "Maybe that contributed in some way, made her pass out or something?"

"Scurvy," cried Lou, before he could help himself. "Barrow suggested scurvy."

"Oh, maybe." Kathy shrugged as if scurvy were an ordinary part of her everyday life. "My roommate accused me of having scurvy once. Anyway, it's really sad. Oh, and Louis—" she reached out and touched Lou's arm with cold, clammy fingers—"I really do appreciate the special journal issue in my `memory'—but that unfinished paper was totally half-baked. I need to revise it for you."

She started talking, and he realized what an idiot he'd been not to pick up on the imposture sooner. A real mathematician would talk about her work all the time, especially with the results the real Kathy was getting, which were remarkable. If they could test the model at the South Pole...

"Wait!" Abby interrupted. "Stop!"

Lou turned to look at her, puzzled. So did Kathy.

"Never mind the Yang-Mills potential! Who was this journalist, and what was she investigating?"

"Oh." Kathy gave Lou a surreptitious look, one of *We'll meet in the office later with some pencils.* "She was real, all right. Her name was Fiona O'Shaughnessy, and she runs—ran—a site unmasking medical fraud. It got a couple of million dollars of funding a year, but she never let on that she was the one running it. She had been investigating Dr. Ortiz for years."

Lou was skeptical. "She was impersonating you all this time?"

"Oh, no, of course not. I only learned about this back in June. But she would have spoken to any doctors under an assumed name, or none at all. It wasn't the first time she did something like this."

Lou snorted. "It's a good thing biologists are dumb, or they could have figured out that all those on-line characters had the same IP address—CaringDaughter, LosingHope..."

"...Miss PoopyPants," Kathy finished with a snicker. "I know. But they are dumb, and she got a lot of information. It would have been a great story, except..."

Except Oriol killed her, Lou thought, suddenly burdened with pangs of conscience. He had still not dared to tell anyone about how Oriol had been there the night the fake Kathy "fell."

His stomach contracted with loathing as Abby started to gush about how great the doctor really was—all the people he'd helped in Mexico, how all of his treatments were free for those who couldn't pay, how he'd even taken a mole off her arm right on campus that she was sure was a melanoma and would have killed her.

"Well," Kathy snorted. "I don't know about that. It does seem as if he was selling false hope."

Lou felt her eyes on him, and he was not about to say anything. He managed to change the subject by offering them coffee back at the house. A real mathematician wouldn't refuse.

Kathy didn't. She sprung up, found her bikini bottom, and crossed the lawn in nothing but it and her sunglasses. With her bone-white skin and jutting bones, she could have been a creature back from the grave. Dolphin seemed afraid of her, hanging back with Lou and Abby.

With a few espressos in her, the mathematician finally admitted who had helped put her up to the whole thing.

"SNAVEL!" roared Lou. "I swear, I'm going to..."

"Oh, be nice," Kathy scolded. "It's really tragic. He and Fiona were made for each other."

"Oh, right!" Abby exclaimed. "You're not the one who snogged him."

"Me? Ugh!" Kathy gulped her strong black coffee, holding out the cup for more. "He kind of stalked me in grad school. I thought he was a creep. But then he met Fiona, and we all became friends. I went right along with the investigation, really—it was a brilliant idea. Don't fire David because of me."

"It's not because of you," Abby began, "it's because—oh, never mind. I'm sure Lou and Lori will take him back."

"I'm just so relieved to have a mathematician," Lou admitted, filling the espresso pot yet another time. "Once we get Sam and David back, we'll be one big happy family once again."

"Right," Kathy agreed. "I meant to ask. When can I start?"

Abby gave her an incredulous look, but after a moment gave up and laughed. "Just as soon as the Infamous Coverups Office can process the paperwork, I suppose."

"Infamous Coverups!" Kathy chortled. "I love it! Are you the ones who kept Oriol's misdeeds out of the papers?"

Lou was about to protest, but held his tongue when he saw Abby's brow knit with suspicion.

"Which particular misdeeds are we talking about, here?" she wondered.

"You haven't heard?" exclaimed the mathematician. "It was probably the last thing Fiona managed to document before she—well, you know. You're going to love this."

THIRTY-SEVEN: CONFESSION

WALTER REFUSED TO SAY any more until they were safely locked away back in the BSL-3. With the air of a condemned prisoner savoring his last minutes of freedom, he helped Lori get her stuff down from the tunnel and pack it up to take home. His eyes fell on the Kindle, opened to the tales of heroic extractions from pitchblende.

"Did you ever think about what it must have been like to be Eve Curie?" he asked in a plaintive tone.

"Eve?" Lori wondered. "What do you mean? Oh—that she was the only one in her immediate family not to have a Nobel Prize in physics?"

Walter nodded, sitting curled up on a lab stool wearing all his protective gear, a perfect picture of biocontainment misery. "How do you think it feels to have dinner at my house? Great-grandpa was the university president. Grandpa is the head of the chemistry department and everyone's favorite professor on top of being a National Academy of Sciences member and the best published of all of the department. Dad works for NASA and runs all the science. Maybe we just get dumber with each generation, I don't know. I'll end up a dropout and probably go to jail besides."

Lori didn't want to reassure him yet. She thought that a good scare might teach him to be a bit more careful in the future about ultraconcentrating anything, even cold viruses. "Well, Walter," she began, as sternly as she could. "Why do you think your virus killed Kathy?"

"It was way too fast to be the rabies construct!" Walter burst out, obviously relieved to get to confess at last. "That takes at least several days to do anything, even to cells in a dish. But the adenovirus works right away, and can cause allergic reactions. I think that was why we were all sneezing. So she could have either had a massive allergic reaction, or it could have spread into her brain."

"OK, but do you have any evidence of this? There was an autopsy. They said she got bonked in the head."

Walter gulped and mumbled something unintelligible. When prodded, he tried again, barely expelling air. "Oriol lied."

"Good," Lori enthused. "Lied about what?"

Walter glanced all around, even up at the ceiling tiles. "She wasn't found in the parking lot. She was passed out in this lab."

"OK, and so?"

"Well, why would he lie unless he was trying to hide the connection to this lab? And then when David turned green, and Claudine's dog died... Oriol had told me all about collies and the blood-brain-barrier problem. He wanted to develop some kind of gene therapy just for collies."

"But David was a fake," Lori reminded him.

"I didn't know that then. So I was convinced that Kathy had something wrong with her—I mean, she was so small and pale."

"With pointy ears and a wet nose? Honestly, Walter, you were just imagining things."

He took a deep breath, but it wasn't yet a sigh of relief. "That's why I was afraid to refuse when Oriol asked me to take care of his mice. I thought he was protecting me."

"Uh huh." Now Lori was getting mad, but not at Walter. "Oriol manipulated you into taking care of his mice by making you think you'd killed Kathy?"

"I didn't say that," Walter objected. "It was my own idea... I mean mostly. But why would he lie?"

"I don't know." Lori didn't want to say it, but the conclusion was inevitable. "Maybe because the bump on the head was a little harder and a little less accidental than he wanted us to believe?"

"Oh, no, really!" Now Walter just giggled. "He may be a bit pushy, but I certainly can't believe he murdered anyone."

"Well, how are you going to die bumping your head in here? Are there even any sharp edges?"

As soon as the words were out, their eyes met and locked, and Lori knew they were both thinking the same thing: sharp edges meant DNA.

With no further encouragement, Walter unfolded himself from his sulking position and went to the back of the room to begin searching. Lori started on the other side, near the microscope, thinking that microscopy was done in the dark and there were lots of protruding bits on the instrumentation.

None of the bits were particularly pointy, though. All she found were a few droplets of dried snot or eye goop, probably left over from their GFP colds. She carefully swabbed the eyepieces with isopropanol, removing the stains and traces of adenovirus, and then cleaned off the objective lenses for good measure.

This spontaneous spring cleaning was interrupted by a cheep of horrified surprise over by the culture hood. "Lori—come quick. I think I found something."

Walter was holding up a long black hair, grasping the end so that Lori could see the ginger at the root. It was a start, but it wasn't enough to get DNA from. She elbowed him out of the way, making him show her where the hair had been.

"Caught on the edge of the culture hood," he explained, pointing.

That was no good, Lori mused to herself. Kathy could have lost a hair just sitting there working. But if she had fallen backwards from there...Lori traced the path, which brought her back to the edge of the bench behind her. It was kind of sharp, but it was clean.

Walter figured out what she was doing right away. "Try sitting in the tissue-culture chair and falling," he suggested. "You know how one side is wobbly."

"Catch me if I fall for real, then, because—Auugh!" The wobbly chair nearly did tip Lori on her head. She looked at the wall where she'd put her hand to catch herself—was there a stain there, or just a smear from her glove?

On the bench, kitty-corner to the wall, was a rusty old power supply from some unknown piece of apparatus. On the back of the power supply was a tuft of black hair and a dark red stain.

"Jackpot," said Lori. "Scalp wounds bleed like crazy."

Walter was quivering like a mouse, but too shy to push her out of the way. When he finally got a look, his face fell. "I don't know, Lori. I barely get any DNA from a whole dish of cells."

"I have the probes, remember." She was already looking for a sterile wipe to pick up the stain. "We only need a few intact cells with nuclei. I also have the degraded DNA kit that I bought to use with the dog brain. We can try it and use the dog brain as a positive control."

Walter found her a tube, shaking his head anxiously. "Why don't you do it? I'll go home and take a sleeping pill. Then if it's negative, call me...and if it's positive, well, I'll just—"

Lori put a stop to that right away. "This is your experiment, Walter." She shoved the tube at him. "You made the virus, now you find out if it killed someone."

Then, like a good principal investigator, she left him all alone and went back to her office. She very much doubted that the adenovirus had done anything, but she hoped Walter's scare would teach him a good lesson.

She was about to take the rest of the day off when she got an email from Lou.

From: grandmechant@gmail.com
To: geek_en_patins@yahoo.ca
Subject: Zombie math professors FTW

Having breakfast with Kathy Greenwood (well, just coffee—she doesn't eat). Oriol is in so much trouble now. Call me.

Superior
Technological
Institute

Weekly
Interaction

California's oldest
student newspaper
weekly@sti.edu

Volume 137, #46   Los Angeles, CA   December 1, 2008

Fly, Birdie, Fly

Ima Bubo, Staff Reporter

Those taking Biology 232 (Advanced Genetics) might have been surprised Monday morning by their substitute teacher. It's not often that one gets substitutes in grad school, though as of this writing it seems that Dr. Bird might be absent for a long, long time.

I dare to say this because I am a Bubo—meaning that I'm a physics major, with nothing to do with biology. I really don't care if I am shunned by the biomedical world, reduced to a lifetime of demeaning postdocs or worse, pursued across continents by vituperative letters from the Great One. The terror he sowed among his lab members was legend—but now, it seems, he has gone one too far.

Someone from Dr. Bird's lab made a little mistake. Or maybe it was a "mistake"—we'll never know. Somehow, though, the wrong version of a paper got sent to a very important journal.

Not a fatal error, you might think, until you see just what was in this version. All of the Bird's Track Changes were visible for the editor to see, and it seems that this most competitive of labs may not always have been completely honest with its readers.

"Just make that part up"—for something called a Western Blot. Oopsie! And that's not all. "Put in the picture from last time"—for a graph of mouse survival. "Never mind the p values, just say <.001 for everything." Oh, my.

Naturally, the student bore the brunt of the blame. She has vanished from our little world, no doubt to surface many years from now as a pole dancer or playwright. But the Track Changes were not hers, and now a bigger, more sinister story is leaking out of the Bird Lab. A culture of data falsification and threats that can get even the most tenured of professors into hot, hot water.

To see the original manuscript, go to the URL below. We also may wonder if it is a coincidence that the founder of that site recently died a violent death.

EPILOGUE

REPEAT TESTING WITH THE samples from Lori, Lou, and Walter didn't show any GFP. They all finally accepted the explanation that the adenovirus had caused GFP to appear in their noses for a few days, sparked an allergic reaction that made them sneeze and bleed, then died out as any cold virus will.

After seeing the blood on the power supply, Lori was able to accept the cause of Kathy's death as being a bump to the head. She wasn't able to amplify any GFP from the sample. Just how accidental the bump was, she wasn't sure, but since Oriol was lying low in Mexico, there wasn't much she could do about it.

Kathy the real mathematician integrated herself rapidly into the faculty. The first paper she wrote was on the migration of DNA through agarose, co-authored with Lou.

Sam agreed to stay in graduate school under the condition that David never darken his door again. This turned out to be just fine, since David planned to leave for the South Pole as soon as the next field crew departed. The idea seemed to excite him.

Lori remained suspicious over Oriol's disappearance, so wasn't too surprised when she started hearing rumors that Moe Deet's green was spreading. The others tried to hide it from her, but pretty soon even the Buboes were talking about it. They finally gave her a picture that they'd stolen from Walter's computer, showing horrible green lumps sprouting all around Moe's eyes and down his neck.

The worst part was, Claudine kept sending messages inviting them all to her and Moe's wedding, seemingly oblivious to the groom's impending demise. Lori knew that she had to go up to the spa and stop the mad old lady from sheltering the green man, then get him to a real hospital that could at least try to do something about the tumors, but she never seemed to get the chance between juggling the grad students and helping to plan David's trip to the South Pole.

Lou finally picked a weekend just before Christmas and dropped a plane ticket on her desk, then carefully helped her pack up all the lamps and tubes they would need to diagnose Moe. He was being so solicitous that she knew he expected her to do the dirty work: ask Moe to submit to a lamp examination, take samples...tell him he was dying. She was the only one who knew enough biology to do it—the only one, of course, except the fugitive down on his Island of Dr. Moron.

It was a beautiful sunny winter day when they arrived in Clonic, birds twittering as they loaded all of their optical and molecular biology equipment into the goat cart. Apart from Lou, Abby, and Lori, David Snavel had also come along—presumably to get away from Sam, who had threatened to go insane if he ever laid eyes on the "green postdoc" again.

She couldn't face anyone at first. Claudine ran out to greet her, and Lori swiftly turned the conversation to work that needed to be done. A few minutes later, sledgehammer in hand, she was attacking Oriol's parking lot as if she were a macrophage going after infected cells. The pieces of cement went into the goat cart or her bike trailer, and she and Miguel hauled them out to the main road for pickup, returning with bags of organic topsoil.

The sun was setting when Lou and Abby appeared, but Lori wouldn't let them interrupt her. Instead she sent them off in human-powered vehicles to pick up the seedlings she'd ordered from the nursery up the road. It was winter, so all of them were plants that would grow best with a chill: camellias, ferns, and a few native plants.

She refused to go to dinner, and was dropping with exhaustion by the time Abby pried the hammer out of her hands and laid it aside in the darkness. "Let me show you the haunted suite, where you'll be staying," Abby said with surprising gentleness.

"Roger asked me to leave *101 Tricks with the Accusative* on the pillow for you," added Lou.

"Ha ha," Lori grumbled. "Lou, I have heard you make grammatical errors that would embarrass a Quebecois."

"Oh yeah? Which of us says `pas personne'?"

"Don't make fun of Roger," Abby scolded in a way that showed she said this at least fifteen times a day—as if Roger would care.

They might have tricked her to come up here, but Lori wasn't going to go to any wedding. She would go straight to bed, finish the smashing in the morning, then tell Moe he was dying and leave.

The haunted suite would have been big enough for two, if it hadn't been for all of Roger's old books scattered and piled everywhere. On the walls were pictures of him at MIT, graduating, getting a PhD. His grad school blanket with the school colors was on the bed, and as Lou had promised, his favorite grammar book was nestled in the folds of the pillow.

Lori sat on the bed and wrapped herself in the blanket, breathing deeply but getting no smell except that of Clonic and animals. As she flipped through the book, wondering if she could still get all of the questions right, a fat gray tabby squeezed through the window and settled next to her. Just as the cat started to purr, a deep rumbling voice came through the wall, giving the impression that the animal had spoken.

"So, you're here at last," said Roger's voice.

"Oh, goddamn it, Claudine," Lori sighed.

"I just wanted to speak with you," Roger pleaded. "It's been so long."

Lori fought tears as she thumbed through the silly little book and stroked the cat. "What do you want me to say?" she managed, trying not to sniffle.

"I've just missed you," said Roger. "And your colleagues are less than comforting, as I'm sure you know."

"Abby is *not* my colleague, even if she does protect me from the granting agencies," Lori snapped. "How dare she presume to speak to you—she hasn't seen you in fifteen years."

"I know...and she doesn't know what happened in Montreal, she has no idea of what we said...I just keep thinking about our last conversation."

Claudine wants to know what happened, Lori realized, clutching the cat as she played along. "Look, Roger, I'm sorry I encouraged you not to take your drugs—but you were right, you were more brilliant without them. What could I do? Lock you in the house? You were as good at picking locks as I am."

There was a long pause and some sort of noises, not sniffling exactly; closer, really, to a woo-woo sort of ghost noise. "I don't blame you," said Roger at last. "It's not your fault. Besides," it added brightly, "being a ghost is not so bad. You get to scare people."

"And you might be getting some green company," Lori suggested.

"You mean Moe? He's not going to die any time soon—unless he staggers off a precipice." The ghost gave a lungless laugh. "Now come on, Lori, make him and my mother happy tomorrow—don't sulk in here with my terrible books."

"I love them," Lori objected, weeping openly now.

"Me too," the ghost admitted, "and they're in terrible disarray from those *cochon* colleagues of yours."

A large teardrop fell on *Question 29: A Secret Between Me and Thee*, which Lori didn't bother to brush away. It balled up on the yellowing paper and sat there, reflecting the light, as she listened to the cat's purr and the faint "Pop!" that was presumably the ghost taking its leave.

Or not—a final whisper came to her through the wall. "Go on, it won't compromise your principles that much to make my poor old mother happy. I won't tell a soul—literally!" it added gleefully, and this time it was gone.

She slept heavily, awakening to a beam of sunlight and the sounds of music and laughter and optical devices. Leaving the haunted suite, she found a gravel path that led to a large grassy area in the rear of the spa. The fence around the lawn had been recently torn down, and sheep and goats nuzzled her as she walked to the main building.

Claudine ran out to greet her, dressed head to toe in tiers of taffeta leaves in all shades of green. Lori felt worse and worse as she was led into the main entrance, which was crowded with people and decorated with flowers and, again, lots of green—palm fronds, leaves from giant ferns, tangles of ivy. Was she the only one who noticed the morbid theme?

She soon lost track of Claudine amidst the throng of spa-goers and a few distant Quebecois relatives no doubt just trying to escape the snow. Soon she would have to get out the lamp, but she had no desire to see Moe, let alone discuss his GFP with him.

Pressing herself against the wall to avoid the throng, she didn't even see Moe come in until he was practically on top of her.

"Auugh!" Lori yelled, convinced he was going to stagger right into her and smash her into the paneling.

Moe stopped, blinked a few times. He was wearing a corduroy suit that was—you guessed it—absinthe green, a big floppy straw sun hat and dark glasses. He reached to take the glasses off, peering into Lori's face as she recoiled in horror.

As the earpieces of the sunglasses brushed against his face, Moe's tumors crumbled and fell off. There was a smell, an odd smell, very familiar, something like—

A squeal came from somewhere else in the room, followed by thumping noises.

David Snavel was rolling on the floor laughing and kicking his feet.

The smell was Play-Doh.

"SNAVEL!" Lori thundered, realizing that not only had she been tricked, but she had been tricked with the same trick he had already gotten away with once.

David looked up briefly, but was beyond words.

Moe clapped her on the shoulder, brushing a few flakes of tumor off his face. "It's good to meet you at last," he chuckled. "Don't blame Dave—we were all just looking for a way to get you up here for the wedding."

Pushing rudely past the green man, she went to stand at the head of the still-writhing David. "Go ahead and laugh," she warned him coldly, "but you're going to be at the South Pole, and I hope you realize that no matter what goes wrong, NO ONE is going to believe a word you say."

Just barely able to restrain herself from giving him a good kick, she pushed through the crowd and out into the oblique sunlight where Claudine, sparkling with green—but only fabric green—smiled for the many cameras as she clung to the neck of a large, horned, kind of scary-looking animal. As Lori got closer, she saw it was only a sheep, but an imposing one; she wouldn't want one of those hooves stepping on her toe.

"There you are!" Abby's loud voice pierced through the crowd, and she reached over to pull Lori into the little group. "Bracegirdle is just about to give his Best Ram speech."

Everyone filed into position—Moe, with bits of Play-Doh still clinging to his cheeks; David Snavel, with his lopsided moustache, still giggling; Lou, with a telephoto lens the size of an elephant's trunk and a huge bag of optics. Moe joined Claudine at the head of the crowd, clutching at the sheep's wool.

Lori had to admit that she didn't think her principles were all that compromised by a wedding speech that consisted of "Beehhhh!," followed by a few sentimental words from Moe about how sheepherding had saved him from madness.

"Now the ring will be presented to the bride and groom by Claudine's son, the, er, late Roger St.-Pierre," announced one of the guests with a Quebecois accent.

Claudine and the formidable sheep turned their faces to one side of the lawn. Others craned their necks but didn't seem to see anything; Moe was pointed in the wrong direction. Finally, Lori saw a small, round piece of metal floating down between the rows of people at exactly Roger's elbow height.

She turned to glare at David Snavel, but the porn-star side of his mouth was contracted into a perfect "O" of awe. Abby, too, appeared rapt, meeting the odd dumbbell-pupil gaze of the sheep as it gave a loud BAAA.

"He's real," whispered David Snavel.